BLINDING SKY

John Brage

Blinding Sky – The Journeyers' Tale Book 2

Written by: John Brage

Book Cover Design by: Donald Semora – www.donsemora.com

This book is the work of fiction. All incidents and dialogue, and all characters with the exception of certain well known historical and public places and figures, are the products of the authors imagination and are not to be construed as real. In all other respects and situations in the book, any resemblance to any persons alive or dead is purely coincidental.

ISBN Number: 978-1-940155-28-9

10 9 8 7 6 5 4 3 2 1

Published by:Castle Top www.CastleTopGames.com

Printed and Published in the United States of America

~

For all who have the courage to be wrong, the humility to embrace it, and the idealism to do something about it.

~

Acknowledgments

I'd like to thank my wife, Natalie, for being so supportive during the process of writing this book. Not only are you a world-class proofreader, but you are the rock upon which our family is based. I literally could not have done this without you.

To Dr. G – I am unbelievably fortunate to have you as a beta. Thank you for knowing the plot of my books better than I do and for seeing those "what were you thinking?" parts that needed literary resection. I truly value your friendship. I realize my coffee debt to you may require me to invade and conquer a South American country (or Seattle).

To Don Semora and Ros White for their tremendous cover art. They collaborated without even realizing they did.

And last but certainly far from least, to all my readers. The feedback and reviews I got on The Protocols of Uma were inspiring and kept me motivated to keep the story moving. I hope you find Blinding Sky as compelling.

CHAPTER 1

The revelation of the Land Bridge community's end sent tremors through Shu's slender figure. Their Journeyers had disappeared. A group much like the Portentists of Atla had risen, and their philosophies had become those with which the community made their decisions. The last thing Shu would ever learn about the Land Bridge residents was their decision to abandon their home. The parallels to her home island were almost overwhelming. And if Atla truly were the last community of Umae on the planet, the mission of its Journeyers had taken on a vastly increased urgency. The data she acquired concerning the ***Aurora***'s search for Haven was meaningless to her, yet she would bear it back to Atla in hopes the Journeyers could understand it. She looked at Min's figure sprawled out on the floor. He was a Journeyer from Atla. She had to try and help him.

Shu knelt down next to Min and placed her palm against his chest. The pulsations of his heart were so fast she almost couldn't tell where one ended and the next began. His eyes were wide open and unblinking. She needed a way to remove him from the Hall. She would not be able to carry him on her own, but she could not bring anyone inside either. Min was already subject to exile. If he didn't return with them to Atla, even if he were dead, there would be no explanation she could provide the other Journeyers that would prevent them from coming here. If that happened, the Protocols would require their exile as well. She could only imagine the difficulties that might create with their vital mission.

Min suddenly gasped and his back arched. His arms and legs stiffened and his body writhed. Then he went limp again, now with his eyelids closed. Shu could see his eyes rapidly darting back and forth. She decided to wait a while longer to see if he would regain consciousness. She didn't want to abandon him unless she had no other choice.

Min careened down a twisting tube, his body summersaulting so rapidly that he could barely discern what was going past him. He shot out of the end of the tube into a vast expanse of nothingness. He finally stopped spinning and lost all sensation of movement.

In the far distance was a single, tiny point of light. He squinted. Another point appeared next to the first. Soon, innumerable tiny lights pierced the black veil in front of him. A deep sense of foreboding tightened his chest and his stomach clinched. Each light grew as they began to move nearer. The armada of lights hunted him.

He was unable to turn to look behind him. He could not even blink. Each light slowly inflated as it approached. His frozen body ached to tremble. The lights stopped and began to rapidly dance around one another, moving faster and faster until Min could hear a sharp buzz inside his head. The lights swirled into a dizzying web of streaks. They left illuminated trails in their wake, like comets, that drew broad circles in front of him. The buzz in his head grew louder and louder.

They all erupted simultaneously and his eyes burned. When his vision returned, he was confronted by countless images weaving about one another. Pyramids shifted back and forth and spun apex-over-base. Journeycraft raced by from all directions, barely avoiding one another. Short muscular men with spears rushed forward, wailing at him, only to change course and go by just as he thought a collision was imminent. Trees and shrubs grew up out of the nothingness, bloomed, withered, and then disintegrated.

He couldn't close his eyes. He couldn't look away. All of these images raced rapidly around one another. There was no pattern, no reason for the way they moved. His panic was slowly replaced by a rising despair. This must be death.

One last tiny light remained in the distance. It did not move. He tried to concentrate on it. As he did, the other figures moved first to his peripheral vision and then disappeared altogether. As his focus grew, he felt himself being drawn towards the bright, distant dot.

It was pure white light. It did not flicker. It was steady, constant. A gentle warmth emanated from it as he drew closer.

Sensing a new presence, his attention was drawn to a group of slender individuals wearing deep red robes and ornate crowns. The Directors watched him, grinning confidently.

What is it you hope to achieve? He had heard nothing, yet the words rebounded inside his head. The images began hounding him once more. The calm was gone and in its place were more screaming men with spears, more Journeycraft and more spinning pyramids. He lurched downwards into his despair.

No! The light! Where? He had become distracted and now it was gone. His eyes frantically surveyed the swirling images for the light, but he could not find it. His anchor was lost.

The men charged at him with spears, stopping just short of impaling him on their deadly points. The pyramids surrounded him, poised to crush him between their massive stone walls. The Journeycraft whizzed by, setting his skin aflame.

He swallowed. Wait. One Journeycraft……something was amiss. The arch of its wings was wrong. Its fuselage was far too broad. It……would not fly. He concentrated on the Journeycraft. It was a falsehood. He was drawn towards it now, and as he was the other images receded. As the huge ship filled his vision, he braced for the collision. It never happened. The ship vanished. The light, his beacon, had returned. The falsehood disappeared.

There was nothing he could do to prevent himself from being drawn into the light. It swept over him, filling him with a great sense of relief. Then, he was gone.

Shu couldn't wait any longer. She would simply have to deal with the other Journeyers. Just as she reached the partition wall, she heard him groan. Min was now on his side, rubbing his face with one hand.

"Are you……?" She wasn't sure of what she wanted to ask. Obviously, and remarkably, he was alive. Miraculously he had survived the panel.

It took him a moment to gather his bearings. He looked up at the display and then turned towards Shu. "What….was that?" he asked weakly.

Shu also considered the display. She couldn't guess what he might have seen. He could have accessed almost anything. Min had answers to questions she had dared never to consider, but did he have the questions themselves? Because if he didn't, he had taken the first irrevocable steps towards madness.

Sol sat staring at the device, seething over the conclusions produced by its data. "I can't believe they would use this substance," he said incredulously. The thought of all of those Umae dying from cycli-toxic shock was smothering him. "The disregard for those individuals . . . .it is appalling. I should have recognized it the moment I stepped off the ***Starshine***," he lamented. "Such a decision. It is just beyond me."

"It isn't your fault," said Jack. "I'm sure your data upload included all the necessary warnings."

"Of course it did!" snapped Sol. "Of course."

"Then the Chroniclers used it knowing the risks," said Eve.

"At least Bal did," noted Sol as he placed the device on the table. "And he would have had to experiment with it for a while to make sure his formula and dosage were correct. He systematically watched them die until he got it right. I wonder if he even told them of the danger?"

"There is no way to know," said Jack.

Sol stood up. "Yes, there is!" he said, a bit more animated.

"Is there another test we can run?" asked Eve.

Sol shook his head. "No, nothing so complicated. Jack, the Guard we spoke with, Max, why don't we just ask him?"

"You had a conversation with a Guard?" asked Eve.

"Yes, believe it or not," said Sol. "One of the Guards Bal assigned to 'protect' us was a rather amiable type. He raises flowers for fun."

Eve's eyebrows arched. "Where was he stationed?"

"He was with us the entire time," said Sol. "We don't know what his usual assignment is."

"How would we find him?" asked Jack. "It would look odd if we just showed up at the Chroniclers' Hall and asked for him by name."

Sol's enthusiasm waned slightly. "It would, wouldn't it? We would need to know where he was stationed at any given time. There is no way to access that information."

"Sure there is," said Jack. "The beacon satellite is constantly relaying data to the Hall. If we could link up to the satellite, we could extract information ***from*** the Hall. But we would have to do it from a Journeycraft."

"I thought the Chroniclers' panel was designed to only receive information," noted Eve. "Is there going to be a technical issue?"

Jack beamed inwardly at Eve's reliance on his opinion. "Possibly," he admitted. "As long as we don't try to retrieve too much data, we won't run the risk of a feedback loop."

"A feedback loop?" echoed Sol.

"Information traveling in the wrong direction within the transfer beam could theoretically result in a chain reaction that could destroy the panel. And everything else in the vicinity," he added. "But we are only seeking a Guard schedule, not…."

"Information about the Cataclysm?" said Eve. "Or the Directors? Now I see why Min has never just accessed the panel directly from space."

A wave of clarity swept over the young Technical Agent. "Of course….." he mused slowly. "It makes perfect sense."

"So you can do it?" asked Sol. "Safely?"

"I could from the ***Starshine***."

"They won't let us board the ***Starshine***," said Eve. "Maybe we can get on the ***Aurora***. We'd need a reason."

"And we'd need a bit of time," added Jack. "The ***Aurora*** is linked to a different beacon satellite. It will take a while to redirect the connection."

"We can tell them that we need to bring Eve on board to do data analysis," said Sol. "She didn't go with us last time. They might believe us."

Jack nodded. "It is worth a try." He began rummaging through their equipment bags, looking for the devices he thought would look the most impressive to the Guards. "Come on."

They exited the pyramid and walked quickly towards the landing area. The Guards were still stationed at the base of the ***Starshine***. One of them turned and eyed the trio as they approached.

"What do you need?" he asked in a hollow baritone.

"Still working up the other ship," said Jack. "We brought our data specialist with us. She needs to run some tests. She didn't go aboard with us last time."

The Guard turned and looked at his companion. The other large man waved them towards the ship.

"Go ahead," said the Guard.

Without delay, Jack activated the egress ramp and the group boarded the ***Aurora***. Once aboard, Jack closed the ramp before increasing the illumination inside the cabin. "I will establish the new link so Eve can retrieve the data," said Jack. He sat down by the main panel and went to work. The ***Aurora*** was able to quickly locate Atla's beacon satellite as it was directly above them. The satellite was protected by an encrypted access code. "Forgot," said Jack under his breath. "We aren't supposed to talk to each other directly. Eve, I'm going to stream the coding matrix onto the display. See if you can give me any suggestions about how to crack it." The display came to life, illuminated by a bright series of dots, dashes, and seemingly random figures. Eve placed her palm on the panel and closed her eyes.

"This is an older encryption method," she said after a moment. "This won't take long." She kept her eyes closed until the stream on the display transformed into a square of neatly-ordered columns. "There it is. Now, let me see if I can tap into the Hall." Jack stood up and let her sit at the panel. She touched various parts of the screen as the columns shrank down to nothingness. Then, a detailed schedule of Guard duties appeared on the display.

"He will be attending the boat wrights at the heartside beach the next two rotations," Jack said. "Let's shut this thing down and get out of here." Eve manipulated the panel for a few more seconds, causing the screen to go blank.

"I hope Max can help us," said Jack.

"I am confident," said Sol, "that he will if he is able."

Min leaned heavily against Shu as she struggled to drag him towards the exit from the Hall. She could barely manage more than a few steps before needing to stop. His breaths came in ragged gasps. Shu tried to haul him forward then grunted as his body nearly pulled hers back to the floor.

"Shu?" a voice called from the hallway. It was Dom.

Shu hesitated. "Dom. Come here," she said. He promptly emerged from the shadows and looked down at Min.

"What happened?"

"Not now," said Shu. "Do you think you can help me move him?" Dom took Min by the wrists and pulled his upper torso up until it rested on Dom's back. Hunched over, he effortlessly began dragging Min's body along the floor. Shu watched with disbelief. "How can you do that?" Dom didn't reply. He dragged Min to the exit, leaning him against the wall. "Where are the others?" asked Shu looking about.

"They went back down to help May and the others up the stairway," said Dom.

"Good. They should be here soon, then." She was catching her breath and sounded encouraged.

"What will we do when they get here?" asked Dom.

Shu sat down next to Min. He was slumped against the wall, eyes closed. "We need to look around the settlement to make sure there isn't anyone here. I don't think we will find anyone, but we need to make sure."

"Why?"

Shu looked up at Dom. He was focused on her, awaiting a response. "Do you always ask so many questions?" she asked finally.

"Is that bad? I want to learn."

"No," said Shu, "it's not bad. The records I found suggest that no one has lived here for a long, long time. There could be a few remaining settlers, though. I just want to be sure."

"How can you teach me if you won't answer my questions?" asked Dom. Again, he was focused intently on Shu. She turned and caught his gaze.

"I will," she said. "But you must learn other things first."

Dom continued to stare. "Shu, you have to trust me, don't you? How can you teach me if you don't trust me? What happened to him?"

His words flowed into her head. She could see only his eyes. His mouth didn't seem to move.

"He accessed the main data panel," she said in a quiet monotone. "I'm sure he saw things."

Dom's unblinking stare continued. "Like what?" he said in a deeper voice.

"Things he wasn't supposed to see. He may have overloaded his mind." Her voice drifted as her head swayed slightly. Dom looked away and studied Min.

"Will he die?"

Shu closed her eyes and then forced them back open. "I . . .don't know."

"Do-omm!" It was Cap calling from near the stairway. "Where are you?"

Dom rose and looked in that direction, clearly annoyed. "Over here!" he answered finally. Once again, Shu rubbed her face with her hands. Min still didn't move.

Cap was soon at the doorway. Shu stood up but stumbled slightly.

"Shu?" said Cap, taking her elbow. "Are you hurt?"

She took a deep breath. "N-no. I'm fine. Just tired from all this activity." She looked over at Dom.

"What happened to Min?" asked Cap.

"His illness is getting worse," said Shu with a quick glance at Dom. For a moment, it appeared as if the boy smiled at her. "He has been coughing a ot more. He was able to do the repairs I needed though. I think the effort overtaxed him."

"So, what now?" asked Cap.

"We need to canvass the settlement before we can leave," said Shu. "We need to make sure there isn't anyone here. I don't think there will be."

"Why not?"

Shu pursed her lips. "I just don't."

Cap frowned but said nothing.

"Where are the others?" asked Dom.

"They will be along shortly," said Cap. "The Charges were eager to get off that landing. They weren't too far behind me on the stairway."

"Divide them up into groups once they arrive," said Shu. "I will take one group to the morningside. Cap, you take Dom and look eveningside."

"You aren't taking me with you?" asked Dom, his eyes narrowing.

"Dom, listen!" scolded Cap. "You must learn to listen to her. She will be your teacher soon."

Dom was almost entirely disinterested in Cap's advice.

"I want you to go with Cap. I have a private matter to discuss with May."

"What kind of private matter?" asked Dom.

Cap hesitated to scold Dom, for he was also curious about this. "Dom! She said it was private." He looked back at Shu. "I'm sure we will find out eventually. What about Min?"

"We can put him in the pyramid where we spent the night," said Shu. "I'm sure Lin won't mind watching him."

"No, I'm sure she won't, either," agreed Cap. Cap lightly patted Min's cheek. "You awake?" Min made no response. "Well," said Cap, "I guess I'll be the one to move him from here." He put one arm under the crook of Min's legs and scooped him up in a cradle carry. "He's not too heavy," Cap noted.

Shu noted a slow grim creeping up on Dom's face.

The group walked back to the stairway. The others were just making it to the top. Pol clutched Joba carefully. Despite the harrowing night and current conditions, the baby babbled with contentment. Shu explained the plan to everyone. They would separate into two groups. One group would be comprised of May, Shu and two Charges just into adolescence. Mac was a tall, well-built boy with a quiet, observant manner. Lise wore her hair in a long braid down the center of her back. Both she and Mac were exceptionally strong and were generally placed near the center of their canoe while rowing. They walked off towards one side of the settlement. Cap, Dom, Lin and another Charge, a young boy named Frell, headed in the opposite direction. Pol and Joba joined the second group.

Cap delivered Min to the pyramid where they had slept the night before. Lin restarted the fire barrels. Pol and her baby sat down near one of them and Pol began singing to her son under her breath. Frell sat down next to them.

"We won't be gone long," said Cap. "I'm not sure what you can do for him," he said glancing at Min. "Just keep him warm. Frell, you can stay here if you'd like." The boy nodded his head, content to listen to Pol's song.

"I'll do my best," said Lin.

"Be careful, Lin," said Dom. She watched him carefully for a moment before kneeling down next to Min. Cap and Dom then exited the pyramid to join their group of Charges.

Eve sat on her cushion, unable to sleep. The roar of the storm had easily bullied its way into their quarters. She got up and walked over to the door. Visibility outside was non-existent. It was as if the pyramid stood beneath a giant waterfall. She couldn't recall ever having seen it rain so.

Sol and Jack were awake as well. Sol joined her at the door.

"Not very conducive for sleep is it?" he asked.

A brief flash of lightning allowed them to better appreciate the nature of the raging torrent. "Quite a storm," Eve said matter-of-factly. She had never been comfortable with small talk. It was pointless most of the time.

"You are wondering if he . . . . .if they, are out in this, aren't you?"

"How can they not be?" she asked. "Aren't you?"

Sol folded his arms, continuing his consideration of the storm. "I have complete confidence that Min will find a way to keep all of them safe," he said finally. "And I know you have a high degree of confidence in him as well."

"Of course I do," said Eve, perhaps a bit too defensively. "I do," she continued, softening her tone. "But can't I still worry?"

"Absolutely," said Sol, placing a comforting arm around her shoulder. "But it would be just like Min to be in the middle of this somewhere, dry as dust." Sol smiled at the thought.

Eve half-heartedly returned his hug and then moved away from the door. She sat back down on her cushions and began rearranging her covers.

"How early are we starting tomorrow?" asked Jack.

Sol also returned to his cushion. "I say we go at first light, or before even. I'm sure Bal will try to tag us with escorts again."

"Good idea," said Eve. "We can't let that happen tomorrow. It is important that the Guard feels comfortable talking to us. If a bunch of other Guards are there, that isn't likely."

Sol rested his head on his pillow. The storm continued to rumble outside. "Dry as dust," he offered quietly. "I'm certain of it."

Cap and Dom walked eveningsidedly, looking for signs of recent habitation. A few of the pyramids had vines climbing up their faces. Several fire barrels still stood at the corners of the pyramids, although a few of them had long cracks in their sides.

As the pyramids gave way to a vast open area, they saw remnants of heavy farm implements on the ground. Large wooden plows, carts, and the remains of clay pots were strewn about. The land itself was overgrown with brightly-colored weeds and clover. In the distance, they could see a broad stand of very tall trees.

"Let's keep going," said Cap.

"There isn't anyone here," replied Dom.

"Probably not, but you never know what we might find." Dom trailed along slowly behind his Rearer.

As they entered the tree stand, it became noticeably darker. The trees formed a thick canopy above them that blocked out the meager light that penetrated the cloud cover. Ahead they could hear a faint roaring sound repeating at regular intervals.

"What's that?" asked Dom.

Cap stopped for a moment and listened. "I'm not sure. Let's go look." Cap picked up his pace and rushed towards the tree line. Dom easily kept up.

As they neared the edge of the tree stand, the roar grew louder. When the trees finally parted, they could see a vast body of blue water that stretched as far as they could see eveningsidedly. Waves were crashing onto a dark brown beach immediately in front of them. The beach extended to the horizon both heartside and emptyside.

Cap stood silently, his mouth wide open.

"Is it another lake?" asked Dom.

"I don't know," Cap said breathlessly. It's....enormous." He began running across the beach towards the water.

Cap stopped once an incoming wave covered his feet. He kicked at the water and bent over so he could better see the weeds and shells that washed ashore. Dom looked at it too, although with much less enthusiasm. He reached down and put his hand in the water.

"It's just water," said Dom.

Cap dipped his hand in the water and took a slow drink. He immediately spat it back out. "It's foul!" he declared. Dom also scooped up some water in his hands. Once the water passed his lips, he grimaced.

"What is that?" he asked.

"I'm not sure. How could the people who lived here use such water?"

Dom looked out at the horizon. "Maybe that's why they left," he offered.

Cap spat again, trying to clear his mouth of the taste. "You could be right," he said. "Let's walk this way," he said, pointing heartside.

They walked back past the reach of the incoming waves and started down the beach. In the distance, they could see a steep rise at the far edge of the tree stand. Once they reached its foot, they found a clear path up the slope. "Maybe we will get a better view up there," suggested Cap. He started up the path with Dom in pursuit.

Cap had underestimated the length and slope of the rise. By the time he reached the top, he was soaked with sweat. Dom stood next to him, breathing easily..

"Are you well?" asked Dom.

Cap was still catching his breath. "You aren't . . . .tired?" he asked.

"I was, but I think I'm well now," he replied.

The rise had brought them up above the canopy. They had an excellent view of the entire settlement area. Back to the morningside were the pyramids. Just eveningsidedly, they could see the old agricultural area they had walked through on their way to the beach. To the emptyside, they saw a tremendous stone wall. It ran all the way into the blue water and extended to the cliff overlooking the lake. Turning back to the heartside, they saw a similar structure.

"Why did they use walls to keep people in?" asked Dom.

"Not to keep people in," Cap said finally. "But to keep them out."

"Who?"

Cap knelt down next to Dom. "They must have been built to prevent the Hek from coming into the settlement," Cap offered.

"Because they are dangerous."

He looked at the wall in the distance. "They are very dangerous. They would hurt us if they could."

"How do you know? Have they ever hurt you?"

"The Chroniclers have taught us that. And the Journeyers have taught them."

Dom was fascinated. "Do the Journeyers teach the Chroniclers everything?"

Cap shrugged. "I don't know. Maybe that is something you will learn from Shu."

"And the Chroniclers make the law?"

"It has already been made," said Cap. "The Chroniclers are the keepers of the law. They tell us what it is."

"And you do what the law says?"

"Yes. The law has served our settlement for many, many ellipses. A few may disagree with some of the laws, but the wellbeing of the settlement is what is most important." Dom turned away from Cap and pretended to study the other distant wall. He placed his hand over his mouth to conceal a broad smile. "Dom," said Cap quietly, placing a hand on the boy's shoulder. "You are finally demonstrating interests beyond yourself. I knew this day would come and I'm glad I got to see it. You won't be a little boy for much longer. I know you are upset because May and I have to go. Don't be. We will be fine. And you are going to become a Chronicler. I know you will do an outstanding job."

Dom turned around, his face now a model of contained grief. "I plan on doing my very best," he said in a low voice. "A lot depends on it."

CHAPTER 2

The Journeyers arose well before any hint of dawn. The darkness outside was almost complete. A few fading fire barrels provided a minimum amount of light as the group made their way through the narrow alleys in between the pyramids. Once they reached the structures closest to the beach, they all stopped and huddled next to a corner of a small pyramid.

"What do we say if we get caught?" asked Jack.

"'Caught'?, replied Sol. "We aren't doing anything wrong."

"It feels wrong," whispered Eve.

"Well, it isn't," said Sol. "There is no reason at all why we shouldn't be able to stroll around the island wherever we want to."

"Do you think Bal will agree with you?" asked Jack.

"Bal. . . .." grunted Sol, making no effort to disguise his contempt. "He can . . . . ."

"Shhh!" hissed Eve. "Someone is coming." The three of them shrank against the stone of the building. They could hear the sound of people talking and footfalls that were approaching their position. They froze and waited.

A group of seven Umae passed nearby, apparently oblivious to their presence. Four were easily carrying a canoe on their shoulders. A red-hooded Chronicler attended them along with two Guards. They walked out onto the sand, stopping well short of the water. The Chronicler spoke briefly with them before moving off down the beach. The canoe-bearers set the boat down near the edge of the lake. The two Guards split up and stood at either end of the group of workers.

"Is either of them him?" asked Eve.

Jack groaned. "I can't say. It is so hard to tell them apart even in the best conditions. Only one sure way to find out." Jack abruptly stood up and began walking towards the men. Eve made a belated attempt to snag him by his collar, but missed. She and Sol then started after him.

Jack waved a greeting at one of the workers who happened to look up and notice his approach. "Well," said the man, "such a surprise! The Journeyers have arisen early!"

The Guards were paying attention but didn't appear overly concerned about his arrival. Jack looked back and saw Sol and Eve hurrying to catch up.

"We don't get to spend a lot of time here on Uma," said Jack. "It is good to be able to walk around a bit and see what is going on."

The worker gestured at the canoe. "Well, we are boat wrights, although you probably knew that. Feel free to stay and watch. We are going to test the worthiness of this canoe."

"Thank you," said Jack. "We may do that."

One of the Guards walked over to where Jack was speaking to the worker. He stopped and folded his thick arms across his chest. It was not Max.

"Do you need something?" he asked in the standard, near-monotone voice employed by the Guards.

"No, not really. We were just tired of staying in our pyramid."

The Guard turned slowly towards Eve and Sol before looking back at Jack. "Does Bal know you are here?"

Jack held out his hands. "Is he supposed to? Are we supposed to tell him where we are?"

The large man frowned and turned towards the other Guard. "Max, come here." The second Guard began walking in their direction.

"Is there a problem?" asked Max. He saw Jack and for a brief instant Jack thought he noted a faint smile on the Guard's lips. His shirt bore the same spear-shaped insignia they had seen the rotation before.

"Can they be here without someone from the Hall?" asked the first Guard.

"We are from the Hall," said Max. The first Guard appeared perplexed by Max's response. "I will speak with them," said Max. "I'm sure there will be no problems. Stay with the boat wrights."

The first Guard turned and walked back to his post near the boat wrights. Once he was a fair distance away, Jack leaned slightly closer to Max. "I need to talk to you."

Max stood passively. "Aren't you?"

"Well, yes. But I need to. . . . . ask you some things."

"I see. Perhaps we could start walking back to your quarters?"

"Yes," said Jack. "That would be fine."

Max waved towards the first Guard. "They are returning to their quarters. I will accompany them. I will return after that." The first Guard waved back. They turned and started walking back towards the island's habitation area. Once they reached the spot where the Journeyers had tried to conceal themselves earlier, they stopped.

Jack and Sol looked around anxiously.

"Is something wrong?" asked Max.

"No," said Sol. "I don't think so." He turned towards Jack. "I'm not sure how to ask what I need to ask."

Max also looked at Jack. "Are you talking to him or to me?"

"You," interjected Eve. "He's talking to you. Let me ask." She paused to wet her lips. "Do you know why you are so . . . . .big?"

She wasn't sure if Max had heard her question. He stood there for a moment, looking at her blankly.

"Yes," he said finally. "You ask about the powder."

Sol lowered his gaze and closed his eyes tightly. "Yes," he said quietly. "The powder."

"How often do you take it?" asked Jack.

"It is provided every morning," said Max. "To all of the Guards."

"How long . . . have you been taking it?" asked Sol.

"I don't. Not anymore."

Sol perked up. "You . . . .don't? Why not?"

"It clouded my mind, made things hard. I couldn't enjoy my plants any more. I stopped."

Sol swallowed and looked up at him. "You know. . . . . ." he began uncertainly.

"Yes," said Max, cutting him off. "I know what happens if you stop. They told us. I stopped anyway."

"On your own?" asked Sol.

"It was an easy decision for me. I don't believe the other Guards even think about it anymore."

"Do the Chroniclers know that you stopped?" asked Eve.

"No, I don't think so. If they do, they have done nothing in response."

Sol patted Max on his shoulder. "I'm . . . .sorry." It was all he could do to face the larger man.

"I'm not," said Max. "I am content. Do not be sorry for me."

"Not for you then. . . ." he replied somberly.

"I should go," said the Guard. "Please return to your quarters, at least for a while. I think Bal will be visiting you soon."

"Not surprising," commented Eve. Without another word, Max lumbered off towards the beach. Eve and Jack turned towards their pyramid, leaving Sol to watch the huge Guard round a nearby corner and disappear from view.

May and Shu walked towards the heartside of the settlement with Mac and Lise. They saw no signs of recent habitation. Nothing that would have been easily bearable was left behind by the residents of the Land Bridge. Shu periodically stuck her head inside some of the pyramids only to have her angst about the settlement's emptiness reinforced. She said very little.

May was fascinated by the settlement, despite its lack of inhabitants. The pyramids were built exactly like those on Atla. The seams between the blocks were still almost impossible to see unless one was right next to the structure. The heavy fire barrels were the same except they were more darkly colored. It was easy for May to imagine that she was back home.

"It looks like Atla here," noted Lise. Mac was taking everything in but remained silent. "What do you think Mac?" she asked, taking his arm.

Mac's face quickly turned a deep red as he freed himself from Lise. He glanced at Shu and May to see if they had noticed. "Yes, sure," he said quietly.

As they reached the perimeter of the pyramids, they could hear the roar of rushing waters. As they reached the top of a low rise, they could see a borderless stretch of blue water in the distance. May squinted at the horizon, trying to see some hint of land.

"Another lake?" she asked Shu.

Shu stared, enthralled by the expanse of water. "No. It is the sea," she said without enthusiasm.

"The sea?" asked May uncertainly.

"Like the lake," said Shu, "but much larger."

Without comment, May began walking towards the water. "Lise, you and Mac are to remain here," said Shu firmly. "May and I will return soon. You will be safe here." Her tone was not necessary. The two Wards stopped immediately upon hearing her order and Lise moved to stand right next to Mac, a smile blooming on her face. The tall young man looked down at his feet but didn't move away.

The two women walked through the abandoned farmland in between them and the ocean. The ground was now littered with thick, wild grasses and thistle plants. They picked along carefully, cautious of any thorn bushes or brambles. Soon, they reached the edge of a rocky rise overlooking a narrow beach. Heartside, they saw an enormous wall that crawled from the sea and extended into the settlement itself.

"What is that for?" May asked.

Shu paused. "It was for protection," she replied.

"From what?"

"From the Hek. The lake protects us. The wall protected the Land Bridge."

May tried to quiet her anger.

"So, all of those people you exiled," said May, her voice rising, "they are all dead now?

Shu turned towards the water. "We don't know. Anything is possible."

"Anything?!?" screeched May. "The island.... this place... is designed to keep us safe from them." She spat on the ground. "You are sending us to die, and you won't even tell us why. What could happen that would be so terrible if we just went back and taught the Wards, and . . . .lived?!?" May's anger transformed into frustration and overcame her. She turned away from Shu, determined not to let Shu see her cry. Shu waited. She had no answers to offer. May composed herself, but still refused to face her.

"I cannot answer that," said Shu quietly. "But I can offer you something. Bal believes it would be wise for the Chronicler Guards to go to the mainland, seek out the Hek, and destroy them. He has been making preparations."

May was overwhelmed by this revelation. "But . . . .kill them? That is forbidden! The Protocols...."

Shu raised a quick hand, cutting her off. "If we do not act, they could use the barge you lost to come to Atla. Bal believes it would be best to take the fight to them."

"And you agree?" asked May.

Shu hesitated. "Bal claims to have found authority within the Protocols for such action. Besides," she continued in a firmer tone, "you helped create this crisis. It would not seem to be your place to criticize our response."

May slowly turned towards her. "So," she began quietly, "suppose I just decide not to go? This is madness! You mock our laws simply because you see fit. I could just tell Cap and the Wards to take us all back to Atla and they would. And you and your Guards couldn't stop us from telling everyone all that we've learned. Tell me, Shu, what could you do about that? What do you think would happen once every Atlan knows what I know?" Her pale face was beginning to glow.

Shu was unmoved. "You would still be eventually exiled. As would Dom." She paused to allow her words to sink in.

May's glow was consumed in a fiery blaze. "But he is to become a Chronicler!" declared May. Shu remained silent. "You . . . .wouldn't!" gasped May finally.

"I do what I must," said Shu. "Such would be a consequence of your choice, not mine. Perhaps you should abandon your plan. I have offered you knowledge of our intentions as a gift, not because I am required to do so. You might want to consider how best to use it to prolong your life."

May turned again, her body trembling with anger. With a deep breath, she stalked off away from the beach, roughly pushing Shu aside with her shoulder. Shu gathered herself as May walked off into the tall grass. She then sat down and watched as the waves rolled up on the beach in the distance.

As Jack, Sol, and Eve entered their pyramid, they found Bal and four Guards waiting for them. Eve took a nervous step behind the two men. "Out early?" asked Bal warmly. "Not a lot going on this time of day."

Sol walked over to his cushion and sat down. "We couldn't sleep. We are anxious for Min and the others to return."

"They should be back by tomorrow," offered Bal. "Cap's rowers are very efficient. Min couldn't be in better hands."

"He is not well," explained Sol. "I would prefer that he be in ***my*** hands."

Bal sat down near Sol. "Of course. But," he continued, "you weren't able to cure him, were you?" Bal's theatrical attempt at concern wasn't lost on the Life Agent.

"No," said Sol. "He isn't curable."

"Why not?"

Sol stared at Bal. "What do you mean, 'why not'?"

"His illness exceeds even the Journeyers' ability to remedy?"

Sol looked over at Jack and Eve who were still near the entry. "He has had this illness for some time," said Sol, turning back towards Bal. "There is a limit to the effectiveness of my treatments."

"He is going to die?"

"No," replied Sol in a harder tone. "We will all die eventually. But so long as he doesn't enter repose again, he should live another 20 ellipses or so."

"So," said Bal, studying a bowl of foodstuffs, "he's going to the moon. What do you suppose he will be doing there?"

"He will go to the Citadel," Jack said. "I was supposed to go with him, but I understand that isn't going to happen now."

"Why would he need you there?" asked Bal. "Isn't he the real technical expert?"

"He is. It is a tradition for a Technical Agent to take his or her replacement to the Citadel. It is the centerpiece of all of our technology." Bal folded his hands in front of him, opting not to eat anything out of the bowl.

"Why can't we talk to him?" interjected Eve. "Explain that."

Bal took a long, deep breath. "I don't have to explain anything," he said coolly. "You keep forgetting that."

"If he is to be exiled to the moon, how do you expect him to get there?" Eve asked.

"I don't follow you?"

"Ever flown a Journeycraft, Bal?" demanded Jack. "If he goes, it will have to be by shuttlecraft. One of us will have to fly the Journeycraft to get him into range. How are you going to stop us from talking to him?"

Bal bristled at Jack's rising satisfaction. "Your ire is misplaced, Jack. Everything is done for the betterment of the Umae. Min will understand."

"Don't count on that," said Jack.

Bal stood up and walked slowly about the room. "So, the boat wrights? Have you taken a special interest?" The three Journeyers looked at one another. "Do you really think anything happens on Atla that we don't know about?" snapped Bal. "Do you?"

Jack's stared at Bal, his fists clenching. The Chronicler stood safely next to one of the Guards.

"Why do you spy on us?" asked Eve. "We simply wanted to walk amongst our people."

"It isn't 'spying'," said Bal. "That word sounds so secretive. But you three, you have been secretive, haven't you?"

"We only wish to understand what is happening," pled Eve. "Something is happening, isn't it?"

Bal folded his arms in front of him, hiding his hands in the wide sleeves of his red robe. "What is happening is this. Once Min returns, he is going to the moon. You and the Cap's Wards are going . . . to wherever it is you are going. Have you found Haven yet? Isn't that what you are supposed to be doing?"

"Yes, and we will find it," said Jack defiantly.

"Excellent," said Bal as he started towards the exit. "The sooner the better."

The Wards began loading the boat for the return trip to Atla. Cap had essentially carried Min down the stairway. The Journeyer barely moved and had merely moaned and grunted as he was transported back to the landing. The Wards regarded him with various degrees of curiosity and concern.

"Are we ready yet?" asked Cap. He was out of breath and his face was dripping with sweat. He would have gladly welcomed a rain shower, but none seemed forthcoming.

May stood silently, watching the Wards finish their preparations. Shu sat in the middle of the boat, her head lowered.

"I think we have everything," said Lin. "Everything is still rather wet. We are in good shape with food though."

Once everyone was aboard, the Wards quickly brought the boat about and began rowing morningsidedly. It was still early in the day, and a thin, wispy mist rose from the lake's surface. The sky was a solid, light gray. The conditions for rowing were nearly perfect.

May shed her lethargy and summoned the Wards to a brisk pace. Despite their harrowing night in the storm, they had recovered enough the day before to answer her demands. The boat cut a sharp trail through the water. By midday, everyone on the boat was warily eyeing the cliff face searching for any possible sign of the Hek.

May's calls bounded off the cliffs, echoing back at them. Min stirred briefly and opened his eyes. He did not attempt to sit up or speak. Lin carefully monitored his condition, frowning each time he would close his eyes.

By early evening, they had reached the narrow, rocky beach where they had camped before. It was the same beach where the Hek had loomed down at them from atop the cliff.

"We can't stay out here on the water," noted Cap as he looked down at Min. "He's going to need a fire. Let's take it in, May." Without waiting for her formal command, the Wards turned the boat and drove it towards the shore. Once the boat grounded on the shallow bottom, the Wards waited for the adults to step into the water before slowly disembarking and towing it onto the beach. Each of them nervously studied the top of the cliff. The absence of anything unusual didn't bring them any comfort.

With the boat secured, Cap carried Min to a spot free of the small rocks that littered most of the beach and laid him down. Lin immediately attended him, standing ready with food and water in the event he regained consciousness. The Wards relaxed a bit and settled in to eat and rest their tired bodies.

"Once you have finished eating," said Cap, "prepare the leantos. We will sleep here tonight."

The Wards muttered amongst themselves. In turn, they each stared up the face of the cliff.

"It will be fine," said Shu. "Even if they come back, they have no way to get down."

"How do you know that?" snapped May.

"May?" Cap's tone was a hybrid of shock and reprise.

"Well, it isn't like we have looked around very much," said May unapologetically. "What if they can get down here?"

Shu approached May and Cap and lowered her voice. "May, you are frightening the Wards for no reason. Please don't do this."

"No reason?" said May. "Again, how do you know?"

Shu stood up straight and lifted her chin. "We are staying here. There will be no more discussion." She then strode off towards her pack.

May was fuming. "May, I know you don't like her," said Cap, "but she is the authority. I think we will be fine."

May looked up at Cap and bit her lip. Her eyes were wet with tears that she wouldn't acknowledge. He reached out and pulled her to him.

"I think I understand now," he said quietly. "This is about Dom, and the others. It is hard, I know that."

She responded by pressing her cheek against his shoulder. "Not now," she whispered. "They aren't going to see this."

"No, of course not," he said, cupping the back of her head in his hand. "We can talk more after our leanto is set up and the others are sleeping."

May remained pressed against him for a moment before pulling away and heading for the boat to get their packs. Cap watched her before going to check on Min. He was still lying on the ground. Lin was seated next to him.

"How is he doing?" asked Cap. Lin looked down at Min, obviously concerned.

"I can't tell," she said. "He doesn't move much. It sounded like he was trying to talk a couple of times, but I couldn't understand his words. I hope the other Journeyers can help him when we get back."

Cap knelt down next to Min. "I'm sure they can," he said, trying to sound confident. Min was taking regular, shallow breaths, but remained almost perfectly still.

"Can he die?" asked Lin. She felt guilty at her inability to prevent the question from escaping her thoughts.

Cap hadn't thought of that possibility. "I don't know. He looks rather frail."

Lin reached out and touched Min's forehead. "I know. He just seems so much . . . .beyond that."

"You will be as they are," said Cap. "You will help them save the Umae."

The enormity of her new position hadn't completely registered with Lin yet. In her excitement over the prospect of traveling in space and learning the technology of the Journeyers, she had forgotten their role. "What if . . . . .I can't?" Cap caught a glimpse of the insecure, frightened little girl he had once known. The inquisitive, determined young woman she had become now shrank at the task ahead of her.

"You can," he said, lightly taking her chin in his hand and guiding her eyes to his. "If it can be done, you can do it. Remember all of the times when you doubted yourself, only to defeat those doubts. This is no different, despite what you might think. Of all of my Wards, if I had to place my life in the hands of just one........"

Lin was heartened by Cap's consolation. But just as she felt encouragement welling inside of her, his words recalled his reality. "Your life . . . ." she replied, wrapping her arms around his neck. She sobbed softly, her body trembling.

"Shhhhhhh….." whispered Cap, returning her embrace. "Listen to me," he said softly. "Everything is a slow transition, remember? Even if May and I weren't staying behind, you would still be going into space. The best we can do is offer you wings. You can honor us by choosing to use them."

Lin sniffled and pulled way. She wiped the tears from her cheeks and tried to force a smile. "I will. I promise."

The Wards quickly raised camp, a task for which repetition had brought them efficiency. The storm from the prior day had drained the clouds. The sky was dark and seamless, but gave no hint of additional precipitation.

Everyone retired to their leantos. Lin volunteered to stay with Min. Cap carried him to his cushion where she tried to make him comfortable. He remained unconscious. His breaths were shallow and slow, but his mumblings had ceased.

May crawled into her leanto and laid her head back on her cushion. Soon, Cap joined her.

"Are you all right?" he asked quietly. He arranged his cushion next to hers and tried to settle in.

"No," she said finally. "How could I be?"

Cap turned to face her. "Afraid? Angry? Both?"

Ordinarily, the ease with which he read her feelings was a source of comfort to her. Now, for some reason, she found his ability to be a little disconcerting.

"Yes," she answered. "Puzzled. I wish I could understand it all." Shu's threat was still fresh. Cap couldn't know of it. She was afraid of how he might react.

Cap turned over on his stomach and watched as some of the Wards made their final preparations for the night. "I don't understand it either."

May positioned herself to watch the same group of Wards. "We have done well with them, haven't we?" she said with a smile. "I think they are as ready for whatever they will face as they can be."

"I hope so. I never imagined they would all be going into space. Do you think we would have reared them any differently had we have known?"

"I don't see what difference it would have made," May said finally. "We don't know anything about what they will be doing. At best, we would have tried to make them inquisitive, assertive and considerate. But we did that anyway."

"Yes, I guess that is true. How are you with . . . .Dom?"

She averted his gaze. He noticed that her lower lip was trembling slightly. "I wish . . . . .well, I don't know," she said, struggling with the words.

"What?"

"I was going to say that I wish we would have known long ago that this would happen, but then I decided that I'm not as sure about that."

He reached out and brushed her cheek with his hand. "He's a good boy. I know he can be headstrong, but from what I understand that will serve him well as a Chronicler."

May closed her eyes and held his hand against her cheek. "And if he weren't going to become a Chronicler……"

"Yes, he would be coming with us," concluded Cap. "Neither of us wants that."

"No, of course not."

Cap sat up and let out a long sigh. "It just occurred to me. This time tomorrow, we will be . . . .out there."

May opened her eyes. "So will Pol and her baby. I hope she will come with us."

"Why wouldn't she?"

The distance in May's eyes grew as she considered his question. "I don't know," she said finally. "She hasn't said much since we've been out here."

"We will convince her. We can find a safe place, I'm sure of it. I can build a boat. Maybe we can go back to the Land Bridge."

She smiled warmly at Cap. For all the ellipses they had known one another, he had always been an optimist. He was determined and confident there wasn't anything he couldn't do. "I think she will for her baby's sake," May offered.

Cap laid his head back down on his cushion. "We should try to sleep. We have an interesting day ahead of us tomorrow."

May watched him as he closed his eyes. She would tell Cap about Bal's plan to attack the Hek later. It would just raise too many questions now, questions she couldn't answer. The sounds from the Wards were quieting down.

She knew she wouldn't be able to sleep at all. She turned over on her back and stared at the top of the leanto, thinking about her little boy.

The anxious insomnia experienced by most of the Wards turned out to be unwarranted. The night passed without incident and the clouds continued to withhold any additional rain. Once the faint rose of dawn could be seen in the morningside sky, the group was up and readying themselves for departure.

Min had regained consciousness. When he did, he saw Lin standing over him, smiling at his apparent improvement. He could sit up on his own but was still very weak. He didn't try to speak much. Lin brought him some water and a couple of pieces of fruit, which he slowly consumed.

Pol stood off to the side, nursing Joba as the Wards stowed the leantos and their other equipment on the boat. Cap and May took Dom aside, speaking with him privately.

"Our new lives begin today," said Cap, forcing a smile. "I know you will serve well as a Chronicler. Be sure and listen to Shu, learn what she has to teach you. You will be in a very important position. Our people will count on you for a great deal."

Dom followed Cap's words but offered no reply.

"Dom," said May. Her voice cracked badly, so she reached out to embrace him. Although he didn't return her embrace, Dom didn't do anything to resist. "I don't want you to worry about us," she said, looking him in the eye. She ran her hand through his cream-colored hair. "We will all be fine."

Dom looked back and forth at the pair of Rearers. "We aren't going to see each other again, are we?" His voice contained the barest hint of emotion.

May closed her eyes and looked away for a moment.

"No," said Cap. "We aren't."

"Is that going to bother you?" Dom asked May.

May nodded her head slowly and pulled him back into her arms. "Yes . . ." she whispered as she started to shake. "Very, very much . . . . ."

Cap wrapped his arms around both of them. If he pulled them both close enough, maybe all of this would change. Maybe they could go back, and he and May could continue to rear their Charges, to rear Dom. But no. He finally released them and stepped away. "The day is not over yet," he said. "It looks as if the boat is ready. We should board." The three of them walked to the boat and assumed their customary positions. May clung to

Dom's limp hand, reluctant to release it. But then she let go and it dropped to his side while he coolly studied her actions. She took a moment to look at the cliff face one more time before beginning her call to the Wards. The boat slowly pulled away from the rocky beach and slid back out onto the surface of the lake.

The air was still and the water's surface was slowly becoming enshrouded in mist. May's cadence was steady, but without emotion. She was able to direct the crew through habit, as her thoughts were elsewhere. Cap tried to distract himself by thinking about what they would do once their exile actually began. He had been so busy with his other duties these last few rotations that he hadn't settled on a definite plan of action.

By the middle of the afternoon, they were within sight of the beach where they had encountered the Hek a few rotations before. May directed them to turn the boat and row towards shore.

The Wards were reluctant to take the boat all the way in. They allowed it to drift along, still some distance from the beach. Their apprehension created an unblinking focus on the top of the rise. "We need to land," said Shu. The Wards turned and look back at May. She nodded, and they resumed rowing. Soon, the boat's keel was grounded on the sandy shore, so Cap and the Wards got out and pulled it the rest of the way in.

"Are we going to camp here?" asked Lin.

"No," said Shu firmly. "We can still make it back to the island by nightfall. The signal drums can guide us. The information I have is important." She looked down at Min who was sprawled on the floor of the boat. "And he requires attention that we can't provide."

The realization of Shu's pronouncement hit Lin hard. She turned and looked helplessly at Cap and May. May leapt from her perch at the back of the boat and ran to her. Both women sobbed uncontrollably as they fiercely embraced. Cap walked slowly over to them and wrapped his arms about them. The other Wards made their way over until all of them were huddled in a large, weeping mass. Dom maintained his spot in the front of the boat.

"Listen . . . ." croaked Cap. "Listen to me," he repeated, trying to sound more authoritative. The Wards did their best to settle down and listen. "I can't believe that another pair of Rearers has ever had the honor of seeing so many of their Wards become Journeyers. I cannot put into words how proud of all of you we both are. This should not be a time for sadness. It is a time for transition. Now," he continued, his eyes welling, "be the ***ones***! Be the ones who find Haven. You are all eagles that May and I now release for our people. Soar. Soar for them and for yourselves."

The Wards surged forward, each trying to grasp a part of their Rearers one last time. Cap pulled their hands to his lips and tried to wipe away as many of their tears as he could. May bulled her way through the group, seizing each Ward in a tight bear hug and kissing them on their tear-stained cheeks. The Wards started hesitantly moving away from them, each secretly hoping that Shu would change her mind and tell everyone to reboard.

As the group cleared, Cap and May saw Dom standing in the boat. "Dom?" called Cap, gesturing. Dom slowly hopped out of the boat and walked over to where they stood. May watched his approach, attempting to etch each step into her memory. As he neared, what few tears she had been able to spare from the Wards rolled down her face. She knelt down, seized him by the shoulders and pressed her cheek against his chest.

"Don't look back, Dom," said Cap. "Eyes forward. Heart forward. Remember what we have tried to teach you. Our people will remember you, I know it."

"Yes, you are right about that," he said quietly.

He stepped back, watching May. She stood directly in front of him, staring into his eyes. She reached out and caressed his cheek. "You are my good boy," she said in a trembling voice. I will never forget you."

"You should go," he said in a low voice. May immediately took a couple of short steps back. Dom turned and started towards the boat.

Pol stood by the gear that had been unloaded for the four of them, holding Joba tightly. Cap and May joined her and Cap made a cursory check of what they had to work with.

"Lin!" called May in a firm voice. Near the boat, Lin turned around and looked back at her Rearer. "You take the call," May directed. Lin tried to tear her eyes away as her tears returned. She wiped them away and moved to the stern of the boat, sitting down in May's customary position.

The other Wards pushed the canoe back into the lake. It drifted slowly backwards as the crew took one last, long look at the pair who had given them so much for so long. Then, Lin called them to bring the boat about, and they began propelling it back out into the lake. On the shore, Cap, May, and Pol watched as the boat slowly slid towards the horizon before disappearing into the mist.

CHAPTER 3

Jack, Eve and Sol spent the morning waiting around the docks. It was the earliest time that the return of Min's group could reasonably be expected. The Journeyers had attempted to distract themselves by providing various acts of assistance to the Atlans, but the anticipation of their Command Agent's return kept them from straying far from the shoreline for very long.

The fog atop the water's surface had been thick all morning. Jack had been tempted to employ a bio scanner to track the boat's approach, but Eve had convinced him that such was not a good idea given how astute Bal had been at discovering their activities. They were limited to simply staring out into the thick mist, their eyes frequently tricking them into seeing things that were not there.

The day passed without incident. The four shipwrights they had seen that morning were still at work on their canoe. Apparently, something about the boat wasn't just right, and the workers had made several trips back and forth to the Shipwrights' Hall in an effort to perfect the craft. While a pair of Guards watched the shipwrights work some distance up the beach, the three Journeyers were surprised that Bal apparently had not sent anyone to watch them. As the light began to wane, Bal and a large contingent of Guards marched onto the beach from the pyramid area. The Guards each bore a large fire barrel, further demonstrating the strength provided by Sol's food additive. Each barrel was then filled with lengths of dry wood and ignited. There were a dozen of them, all spaced along the beach in roughly equal intervals near the docks. As there was still no rain, the flames burned high and bright, creating a line of beacons along the edge of the island. A dozen Umae followed behind the Guards rolling large wooden drums along the ground. As soon as the fires were lit, they each righted their drums and began rhythmically pounding a beat that rolled out into the darkness.

"Well, if they are coming tonight, they shouldn't have any trouble finding us," offered Eve.

"But why so many Guards?" asked Jack. "I counted twelve. They brought the barrels but don't appear to be leaving."

Bal moved from Guard to Guard, speaking with each briefly as he made his way towards the Journeyers.

"So, do you think we will see them tonight?" he asked in his usual annoying, upbeat tone.

Jack stood up and moved to greet Bal. A couple of the Guards watched closely but didn't move.

"Min is always very efficient," he said. "If they listened to him, they should be back tonight."

"If . . . . . .," said Bal. "But we will see."

Jack looked at the long line of barrels, each attended by a Guard. "So, are there enough barrels, what with the drums as well?" he asked.

"The barrels are important," said Bal. "Sound can be difficult to pinpoint on the lake."

Jack turned and looked back at the water. "What happens when they get here?"

"Why, they will be welcomed home," said Bal.

Sol and Eve walked over and joined them. Bal made a quarter bow and lowered his head slightly. "Good evening. Jack and I were just talking about the return. I am rather excited myself."

Eve's reply was cut off by a call from one of the Guards. "There they are!" he bellowed. Everyone turned to look. The long canoe was barely visible at the far edge of the firelight. Eve squinted, trying to make out Min's form in the boat. She finally saw him as the craft began pulling alongside the dock.

"Min disembarks first," snapped Bal. "The others remain on board until he has been removed and taken to his quarters." The Guards began to scramble, clearly familiar with their respective assignments.

"What are you talking about?" protested Jack.

"The other Journeyers will also be restricted to their quarters, now!" said Bal. Four Guards promptly strode towards the Journeyers.

Eve nimbly sidestepped them and ran towards the dock. Jack was also able to elude them. Sol was not. His agility had decayed as his number of ellipses increased. He made no effort to avoid them. Seeing this, Jack gave himself up and a pair of Guards held him by the arms. Eve managed to make it onto the dock before any of the other Guards could cut her off. There were still three Guards on the dock between her and the boat. Two of them moved to block her way. Without hesitation, she dove into the water and disappeared.

The Guards stood on the edge of the dock, looking down into the dark water, unsure as to what they should do. The Wards on the boat had stayed seated, too frightened to react. Shu and Dom sat calmly, apparently disinterested in what was developing around them.

Eve surfaced right next to the canoe. She tried to pull herself up on the edge of the boat, searching for Min. He was right in front of her.

"Min!" she gasped, the cold lake water dripping down her face. "They said I wasn't going to be able to talk to you again." Her speech was broken by breathless emotion. He weakly reached out and took her hand. "You . . .are you hurt?"

Min leaned against the bench next to him.

Eve began trying to pull herself into the boat, but lacked the strength. Mac and Lise were seated near Min and assisted in hauling her roughly into the boat just as the Guards who had been blocking her way earlier arrived on the dock on the boat's opposite side. She threw her arms around Min's chest and held on to him as tightly as she could. She released him, taking his face in her hands. "Min." She had tried planning her words to him for several rotations now, but she hadn't anticipated these circumstances. She pulled his face close to hers, looking deeply into his eyes.

Min coughed. One of the Guards was boarding the canoe, causing it to rock perilously. Min took her by the collar and held her face close to his. He was unable to prevent the Guard from hoisting her in the air and lugging her back to the dock. As he carried her over his shoulder back towards the beach, she continued staring at Min until the Guard was too far down the dock and she could no longer pick Min out of the crowd. Shortly after that, another Guard removed Min from the boat and carried him off as well. Dom and Shu stood up and stepped onto the dock. Shu took Dom by the hand and they walked off in the direction of the pyramids. They passed Bal, neither so much as acknowledging his presence.

Eventually, the Wards were allowed to disembark. Bal gave the remaining Guards directives. They escorted Jack and Sol back to their pyramid and then blocked the door for the rest of the night. The two men were alone in their efforts to determine what had just taken place, as neither Eve nor Min had returned by morning.

Cap stood on the beach, watching as the boat faded into the mist. He remained until he could no longer hear Lin's call, a small part of him still convinced that the canoe would return. May moved near him, taking his arm in hers and leaning up against his side.

"Well.......," he muttered, unable to take his eyes off the lake. "We need to make some decisions."

May looked over at Pol. She was also looking out over the lake. Joba was sleeping, deeply nestled into her layered garments. "We need shelter," said May. "We need to find a safer place."

"It will be too difficult to travel in the dark, especially for her and the baby. I think we will be all right if we stay here until the first light of dawn. I don't think they come here very often."

They.

May's memory of the wailing men, standing atop the rise just above them waving their spears, was refreshed by her surroundings. She turned around and looked at the hill, barely able to see the top due to the darkness. "Why not?" she asked finally.

"Because we had never seen them here before," he offered. "Why would they come here? There isn't anything unusual about this beach. And it isn't as if water is in short supply."

"They saw us here," countered May. "Doesn't that make it unusual?"

Pol began to slowly walk in their direction. "We have no society now," she said listlessly. "Joba and I will wait here for the end."

"No!" protested May. "Don't do that! Don't even think that! We will come up with a plan. You and your baby will come with us."

Pol pulled back a layer of her clothing and smiled at the tiny bald head that was revealed inside. "But . . .where?"

"I know," said Cap. "The best place would be to go back to the Land Bridge, but we don't have a good way to get there. It is really only accessible by boat. I can build one, but it will take a long time. I'll need a sheltered spot to do my work. In the meantime, we will stay inside the Garden."

"The Garden?" May scowled at him. "We can't get in."

Cap reached into his tunic and withdrew the metallic key he had used to access the door before. "Yes, we can."

"You ***stole*** the key?" asked May incredulously.

"I didn't steal it. They never took it back from me when we returned from that last trip. I never mentioned it."

"There is a garden?" asked Pol. "Where?"

Cap pointed in the direction of the rise. "It is that way. It will take us quite some time to get there. I don't think we should risk traveling in the dark. If you fell . . . . ."

Pol unconsciously pulled Joba closer.

"First light then," said May. "Should we camp here?"

"Take out the minimum amount of equipment necessary to stay warm," said Cap. "We need to be ready to go as early as possible. We'll sleep right at the base of the rise."

Pol watched May, seemingly content to follow along with whatever she decided. When May started in the direction of their gear, Pol walked after her. They made a hasty camp at the bottom of the hill. They didn't dare a fire. At Cap's direction, they left most of their equipment stowed away. They each took out a covering and used their packs as pillows. Pol nursed her baby for a bit before cleaning him. She then made sure he was safely wrapped inside her clothing before she settled back and tried to sleep.

Cap had no intentions of sleeping. There was far too much to do, too much to plan. He was angry at himself for not thinking all of this through before, but the reality of exile hadn't really hit him until he saw the boat sailing off onto the lake. He sat with his arms resting on his knees, slightly rocking back and forth. May watched him for a long time before she managed to drift off.

Cap awakened with a start. It was pitch black. His eyes needed time to adjust. A short ways away, he could hear Joba crying and Pol trying to sooth him.

"What is wrong?" asked May.

"I . . .I don't know," Pol said nervously. "He woke up and started crying. I tried to nurse him, but he wasn't interested."

Joba opened his mouth wide, took a deep breath, and let loose with a bellow that belied his tiny size.

"Shhhhhhh……." Pol tried rocking him and patting his head. He continued to bawl.

"Let me take a look," said May. She leaned down as close as she could to get a better look. "There . . . .there . . . .," she said gently. "Can I hold him?"

Pol froze. She was the only person who had ever held her baby. Reluctantly, she handed him to May.

"What's wrong little man . . . .?" She stroked his cheek with the back of her hand. She immediately flashed a concerned glance at Cap.

"What?" asked Pol, a hint of desperation creeping into her voice. "What?" She frantically looked back and forth at the two Rearers.

"Cap," said May, "he is burning up."

Pol started to cry. "Help him! Can't you . . . .help him?"

May checked his swaddling and tried to rock him. "The only thing I know to do is to either cool him off in the lake or give him some Sweet Flower juice."

"Sweet Flower juice?" said Pol. "What is Sweet Flower juice?"

May looked down at the baby. Despite his fever, he continued to bawl. "It is taken from a plant. We use it for a variety of things, including fevers."

"You have some? Where is it?" she asked anxiously.

"No, we don't. Not here," replied May. "But I think the plant grows in the Garden." She turned towards Cap. "Cap, I can't remember a baby this hot. We need to go."

"Of course," said Cap. He quickly began gathering up the coverings and replaced them in their packs. "You carry the baby, May. I'll carry your pack." Cap noted the insecurity on Pol's face. "May is used to making difficult treks. You aren't," said Cap firmly. "Do you want to risk falling with him in the dark?"

Pol took another quick, deep breath before shaking her head.

"All right," he said as he started up the hill. "I'll try not to get too far ahead, but I want to make sure nothing is out there."

Carefully cradling the baby, May followed him up the hill with Pol close behind. Joba let out another pain-fueled cry. The sound swept away from them, crossing the plain Cap knew was directly ahead. He stumbled along in the dark, wishing the baby would be quiet. His eyes were focused forward, anxiously searching the night for the flickering glow of torchlight.

The first thing Min became aware of was the sound of his heart pounding in his ears. He tried to raise his head, only to feel it swirl with pain. His body was wracked by a fit of heavy coughing, so he put his head back down on . . . . what?

His vision slowly penetrated the darkness. He was inside, lying on a mat on the floor. In the distance was a fire barrel casting a dim light into the room. The rest of the chamber was sparsely furnished.

"Min?" A voice crept through the near-dark. "Can you hear me?" He could hear footfalls coming towards him.

Sol. He looked down at his Command Agent and tried to smile. "Let me take a look at you," he said softly, trying to get Min to roll over on his back. Sol fitted the membrane glove onto his arm and held his palm against

Min's forehead. "What happened to you?" he asked finally, his voice laden with concern. "You neural pathways are firing at an extremely elevated rate. When I checked you before you regained consciousness, it was even more elevated." The pain spiked through Min's temples. Again, he began to cough spastically. "Easy, friend. Easy," implored Sol. "See if this helps." He held out a small glass container and removed the top. "Open". Min did as he asked and Sol poured the contents into his mouth. It burned the back of his throat like vomit causing him to scowl. "I know, it is awful," said Sol sympathetically. "But it will make you feel better." He was right. Almost immediately, the pounding in Min's head relented and he was freed from the need to cough. Sol helped him sit up. "Now, what happened to you?"

Before Min could respond, Bal stepped forward from across the chamber. Several Guards attended him. "We need to talk," he said, looking down at Min. "Is he going to be all right?"

"I'm going to be fine," answered Min. "Is there any water in here?" Bal snapped his fingers at one of the Guards, prompting him to leave the chamber.

"I need to know what happened to him," said Sol. "His body has recently absorbed a massive electrical charge."

"I wasn't there," said Bal brusquely. "And Shu is unavailable. If he isn't going to die, then he needs to leave. I made an exception to his exile to allow you to attend him." He leaned down slightly to get a better look at Min. "I haven't decided how to deal with Eve's exile yet."

"Eve's?" protested Sol.

Bal smiled. "Min violated the Protocols by speaking with her. She will be sent to the mainland. It is a consequence of his choice." The pleasure in his voice grated on Min's gut like rough stone.

"You can't," said Min. "The Protocol says I can't speak to anyone. I didn't speak with her on the canoe. She spoke to me."

Sol stood up straight. "You think yourself clever, don't you?" said Bal. "Well, it doesn't matter. You are going to the moon. She is not."

"That remains to be seen," said Min. "Since I was going to be exiled anyway, I got a scan of the Hek's protein templates while I was gone. Once I'm on the moon, I can use that data to perform a very accurate calculation as to the proximity of Critical Closure. That will determine where Eve ends up."

Bal could feel the heat rising up his neck, but he mastered it. "You press my exception for Sol's presence," he noted. "Perhaps this violation should result in his exile?"

"I'm not talking to him," said Min cooly. "I'm talking to you."

Bal gritted his teeth. "I do as I please! Once you have that information, you will relay it to the Chronicler Hall. I will then advise your crew. They won't be allowed to board either Journeycraft until you have contacted me." Sol glared at Bal. Min remained composed. "Not so clever, are you Min? Besides, the other ship has found Haven. The other Journeyers have work to do."

"How do you know that?" asked Min.

"The information from the Land Bridge confirmed it."

Sol guffawed. "You figured that out from the data, all by yourself?"

"No," Bal replied flatly. "Eve did."

Min paused to consider what he had just heard. "Why did they come back then?" he asked. "If they were so close."

"One of their members was ill," explained Bal. "Another had some sort of behavioral abnormality. Eve believes they were trying to bring the data back themselves because it was so vital. They had attempted to get word to the Land Bridge about their discovery." Bal's eyes narrowed. "By the time the message arrived, the settlement was abandoned."

"He's telling the truth, Min" offered Sol. "Jack and I reached the same conclusion when we went aboard the ***Aurora***. Where are Eve and Jack now?" asked Sol.

"Eve is aboard your ship, still studying the data from the Land Bridge. Jack is aboard the ***Aurora***, preparing it to transport Min to the moon."

"He can't fly it there by himself," protested Sol. "Someone will have to fly the craft back after he takes the shuttle."

"Do you still think me foolish?" interjected Bal. "The ***Aurora*** landed here the first time without any crew at all. It can do the same again."

"Only if we tell it too," said Sol defiantly.

"Jack already is," said Bal.

"You are sure of that?" snapped Sol. "He could be directing that ship to do just about anything and you'd never know."

"I am," replied Bal, a low iciness in his voice. "I am because I told him if that ship doesn't return within a rotation, we are going to execute you right in front of him."

Sol started towards Bal but Min managed to weakly grab a hold of his pant leg. Three of the Guards instantly reacted, interposing themselves in front of Bal. Min slowly struggled to his feet. "We don't have a lot of choices here," he said. "Can you fix me?"

Sol turned and looked at his friend. "You know I can't or I would have," he said. "The electrical shock greatly exacerbated your condition. The medication I have will only offer temporary relief. You will receive a diminishing benefit with each successive use." He placed the vial in a small bag and handed it to Min. Sol glared at Bal. "But he will need to rest for a few rotations before he goes to the moon. If he doesn't, he will die."

Bal considered this demand. "I'll allow it. But simply because I can. He will remain in quarantine until then."

"Do I have any repose options at all?" asked Min. Min was gathering information for later use. Sol had seen him do this on innumerable occasions.

"If you go into repose, you have about a five percent chance of coming back out again."

"Understood." The two men faced each other. The time for words was nearly past. Min extended both hands and Sol gripped them tightly. Each did his best to fill his mind with one final image of the other. "You happened with me, old friend. Go find Haven. Our goodbye does no justice to the time we shared."

Sol stared into Min's eyes until Bal began to fidget. "Indeed it does not. And you happened with me." He slowly released Min's hands, turned, and exited the pyramid.

It was a wonder May hadn't fallen. Even after her eyes had adjusted fully to the darkness, she could barely see anything. She clutched Joba close to her chest, feeling his heat through her shirt. He continued to bawl, his cries fanning out into the darkness. May heard Pol struggling along behind her. Pol had stumbled several times but had repeatedly risen and fought her way forward. Her knees stung with the wetness of her own blood.

Periodically, Cap would guide them forward by making a clicking noise with his mouth. May would follow the sound while making sure Pol was close enough behind to follow her. Finally, Cap was directly in front of her. She knelt down and took a look at Joba. Pol staggered up and fell to the ground, gasping for breath.

"We are almost there," assured Cap. "We are nearly to the trees. After that, it is just a short distance."

May pressed her lips to Joba's cheeks. "He is still very hot," she said anxiously. "We can't stop."

Without a word, Pol pulled herself to her feet and began to move, despite the fact that she had no idea where to go. Cap and May quickly moved passed her. As Cap had promised, they soon reached the trees. What little they had been able to see while on the plain was taken from them now. The way ahead was utterly lightless. Joba's cries seemed to reflect off of the nearby trees, bounding back at them from every direction. Cap stopped again, causing May and Pol to run into him.

"We need to hold hands now," said Cap. They each felt around in the darkness until they were all joined. They slowly made their way ahead, stumbling over tree roots that rose like snares from the forest floor.

One such root caught Pol's foot, sending her hurtling to the ground. She nearly pulled May and Joba down with her. Pol cried out in anguish.

"Pol?!?" said May in the darkness. "What happened?"

"F-foot . . . ." she replied. She began to whimper.

"Can you stand?"

"N-no. Go on. Take . . . Joba."

Cap pulled May close. "Can you stay here with Joba by yourself for a short time?" he asked. He knew what she would say.

"Of course. What are you going to do?"

"The Garden is very close. I will take her there and then come back for you."

"Are you sure you can find it?"

Cap's confident nod was lost in the darkness. "I have been there enough times. I can get there. It won't be long." He stooped down and hauled Pol to her feet, slinging one of her arms over his shoulder. "Lean on me. We will be there soon." May could hear their footfalls as Cap dragged Pol towards the Garden.

Once again, May pressed her lips to Joba's cheeks. They were hotter than they were before. Joba's cries were weakening and she could feel his tiny lips quivering. "Now, now . . . . ." she began softly.

Far off to her heartside, she heard a long baying sound. ***Wooooooo.........*** She crouched down, pressing Joba to her chest in an effort to quiet him.

Wooooooo........... wooooooooo...........

The sound was a bit closer. She squinted into the veil of night but couldn't see anything. She tried to take a few steps forward.

Something grabbed her arm and she screamed.

"May! Shhhh!" whispered Cap. "Come on!" He pulled her along while she tightly gripped Joba with her free arm. The Garden wall seemed to appear right in front of them. Cap led her along the wall until they reached the entryway. Once they were inside, May sat down and wrapped Joba with both arms. Cap operated his metallic key, closing the huge wooden door.

"J-joba?" called Pol.

"He's fine," said May. "He's here." May heard the telltale sound of flint striking stone and a torch quickly came to life next to her. Cap looked down at her and the baby with great concern. A dozen paces away, he could see Pol sprawled on the ground.

"I'll try to find the Sweet Juice plant," said Cap.

"Hurry." She watched him as he maneuvered his way through the various plants growing inside the stone walls. He stopped for a moment before making a quick return.

"Here it is," he said, holding a long, thin brown stem. "What do I do with it?"

"Cut the tip off of one end, far enough down to make the juice flow. Then give it to me."

Cap withdrew an edged piece of flint and began sawing at the stem, removing a tiny portion of its top. He then handed it to May.

"Now, Joba," she said reassuringly. "Try this sweet boy........." She held the open end to his mouth, watching as its thick juice dripped from the opening. Joba was still crying weakly, but the juice trickled in between his parted lips. May continued until the stem was dry. She then stood up and carried Joba to his mother. "You need to nurse," she said. "It will calm him and make sure the juice stays down. Try it for as long as it takes. Don't stop until he has done it."

Pol sat up as best she could. She eagerly took Joba into her arms and held him to her breast. May walked back to where Cap was and sat down next to him.

"Did you hear that noise?" she asked.

"Yes. Did you see what it was?"

"I couldn't see anything," said May. "What was it?"

"I don't know, but we are safe in here."

"Are you sure?"

"Yes, if they . . . . " He caught himself when he saw May's eyes widen. "If they could get in here, they would have already."

"It's them, isn't it?" asked May. "The Hek."

"We don't know that," replied Cap. "It was probably just an animal."

Joba was quiet now. From the smile on Pol's face, it was apparent that he was nursing.

"Will he need more?" asked Cap.

"Yes, each time before he nurses. To be safe, we should do it for the next rotation."

Cap was relieved. "There isn't any way to build a lasting fire," he said. "But we don't really need one. When morning comes, we will decide what to do."

"That sounds . . . . . ." May abruptly stopped speaking and sat as still as she could. From just beyond the stone wall, she could hear voices. They had the vagueness of distant speech. Cap cocked his head to listen.

They heard it again. A voice, followed by another in response. They couldn't understand what was being said. It sounded as if the speakers were right next to them. Pol continued to nurse, oblivious.

Cap put a reassuring arm around May and continued to listen. More voices. Too many to count. And a high yipping sound.

Joba choked and broke off from his mother's breast. The interruption upset him and he began to cry.

Cap and May both looked frantically from the infant back to the stone wall. The voices were all competing with one another now. A whiny yipping noise seeped in from outside. Something began to thump loudly on the doorway.

Pol wrapped her arms tightly around Joba. This only distressed him more, amplifying his wail. Cap searched the area around him before seizing a long-handled wooden hoe. He moved in between May and the door.

The voices continued as one steady murmur. There were a half dozen solid thumps on the door, then nothing. The yipping gave way to a series of barks.

May found herself unable to move. Pol finally managed to get Joba to take her breast again, and he fell silent. Cap threw several handfuls of dirt onto his torch until it went out. The four of them sat quietly in the darkness.

One distinct voice sounded and the barking stopped. There was a discussion of some sort near the door, but eventually the sounds outside the walls faded away. After sitting hunched on the ground until their knees ached, Cap and May slowly crawled over to where Pol and Joba sat. They all huddled together. Only Joba was able to sleep.

Min sat on the ground of a wide, flat plain. Heavy fog obscured his view in every direction. The sky was a dark gray, heavy with rain. The clouds rumbled to one another, planning the coming storm.

He struggled to his feet. "Hello?" The thick mist absorbed his voice. There was no response. Cupping his hands to his mouth he called again. "Hello?!?" Still. Nothing.

The rocky ground gnawed at his bare feet as he walked along. Looking behind him, he saw his footprints filling with blood.

"Is anyone there?!?" No answer. The soles of his feet were slashed and gouged. He could not feel anything. He prodded at his wounds, to see if it would hurt.

Woooooooo . . . . .woooooooooooo........

The strange sound sliced through the air, encircling him. He slowly spun, trying to determine where it had come from.

Wooooooo . . . . .woooooooooooo . . . .

Was it the same noise? Or was this one from a different direction? He could not tell. The second sounded . . . .hungry.

Wooooooo . . . . .woooooooooooo . . . .

This one was closer. Much closer. He wanted to run back in the direction from which he had come. But where had he come from? He began searching for some clue, but the fog obscured everything. His footprints were gone. He saw only gray. He looked up. The sky rumbled. It sounded like a gigantic barrel rolling atop the cloud cover. The noise reached the edge of his hearing and then turned around, coming back towards him.

He began to run.

His feet were slippery with blood. He found himself on the ground with no memory of falling. After pulling himself up, he ran again.

Ahead, the fog was beginning to lift. He saw a neat row of pyramids, ordered by height from one side to the other. It strengthened him and he ran like he could not before.

Woooooooooooo..........woooooooooooo................

It was right behind him. He pushed aside his fear enough to turn and look. The fog had completely cleared away now. In the distance he saw at least 50 men running after him, all bearing long spears. They were short and thick and hairy. They were shrieking at one another. Ahead of the men were a dozen medium-sized animals running on all fours. They were brown and black and gold and white and easily covered the plain with their long tails streaming behind them.

Woooooooooooooo . . . .woooooooooooooo . . . .

It was the strange animals who were making the howling cries as they ran. They were quickly gaining on him as the men and their spears gave chase.

He saw his people standing by the pyramids, working. They tilled their fields with long, wooden tools. They were short and lean. Their hair was creamy yellow. He tried to call to them, but he couldn't make a sound. He was almost there.

As he reached them, he tried to warn them of the danger. There were men and women working. Children sat and tried to build tiny pyramids with small stones. He grabbed one of the men by his shoulder, trying to turn him so he could see. The man pushed him away, easily knocking him to the ground. When Min tried to get up, he saw that he was now very far away from his people and their pyramids.

The animals sprinted by him, baring their yellowed teeth. They howled and barked as they charged. Their masters were on their heels. They were squat and muscular and covered with hair. They ignored him. Their spears had grown and were now three times as long as he was.

"Noooooooooo!!!!!!" He shouted with all of his might, but his voice was a mere ragged squeak. The animals and men flowed by in waves, kicking dirt on him as they passed. In the distance, his people continued to calmly go about their work. The cries of the men-with-spears made a deafening hum punctuated by howls and barks. He could no longer see the ground, there were so many. One woman finally looked up, puzzled by the approaching mass of animals and men. She shrugged and continued to dig at the ground as the men and animals closed on the people, spears poised to strike, teeth bared to rend and tear.........

Min shot upright from his mat, screaming. Once again, his heart pounded away inside his skull. His clothes were soaked and he gasped for air. He collapsed backwards onto his mat and sobbed. Outside, the thunder assaulted his ears and he could hear the rain's hiss on the stones. No one, he was certain, had heard his cry.

CHAPTER 4

The long, tense night had finally taken its toll. Cap awakened just after dawn. The others were still huddled next to him. May and Pol were sleeping. Joba's eyes were open, but he was content to lazily nuzzle his mother's chest.

Cap noted the thickening clouds. It had been a few days since the last substantial rain. The sky was well overdue. He stood up, trying to remain as quiet as he could.

Aside from the calls of a few morning birds, he heard nothing from beyond the walls of the Garden. He crept over and inspected the wooden door, satisfied that it was completely intact. He retrieved the packs and moved them under a slight overhang where the tools were stored. It would storm soon and he wanted to keep their equipment as dry as he could.

Staying in the Garden indefinitely wasn't possible. At some point, someone from Atla would return to tend the crops. While he was uncertain about the complexities of the law, he suspected that an encounter between islanders and a group of exiles would not sit well with the Chroniclers. He couldn't risk the fate of any other Atlans. Besides, the Garden could not offer him the one thing he needed most – a tree suitable for fashioning into a canoe. He was still convinced that a return to the Land Bridge was the most prudent choice for his group.

Before he could start on the canoe, he would have to find shelter from the rains. The overhangs in the Garden weren't deep enough. It would be impossible for him to keep a fire going long enough to burn away the interior of a tree. He would have to find his workplace somewhere outside the Garden. The memory of the murmuring voices from the night before returned.

May stirred and then sat up. She brushed Joba's cheek with the back of her hand and smiled. She stood up and joined Cap.

"He is much cooler," she said quietly. "The Sweet Flower juice worked better than I could have hoped. Have you been awake long?"

"Not too long," said Cap. "I didn't drift off for a long time. I haven't heard any strange noises this morning. I think they have gone."

May looked over at the heavy wooden door. "They?"

He rested a comforting hand on her shoulder. “That had to be the Hek that we heard last night,” he said. “The other noises must have been made by those animals they had with them on top of the cliff.”

May took a step closer to him. “So, we are trapped in here?”

“No,” said Cap, his voice tinted with defiance. “We will get out. I plan on building a canoe.”

“A canoe?!?” said May. “And just how do you plan on doing that?” The two of them surveyed the trees that grew inside the Garden. All of them were enormous nut trees of various types. Some of them reached much higher than the walls themselves. They were all much, much bigger than any trees they had ever seen the Atlan boat wrights work with.

“I’ve been thinking about that. I will have to slip out for a little while each day until the canoe is done. I will work on it some ways away. There has to be a cave or something nearby.”

“That’s foolish,” protested May. “What if they find you?”

“We don’t have any other choices.”

May checked to see if Pol was still sleeping. “I need to tell you something. Bal intends to bring the Guards ashore. He is going to attack the Hek.”

“What?!?” asked Cap. “Why would he do such a thing?”

“Shu told me that they are concerned about the Hek having the barge. They are afraid the Hek might use it to go to Atla. I guess they believe that if there is going to be a fight, it should be here and not there.”

“Shu told you this? I thought the Protocols forbade that.”

“She told me such actions were our fault, for losing the barge in the first place. She thought the information might give us more options.”

“We don’t even know how many Hek there are. I’d still prefer to be at the Land Bridge. The Chroniclers won’t take us back. I don’t see any reason why we should rely on their decisions anymore.”

“So many things we need to do in order to live,” said May in a heavy voice. “It just seems so…..”

“No!” snapped Cap. His retort startled her and she stepped away from him. “We are still alive and will continue to be. Give my plan a chance. Give me a chance.”

May drew a deep breath. “You have never let me down before,” she said finally. “When do you plan to start?”

Cap looked up at the clouds. “It will be storming soon. Maybe if the Hek understand that, they won’t be out wandering around. I can look for a good tree in the rain as well as I can any other time. As soon as it starts, I will go and look for a while. I will also need to look for a place to do the work."

She frowned at him. "I've seen you do a lot of different things, but you have never made a canoe, have you?"

He hesitated. "No. But I have watched the boat wrights many times. I am confident I can do what needs to be done."

From across the Garden, they noted that Pol was awake. She was cleaning Joba's undergarments. He was flat on his back, completely naked, happily flailing his arms and legs.

"He is so much better," said Pol smiling. "Thank you, May. You saved him."

"Don't thank me," said May with a wave of her hand. "He is a dear. I'm glad he is better."

"Will he need some more of that juice?" asked Pol.

"It might not be a bad idea," said May. "Once you have him cleaned up, I'll show you how to prepare it."

"I would like to learn that," said Pol. She returned her attention to the infant.

"I'm very worried about Joba," said May in a hushed voice.

"I thought you said he was better," said Cap.

"He is. It's not that. This is just no place for a baby. Keeping him warm and dry is going to be very difficult."

"It will be," confirmed Cap. "But I know you can find a way to do it. You are the best infant Rearer there is."

"So, what is the plan for now?"

"I think we should eat. You and Pol can attend to Joba while I try to arrange the leantos to provide us with some shelter from the rain. Once that starts, I'll go tree-hunting."

"We can just do what we can do, right? Isn't that what we taught the Charges?" asked May.

"Yes," said Cap. "But we can do more than we think. We taught them that, too."

Max assisted Min on his walk to the ***Aurora***. Min's legs were wobbly and he leaned heavily on the Guard. As they approached the landing area, he could see Sol and Jack surrounded by a large contingent of Guards and Chroniclers. Eve stood apart, unable to tear her eyes away from him. The egress ramp on the Journeycraft had already been lowered. The ship was ready to swallow him up.

"Remember," said Bal sternly, "once you have reached the moon, the ship is to be returned." Min meekly lifted his head, recalling Bal's threats from the night before. "It is time," said Bal. Max assisted Min to the base of the ramp where his gear awaited him. "We may not board your ship," said Bal. "That is the law. And they may not assist one in exile," he added, pointing to Min's crewmates. "You will have to board yourself." His last directive dripped from his lips like venom.

Without Max's help, Min couldn't stand. Sliding down to all fours, he reached out, grabbed his pack, and began dragging it behind him. Crawling upwards, each successful movement forward left him gasping for breath. He began to cough. Sol had to turn away to avert his eyes. Jack trembled with an anger he dared not release. Eve kept her eyes on Min. Seeing him like this was almost unbearable, but she didn't want to miss what might be her last chance to ever see him at all.

Once he caught his breath, Min struggled forward a bit farther up the ramp. Min refused to look back. After a couple dozen short efforts, he reached the top. The ramp slowly began to rise, sealing him away from his crewmates.

"Journeycraft ***Aurora***," he said quietly, "Command Agent Min. Reduce gravity to 50%." The tether beam system insured that every Journeycraft "knew" who had command authority. Both the ***Aurora*** and the ***Starshine*** would soon be advised of Eve's new authority. Min could hear the faint hum of the residual batteries kicking in. Almost instantly, the burden of his own body lessened by half. He pulled himself to his feet and walked slowly over to the ship's Alpha panel. "Voice data only. Ship status?"

"Journeycraft ***Aurora*** is fully functional. There are no impairments to any vital systems."

"Good boy, Jack," Min muttered. "How about non-vital systems?"

"Residual batteries at 88%." The ship's voice communicator was metallic and lacked the warmth of intonation.

"Calculate course for lunar intercept and stand by for launch command." He pulled his pack into his lap and secured himself into his chair. He removed the small bag containing Sol's medicine. His hand felt an irregularity in the bottom of the bag. There was something else inside. Upon removing the bottle, he saw a small metallic object. It was a simple metal sphere on a chain, its two hemispheres hinged together and closed with a tiny clasp. He flipped the clasp open and the two hemispheres unhinged. A holographic image of him and Eve standing on the bridge of the ***Starshine*** flickered to life from inside the sphere. Min couldn't name the exact occasion of the image, but that didn't matter. He put the pieces of the sphere back together and slipped the chain around his neck.

"Engage lunar intercept." He noted that Jack had already entered the necessary directives for the ***Aurora***'s return trip to Uma.

Again, he could hear the faint hum of the batteries as the ship began exercising his commands. The inertial neutralizers prevented him from feeling any force at all as the ship was easily lifted upwards by its vapor boosters. He resisted the urge to go to one of the nearby portals. Jack and the others would have moved a safe distance away from the ship prior to liftoff. He wouldn't be able to see anything until they were all just indistinct dots on the ground. He absently toyed with the locket hanging around his neck. Eve's memory would stay with him, regardless of their respective fates.

Those fates were still undetermined. Nonetheless, he entered directives into the panel conveying Command Authority to Eve. Regardless of what the data concerning the Hek's protein templates told him about Critical Closure, she would need it either to pass it to Jack before joining Min on the moon, or to lead the two Journeycraft on one last attempt to save the Umae. He wanted desperately to be with her again. He wondered how he would feel if she could only come to him because their race was doomed to extinction.

The ship entered the thick cloud cover, soon exiting on the far side of the grayish mass of vapor. The space beyond was a black sheet adorned with tiny, unblinking gems. The yellow sun blazed on the far side of the planet. On the near side, the smooth, bright face of the moon reflected the sun's light back at Uma. Uninhibited by the planet's gravity, the ***Aurora*** quickly covered the distance to Uma's tiny orbiting partner.

"Begin landing sequence, destination Citadel."

"There is no response from the docking bays at the Citadel," the ship announced after a moment.

Min sighed. That didn't provide him with any encouragement that the Citadel's systems were functioning like they were supposed to be. He thought about hailing the Citadel directly. But that call, like all communications from a Journeycraft, would route through the tether beam and back to the Chroniclers' Hall on Atla. Min didn't want Bal to have the opportunity to have any information about what was happening up here. It was for this same reason that he couldn't just send the results of his Critical Closure analysis directly to one of the Journeycraft. Calls from the Citadel followed the same path. The only way to change that was a lengthy refitting of all the communications arrays in both the Citadel and the target Journeycraft. The Protocols had forbidden any electromagnetic communications that the Chroniclers weren't privy to. There was no way to prevent Bal from being the first person on Uma to know the results.

"Redirect," he told the panel. "We will have to land on the surface."

The ship banked slightly, locking onto the requested course. "Proximity of landing zone?"

Min took a deep breath. The less walking the better. "200 paces." He then sat back in his chair and closed his eyes.

"Proximity modification alert." Min's eyes snapped open. He wasn't sure if he had dozed off.

"Why?"

"Debris detected in the proposed landing zone."

"Debris? How far out?"

"Landing zone should be modified by at least 100%."

Min tapped his finger on the panel in front of him, considering the ship's advisory.

"Get as close as possible without compromising safety," he said finally. He stood up and glided towards the equipment pantry. He removed a vacuum suit and began putting it on. The reduced gravity made things much easier for him. He was hopeful that the Citadel's systems were functioning well enough to do the same thing there. He had no way of knowing how long it had been since anyone had been there, or what the maintenance situation was.

"Landing parameters modified."

Min snapped his helmet in place and waited. He could feel a very faint jostle as the ship came to rest on the lunar surface. "Egress ramp down."

The ramp opened from the belly of the ship. Min put his pack over his shoulder and floated downward in three steps. He couldn't help but note how much easier it had been than his boarding process.

In the distance, he could see the Citadel rising from the surface. In the foreground sat a lone shuttle very similar to the ones on the ***Starshine***. Beyond that, he could see what appeared to be twisted pieces of metal scattered between the shuttle and the base. Min stepped off onto the powdery surface and began walking towards the Citadel. The ***Aurora*** waited for a few moments until Min was clear before raising the ramp and beginning its return trip to Uma. The debris, a shuttlecraft……he hadn't even made it to the Citadel yet and the mysteries were already multiplying.

No sooner than Cap had finished rigging the leantos, it began to rain. It started out as a steady drizzle that lasted all morning and into the afternoon. After that, the sky rumbled with long, deep growls and the rain started falling in sheets.

The leantos proved to be remarkably effective in providing them with shelter from the rain. However, as Cap noted to himself, the materials from which they were made were not going to last for too long in such weather. Repairing them was yet another task for which Cap would have to find time.

Once the storm intensified, Cap decided to leave in search of the tree from which to construct his canoe. He scrambled out from under the leanto and ran to the massive door in the Garden's wall. He deactivated the lock and stepped outside into the woods.

The trees in this area of the woods were far, far too tall and thick. He still hadn't determined how he was going to fell the right tree once he located it. He guessed that even an experienced team of boat wrights with all of the right tools would need several rotations to bring down one of the huge trees near the Garden. Cap headed deeper into the forest in search of a smaller tree. That part of the woods was unknown to him as he had never had any reason to travel beyond the Garden before. The rain limited his vision so he tried to take care and note landmarks along the way.

As he walked along, the canopy thickened considerably. Even the torrent pouring from above had difficulty penetrating the leafy roof overhead. The ground was relatively firm although still covered with twisting roots that rose up from the forest floor.

Although he was thankful for the cover from the worst of the rain, the woods were very dark. He slowed his pace, determining that getting a good look at a few trees would be better than trying to get a glance at as many as possible, particularly given the darkness.

By the time he was ready to rest for the first time, he still hadn't found anything even close to what he was looking for. The old trees in this part of the woods were too large and the canopy had prevented any smaller competition from springing up at their feet. He stopped, turned around, and began walking back in the direction from which he had come.

The forest was completely new to him. He didn't recognize anything that he had seen before. He knelt down from time to time to search for his own footprints but found nothing. Flashes of lightning periodically lit the blackness overhead, exposing the tiny gaps in the canopy. Even though they briefly allowed him to see a bit farther for a split second, they didn't reveal any clues about which way he should go.

Finally, he decided to keep walking until he was free of the trees overhead. That may not take him to the Garden, but it was likely that he would be able to regain his bearings once he was in more familiar territory. He planned to follow the edge of the forest until he saw something he had seen on one of his numerous prior trips. Then he would easily be able to make it back to May, Pol, and Joba.

As he picked his way over the roots in the darkness, the wind suddenly picked up and the rain stopped abruptly. The sky flickered with repeated bursts of lightning. One burst of wind nearly knocked him over. He steadied himself against the gale and pressed forward. The wind began to swirl, making it almost impossible for him to stay on his feet. His foot slid off of a tree root, sending him toppling backwards. His head smacked the wet ground, leaving a cascade of stars weaving in front of his eyes. He sat up slowly and saw a huge root just next to where his head had hit. After clearing his senses, he noted that the wind was continuing to gain strength. He would need to find shelter.

Cap began to crawl across the ground, trying to make himself a more difficult target for the wind. The canopy overhead was swaying violently and the sky was alive with light. A bolt of lightning struck nearby, deafening in its explosive power. He quickly crawled forward, searching as he could with each periodic flash of light.

In a small clearing, there was an opening in the ground. It looked as if the earth had been split open by a huge stone axe. He stood up and scrambled over to the edge. It was deep, and its sides were fairly steep. It would provide excellent protection against the storm.

As he crouched down to begin his descent, the wind buffeted him without warning causing him to lose his balance. He tumbled down the side of the crevasse, landing hard on his back at the bottom. The breath raced from his chest, leaving him gasping. Cap tried to push himself up, still struggling for air. His head reeled from the loudest sound he had ever heard. A titanic bolt of electricity struck a tree near the edge of the opening. Smoke and flames rose from the base of the tree as it groaned in protest. The wind conspired by pushing against it with all of the fury the storm could offer. As it began to tip, the tree was betrayed by its own massive girth. With a series of loud cracking sounds, the tree at first simply listed to one side. As gravity took hold, the treetop accelerated towards the forest floor, directing the trunk directly at the opening in the ground.

As Cap looked up, a brief flash of lightning illuminated the massive tree as it crashed down towards him. Instinctively, he raised his arms in an effort to cover his head as he rolled to one side. The tree landed squarely atop the opening, with Cap underneath. The howl of the wind had only the occasional roar of thunder as competition for the rest of the night.

May, Pol and Joba huddled under a leanto, trying to stay dry. The wind whipped in over the top of the Garden walls, tearing at the fabric of their shelter. The sky was etched repeatedly by vicious forks of lightning. Joba wailed, but the two women could barely hear him over the storm's din.

Above all, May hated feeling powerless. If she were alone, she realized that she would likely run outside in an effort to find Cap, and would equally as likely not make it back. For now, Pol and Joba were her anchors to the Garden, and safety. She had every confidence in her fellow Rearer, but she also knew that he had never seen a storm like this one. Biting her lip, she realized there was nothing she could do. She ***was*** powerless. But when the storm ended, she would head off into the forest, regardless of the danger.

For the first time in his life, Min was entirely alone. He thought of the symbols that were carved into the side of many of the pyramids back on Uma. One was of a single vertical line, solitary in its character. Min had become that line, standing on a lunar plain that was absolutely silent.

"Set ambulation at 90% assist," he said, speaking inside the sphere of hard plastic encircling his head. He took a few steps forward. It was as easy as swinging his legs from a high stool. His suit was doing most of the work as he began moving towards the shuttle in the distance.

Despite the assistance of his suit, he was becoming winded by the time he reached the shuttle. Min couldn't see any obvious damage. All of its doors were closed. The access panel was a bit beyond his reach.

"Booster lift, 10%," he said cautiously. It had occurred to him that he didn't have an exact value for his mass or the mass of his suit. The suit unsuccessfully attempted to lift him off the ground.

"20%." His feet were barely raised from the ground, but he still couldn't reach the panel.

"30% then stabilize." His suit lifted him up a bit higher and then held him in position. He plugged his voice matrix into the access panel. "Authority Command Agent Min." The door to the shuttle immediately slid open and he pulled himself inside.

Everything looked normal. There was no damage that he could see. This was plainly one of the shuttlecraft from the ***Aurora***. The odds of it coming from anywhere else were essentially zero.

Whoever landed the shuttlecraft had to have gone inside. He went back to the door. "Initiate command contingency and reseal," he told the shuttle. The doors slid shut and he could hear the shuttle re-pressurizing the inside of the cabin. He unfastened the top of his suit and rolled it down to his waist before removing his helmet. "Jack," he muttered quietly as he removed the pendant Eve had given him, "it is hard to fool someone who taught you everything you know." He flipped open the pendant, smiling as the image of him and Eve sprung to life. After absorbing the scene for a moment, he removed a tiny, cylindrical tool from his pouch. "Classic bioscan relay device," he continued. "Not that I'm untouched by your concern." With a brief application of the tool, the back of the pendant swung open, revealing a tiny electronic mechanism. Min didn't have to do any analysis to know that the pendant fed his bioreadings to the ***Starshine***'s beacon satellite. The crew of the ***Starshine*** wanted a way to know if he was still alive.

Min still had to process his data on the Hek inside the Citadel. Then he would have a very good estimate as to how much time was left before Critical Closure. If it had been reached, there was no point in the ***Starshine*** going back into deep space. They could simply come and get him. If it hadn't, they would have to go back to where the ***Aurora*** had detected the likely presence of Haven. At that point, Min would be forced to decide who the next Command Agent was going to be. That would depend on how much time they had left. While he hoped that the analysis would show an abundance of time remaining, he wasn't sure what he would do if the window for action were moderately sized. That would require him to make a judgment call independent of his feelings for Eve. He almost preferred a finding that the Looming had begun.

Min quickly linked the biosignal to the shuttle's panel. Now the shuttle would also "know" whether or not he was still alive.

"In the event access is gained through code abath-del-mot-ferro, activate Beta Process upon initiation of engines," he said finally. "Lock out all other access codes except that one and mine." The Beta Process would disable the shuttle. Until he knew exactly what had happened to the ***Aurora***, he didn't want anyone taking this shuttle without his approval. He also didn't want to unnecessarily trap anyone on the moon if he were to suddenly die before releasing the restriction he had placed on it. "If I'm dead when the shuttle is accessed, cancel Beta Process directive." He slowly pulled his suit back on and donned his helmet. Activating his suit's boosters, he carefully lowered himself back to the ground.

The Citadel was a short ways away. He hadn't been here since he had, biologically, about 25 ellipses. Hab had brought him here soon after Hab had become Command Agent, and Min had become Tech Agent, of the ***Starshine***. It was a tradition for each former Tech Agent to take his or her replacement on a tour of the Citadel. Min had been looking forward to taking Jack, but that simply wasn't going to happen now.

Hab and Min had spent over one hundred rotations together in the Citadel. It was a time Min would never forget. He could not have asked for a better mentor. Hab had an exceptionally keen technical mind, yet he was a patient instructor. In Min, he had found an intellect exceeding his own. Hab had pushed Min, forcing Min to grow past the temptation to simply get by on his natural gifts alone. For that, Min was deeply grateful. Min felt he had found himself an equal in Jack. Jack was young and overly anxious to prove himself, but he was brilliant. The ***Starshine*** and her crew were in good technical hands. Min had no doubt that Jack would one day become a Command Agent. But every Command Agent had to learn on the job. Was Jack ready now?

The area between the shuttle and the Citadel was littered with metal debris. It was obviously the remains of another shuttle. Any doubts as to where the first shuttle had originated were now gone. The debris made a trail directly towards the Citadel. Min picked his way through the debris until he reached the exterior of the structure. He turned and looked back at the twisted metal. There was no ground scar from a heavy impact. There didn't appear to be any obvious damage to the exterior of the Citadel. He also didn't see signs of an explosion. Most of the debris was concentrated near the exterior wall. If a shuttle had struck the Citadel with any significant velocity, the damage to the base's exterior would have been obvious. The shuttle itself was demolished. This scene didn't make any sense. He'd have to search for more answers inside.

Growing fatigued, he walked to the access panel on the side of the structure and entered his command code. A door slid open in front of him. Min stepped through and sat down to rest as the door slid shut behind him. While it was completely dark inside, the ambient air temperature was elevated. That is what he would have expected for an empty Citadel. The building's Alpha panel would have terminated all illumination once its bioscans determined there were no Umae inside. The temperature would be maintained to extend the life of the devices within. He reached up and removed his helmet and set it down on the floor next to him.

The air in the passageway smelled fresh. "Authorization Command Agent Min. Is voice command online?" he asked.

"Voice command is online," came a robotic voice from somewhere in the darkness.

"Reduce gravity to 50%." He could feel the tug from the floor weaken as he activated his hand lamp. The hallway was empty. After resting for a few more moments, he stood up and removed his suit. "Is there anyone else here?"

"Unknown," replied the voice. He could tell that it was emanating from a panel just down the hallway.

"Unknown? Are bioscans online?"

"Yes."

"Why is it 'unknown'?" Min realized he had just asked the panel why it didn't know something it didn't know. His mind was boggy from fatigue.

"Unknown."

"How long has it been since an Umae has been here?"

There was a delay as the panel processed the response.

".226 ellipses."

"How many Umae?"

"One."

"Where is he or she now?"

"Unknown."

"Before that, how long?"

Again, a delay. "816.23 ellipses."

Min couldn't believe that. "Verify response." That figure had to be incorrect. If it were, he and Hab had been one of the most recent groups of visitors all those ellipses ago.

"816.23 ellipses."

"Are beacon satellite uploads intact?"

"Affirmative."

So, a lone Umae had been here just less than three-tenths of an ellipse ago. Now the panel didn't know if he or she was still here or not. One Umae. Two shuttlecraft. That meant that there were likely fatalities when the second shuttle was destroyed. Much worse was the second bit of information. Under the protocols devised by the Directors, there were 240 Journeycraft involved in the search for Haven. None of them had been here in over 800 ellipses. Not all Journeycraft that returned to Uma came here though. There would be Technical Agents with their students, and then the occasional ship in need of some unusual repair. But even so, Min estimated that still comprised maybe twenty percent of the ships. Yet of those 48 or so ships, none had been here in over 800 ellipses. Given the amount of time that had passed, the only reasonable conclusion was that those Journeycraft were somehow lost. Min staggered slightly and leaned against the wall.

"Maintain illumination by 75% within 50 cadens of my position." He effectively placed himself at the middle of the only light source currently operating in the base. Hopefully if someone else were here, that would draw them together. Min took a moment to compose himself. He remembered that the Citadel's Alpha panel was farther towards the center of the structure, so he started walking in that direction. It was as if he had just been here the rotation prior. His memories of the place were just as what he was seeing now.

He rounded the last corner before reaching the panel and abruptly stopped. At the end of the corridor just at the edge of the light was an Umae seated at the panel. He rotated in his chair slowly until he faced Min. He then stood up and began walking in his direction. He appeared to be about Eve's age.

He smiled. "Welcome to the Citadel. May I ask your name? I am called 'Olm'."

Dom accompanied Shu into the Chroniclers' Hall. It was almost identical to the Hall he had seen at the Land Bridge. The central chamber had an enormous panel at one end with a series of thick cables extending up to the apex of the pyramid. Shu took Dom to one of the chambers that branched off of the main area.

"You will live here," she said. The interior of the chamber was rather small with only room for a cushion, a chair, and a simple table. Dom made a quick survey of the space.

"Does yours look like this?" he asked.

"They are all the same," she said. "Regardless of the rank within the Order."

"But you are, what? The 'Chief Chronicler'? Is that your title?"

"Yes. I am the Chief Chronicler and Bal is my Adjutant."

Dom looked about, not seeing Bal in the area. "Are you his only superior?"

"That is an odd question," noted Shu. "Why do you ask?"

"I'm just trying to understand the hierarchy."

"He is my second-in-command," confirmed Shu.

Dom walked over to the chair and sat down. "Who decides the hierarchy?" He ran his finger over the grain of the wood on the tabletop. Shu had no idea that Dom had such a broad vocabulary.

"We decide our own hierarchy," said Shu. "There is a Chief and an Adjutant. The remaining hierarchy is determined by the age of the Chronicler."

He frowned, less than pleased by that discovery. "So . . . .the other Chroniclers made you Chief?"

"No. One of the tasks of a Chief is to designate the person who will become Chief in succession. I was designated by a Chronicler named Ree."

"Ree? What happened to her?"

"Ree was a man," explained Shu. "He died just over an ellipse ago."

"And he made you Chief? Why?"

She sighed, conflicted by his stream of questions. She was heartened by his curiosity but could see that his persistence could easily wear thin after a time. "I suppose it was because he believed that I was best-suited for the position," she said finally.

"Bal has many more ellipses than you do."

"Yes, he does."

Dom looked up from the table. "He probably hated that, didn't he?"

"Who hated what?" interjected a voice. It was Bal. He was standing behind Shu near the entrance. As usual, a small host of Guards attended him. "As you may have noticed, there have been some changes since you left."

"Oh?" said Shu.

Dom studied the Guards and smiled. "Don't worry Shu," he said in a deep, slow voice. "It will be fine."

Shu blinked slowly. "Fine," she said distantly.

"Perhaps you should devote your time to your new student?" suggested Bal. "I'll take care of everything else."

"Yes," agreed Dom.

"Yes," echoed Shu.

"Now, you must go," demanded Bal. "I am awaiting important information." The Guards began to herd Shu and Dom towards the exit and Bal sat down in front of the panel, waiting for Min's message. Dom locked eyes with Bal as he walked passed.

Hierarchies, you fool. Soon, you will know all about hierarchies. I will teach you.

CHAPTER 5

Bal was alone in the Chroniclers' Hall, seated in the Chief Chronicler's chair. He had had the Guards move it so it faced the Alpha panel. Soon he would go out to the remaining Journeyers and advise them as to what Min's calculations concerning Critical Closure had revealed. Bal already knew what the message was going to be. What he didn't know was how long it would take Min to get to the moon, do his calculations, and then relay the result. Bal didn't want to approach the Journeyers too soon, for that might upset his plans.

He had remained patient for so long as his plot unfolded. The Chroniclers were fools, albeit fools in charge. Once he reached that obvious conclusion, Bal had orchestrated a series of events intended to place the Atlans under his worthy rule. The portents revealed as his plans developed only served to reinforce his belief that his course was proper. The discovery of the formula from the Journeyers made him master of the Guards. Earl had handed him supervisory authority over them, providing ample cover for his experiments. Just when his control of them was nearly complete, the earthquake gave him the opportunity to remove Earl permanently and become the primary authority in both law and practice. But Earl was more clever than Bal had anticipated, naming that stupid girl as his successor. The outbreak of the plague and the arrival of the empty Journeycraft had almost sent the people into a blind panic. He wanted them to be afraid, but manageably so. The arrival of the second ship was more fortuitous than he could have imagined. The plague had been eradicated and the authority of the Chroniclers, his authority, had been firmly re-established. Now he simply had to get rid of the remaining Journeyers and his plans were complete.

Eve, Jack and Sol stood near the landing area, accompanied by a band of Guards. Lin and the other Wards had left to gather some of their personal belongings and were just now starting to return. The young Umae sat on the ground shifting uncomfortably, anxious about the journey ahead. Once more, Lise sat very close to Mac. Noting her anxiety, he allowed her to do so.

Bal approached from the direction of the Chroniclers' Hall. He was looking up, searching the sky for any sign of the Journeycraft. The Journeyers watched him uneasily. His appearance surely meant that he had heard from Min.

"How much longer do you think it will be?" said Bal to Jack.

Jack stood silent, staring coolly at Bal.

"It won't be much longer," offered Eve. "Unless there was some sort of mishap. The chances of that are practically zero."

"There won't be any mishaps," said Jack. "I checked the ship myself." He looked up just as the Journeycraft broke through the cloud cover and came into view. Satisfied, he continued glaring at Bal.

The ***Starshine***'s friction thrusters made their characteristic hissing sound as they slowly lowered the ship towards the landing area. Eve ushered the Wards to one side of the platform, well beyond the range of the heat emanating from the ship's hull and the noise from the thrusters, and began explaining the plan to them as the ship started its landing sequence.

"Initially, all of you will board the ***Starshine***," she said pointing to the ship. "Once it takes off, you will enter repose sleep. At the appropriate time, you will be awakened so you can be evaluated and commence training."

Sol looked on with approval. Eve was a natural leader. He had always suspected that. "It is preferable to engage in repose first, and then train," he explained. "Long periods of repose can sometimes interfere with memory and learning. If we did the training first, we might have to do substantial retraining once you awakened."

The students remained silent, unsure of anything they had just heard other than which ship they would be boarding.

"What will you be doing while we are asleep?" asked Lin. Eve glanced at Sol and bit her lip.

"I ....don't know yet," she answered quietly. She looked over at Bal. He was still studying the Journeycraft. The ***Starshine*** had finished landing and had already lowered its egress ramp.

Bal turned abruptly towards Eve. "A word?" he asked. Eve and Sol eagerly walked in his direction.

"Wait!" called Jack. He had been inspecting the gear brought by the Wards. He started after Eve and Sol.

"No!" insisted Bal. "I've no need to speak with you. Your insolence may be permitted when you are with your fellow Journeyers, but I will not tolerate it." Jack scowled but kept coming.

"Jack," said Sol firmly. "Do as he says. We will tell you everything soon enough." Jack stopped, his face a mixture of anger and disappointment. He sneered at Bal before turning and heading back towards the Wards. Bal waited until Jack was outside of hearing range before speaking.

"Min offered grave news," he said in a hushed tone.

"Oh no….." Sol covered his face with his hands. They had failed. Critical Closure had past. Eve slid downwards into a pit of guilt. She was ashamed of the part of her that was relieved, the part that celebrated her opportunity to be with Min once more.

"Critical Closure has not yet been reached," continued Bal.

"But……" began Eve. "You said the news……"

"He said it is very, very close," said Bal. "How did he describe it?" He folded his arms, apparently lost in recollection. "Oh yes. A 'Looming', I believe. He said you would understand."

"Stars……," cursed Sol quietly. "Time is of the essence." He turned towards Eve.

Eve's eyes were lowered as she struggled with her composure. Her life with Min had just been torn from her forever. "Did he say….. anything else?"

Bal let the silence draw out a bit. "He said he was going to enter repose," he said finally. He let that comment float out, inviting further inquiry.

"Repose?" said Sol. "But, he can't………"

"Why would he do that?" interjected Eve. "Why would he?"

Bal hated to provide them with any information that might make them feel better, but his success depended on it. "He said it was the only way he could ever be with you."

Eve was frozen. If The Looming had begun, they would need to arrive at the planet the ***Aurora*** had detected as soon as possible. Even if they found it quickly, and it was suitable with little or no modifications required, it might not matter. Critical Closure could still happen while they were gone. Then it wouldn't matter how long it took them. But, they had a chance.

"Be with me?" she repeated.

"He said he knew he would die soon. He also said that he knew the chances of him surviving the repose weren't very good. But," he continued, looking at Sol, "he said that the best Life Agent he knew could still find a cure. He said you would understand that as well."

Sol swallowed hard. "Eve, we need to go. There is still a chance that everything can still turn out the way it is supposed to, but only if we hurry. You know that."

Eve was focused on something far away, deep in her memory. "I don't want to see him in repose," she said. "I'm afraid that is how I might remember him forever. You are right. We do need to go. And we need to do that now."

Bal looked at the collection of Wards standing ready near the egress ramp. Jack stood with them, impatiently rocking back and forth. Sol and Eve turned and started towards the ship. "Get them aboard," called Eve to Jack. "We have a planet to find."

"And a disease to cure," added Sol quietly.

The storm finally broke shortly before the faint light of dawn arose in the morningside sky. The leantos held out, but they wouldn't be of any use for the next storm. The water had over-saturated the plant fibers comprising the fabric which was now starting to stretch and sag.

May and Pol had managed to keep Joba dry for the most part. Hidden away from the tempest inside his mother's wrappings, he had actually slept through most of the night, waking only occasionally to nurse. May and Pol had huddled closely together, providing each other with the quiet assurance of companionship sought by those facing a common menace. Pol had eventually dozed off, leaving May alone to worry about Cap.

After the rain stopped, May waited for a while to see if Cap would return. When he didn't, she awakened Pol and made preparations to look for him.

"How will you know where to look?" asked Pol anxiously. "He could be anywhere."

May was sorting through the packs, trying to find any useful equipment that was still relatively dry.

"He went deeper into the woods," she said. "I'll follow a line in that direction from the Garden. I can't just stay here and do nothing."

"We will go too," said Pol, starting to rise.

"No!" said May firmly. "The safest place for you and your baby is here, inside these walls." May thought back to the strange noises Cap had attributed to the Hek.

Pol sat back down. "How long will you be gone?" Her voice was nearly strangled by the prospect of being left alone with her baby.

"Not long," said May. "He will probably get back here before I do," she added, trying to comfort herself.

"But won't he go and look for you then?" asked Pol.

A likely possibility, thought May. "Tell him not to," she told Pol. "I don't plan on walking that far. I will just go for a while and try to call to him. I will be back before mid-day."

"What should I do in the meantime?"

May began walking towards the door. "Just take good care of your boy," she said smiling. "He's beautiful." Once she reached the door, she began searching through her pack. With a frustrated grunt, she beat against the door with the side of her fist.

"What's wrong?"

May stepped back and stared at the door. "Cap took the key with him." While Cap's action didn't surprise her, she was nonetheless angered by it. "We can't get out."

Pol looked around at the inside of the Garden walls. Many of the plants had been knocked down or otherwise damaged by the storm. She was relieved that she and Joba would not be left alone.

"Maybe we can fix some of the plants," she suggested. "While we wait?"

Up above, the women heard a dull, distinctive rumble. Looking up, they saw a pair of dark-colored objects moving across the sky, difficult to detect against the background of the cloud cover. May shielded her eyes. "The Journeyers are leaving," she said.

Pol sat in silence, staring up at the pair of faint dots soaring against the gray cloudy backdrop. Joba stretched against his swaddling and then began to fuss. Pol rubbed her cheek against his and began to rock him. May continued to watch the ships until they were swallowed up by the ashen shadows of the sky.

Cap awakened, unable to see anything. Disoriented, he was uncertain if he was enveloped in darkness or if he had lost his sight. From somewhere above him, he could hear the calls of morning birds.

So, he wasn't dead. The pain shooting through his head nearly made him wish he were. He closed his eyes tightly and opened them again. He was face down and his head was surrounded on three sides. He could feel the cool clamminess of mud on both of his cheeks. There was something heavy, and hard, pressed against the back of his head. Only his face was clear, and his nose filled with the scent of damp earth.

Whatever was on the back of his head extended almost to his waist. He was unable to lift his head upwards, so he tried to slide backwards. His arms were relatively free and he was able to push against the dirt on either side, but he couldn't move. His head was lodged into a tight, vice-like space. No matter how he pushed or twisted, he could not extricate himself.

He thought back to the night before. The lightning was striking all around him. He had seen the crevasse in the ground and tried to make it there for cover. An explosion had felled a large tree just as he tumbled inside. The last thing he remembered was the vision of the tree coming down on top of him.

He could not see how he had survived. The only possibility he could imagine was that the bottom of the crevasse was in the shape of a sharp "V". The width of the tree was such that it was narrow enough to strike him a healthy blow, but too thick to reach the bottom of the crevasse. The walls of the crevasse had stopped the tree from crushing him entirely, but now served as two walls of his three-walled prison. There was no way he could move the tree. His only other hope was to dig his way out.

He began to blindly claw at the dirt to either side of him. The clay soil resisted almost every effort he could make. His hands were useless for such a task, his fingertips splitting, his nails starting to break away. From what he could gather, he had made no progress at all.

There remained only one other option. If he stayed here, he would die at the bottom of the crevasse. He needed someone else to get him out. May would be unable to help him as the key to the Garden's door was still inside his pack. He now regretted taking that step to prevent her from following him. Cap began to call out.

"Help! Help me!" Every cry made his head pound more. He had to stop and wait for the pain to subside so he could try again.

"Help! P-please!" His repeated calls left him nearly breathless. Everything was beginning to spin. He called out one last time with all of his remaining strength.

"Help me!"

His mind swirled towards the same darkness that surrounded his face. Air from his stomach forced acid into the back of his throat. The thumping inside his skull sired a wave of light that drowned his vision.

The sounds of the birds stopped. For a split instant . . . .had he heard something? Voices? His focus vanished and he slowly sank into a turbulence that rivaled the storm from the night before.

Dom and Shu walked a short ways up the path towards the lake. Dom stopped and directed Shu to sit on the ground.

"Stay here," he said in his low voice. "Tell no one where I've gone." Shu looked up at him moonily and weakly bobbed her head. "Count to five hundred, and then return to the Chroniclers Hall." Shu tried to force the haze from her mind, searching for the numbers.

To his heartside, Dom could see a large number of people moving towards the launch pad. The so-called "Journeyers" were leaving. Under other circumstances, they would have served his purposes perfectly. However, he had decided they might be more of a hindrance than they were worth. He lost nothing by allowing them to leave on their ship.

He turned to his empty side and began walking along a main pathway between the various pyramids. Once he reached the beach area on the heartside of the island, he stopped and sat down on the ground. Ahead of him, his eyes saw only water. But he could sense his agents. Some of them were not that far away at all. He crossed his legs, closed his eyes, and reached.

His mind peered through the darkness. They tugged at him, so he followed. Some were buried deep in the mud. Eventually, they would prove useful, but he didn't want to wait. There were others who were nearly ready now.

Many of them soared through the sky, scanning the ground. Others crawled through the grass on their feet, or on their bellies, sniffing the air. They all felt his presence, their bodies charging with excitement.

I will tell you what to do. I will tell you what to find. Once you find it, wait for me to give you further instructions. Then we will act, and swiftly. Once we claim this as our own, we will have to only wait for the other. Then the planet will belong to us.

The ***Starshine*** exited the cloud cover high above Uma. Eve watched as the last glimpse of solid ground disappeared beneath the solid gray sky. She turned and sat down in the seat reserved for the Command Agent. It was the last position she had wanted to find herself in. Consistent with what Bal had told them, Min had conveyed Command Authority to her. The ***Starshine*** was her ship now.

Lin hesitantly approached. "Eve? I'm curious. Is it all right if I ask what we are doing?"

Eve thought about the best way to answer that question. "Critical Closure hasn't been reached," she said finally. Lin stared at her. "That means that we still have time to find Haven and get back in time to save our people. But we need to hurry." She patted Lin's hand. "***You*** need to hurry." Eve had decided some time ago that if things worked out the way they had, she would need distractions. Her focus, as much as she could determine it, would have to be on the students.

Then there was Min. She imagined him on the moon, all alone. He was in repose because it offered him the only chance, however slight, of a life with her. A growing part of her wished that Critical Closure had come and gone already.

She stopped for a moment and gathered herself. She doubted that Min had ever felt that way, but she was comforted by the slight possibility that he had.

Min studied Olm for a moment before responding.

"I am called 'Min'," he said. "I wasn't expecting anyone to be here. I guess the bio-sensors have been damaged."

"Oh?" replied Olm. "I have never had any reason to use them. I wasn't aware there was a problem."

"How long have you been here?"

A trickle of sweat made its way down the side of Min's face as he awaited Olm's reply. "Are you all right?" asked Olm. "You don't look well."

"I have a terminal illness," he said plainly. "I become fatigued rather easily. That is why I reduced the gravity."

"I see. So, you have command authority."

"Yes," said Min. "I assume you don't."

"No. I was the Tech Agent on my ship. It will be nice being able to access the command level systems finally."

"What happened to your ship?"

"It is a long story," said Olm. "Perhaps we should sit. Here, let me help you with your gear." Olm reached down and picked up Min's pack before the pair moved back to where Olm had been seated earlier.

Min casually looked over the panel after lowering himself into a chair. "It appears to be in excellent condition," he said. "Have you done much to it?"

"Yes, I have done a number of upgrades since I have been here. Some of the equipment was damaged somehow. It required fairly significant repairs."

Min continued to study the panel. "You have done fine work. I can't see any sign of damage at all."

"Thank you."

"So, tell me your story. How long have you been here?"

Olm sat back in a chair. "Not quite an ellipse. When I came out of repose, the rest of my crewmates were dead. There had been some sort of malfunction in the repose support systems. I wasn't sure what to do, so I came here."

His tone seemed to Min rather matter-of-fact considering the subject matter of his story. It also didn't explain the existence of the two shuttles, one of which was obliterated. Min needed to hear more. "You just abandoned your ship?"

Olm took a deep breath. "Before I came here, I tried to identify the nature of the problem with the repose units. I determined that their failure was due to a severe imbalance in the fusion generators. The imbalance was critical and I didn't have time to effect repair."

Min leaned forward slightly. "What did you do?"

"I set a course for the sun and took a shuttle here."

Min sat back in his chair again. "You sent your Journeycraft into the sun?!? Why?"

"I hadn't been Technical Agent for very long," Olm said in the same flat tone. "I didn't know what else I should do."

"I see," said Min finally. "Were you coming here anyway, to the Citadel, before going to Uma?"

"To Uma? Yes," said Olm. "We were coming here."

They must have been stopping for his introduction to the Citadel, thought Min. His former mentor was bringing him. "I'm sorry to hear about your loss," said Min. He was feeling a bit guilty about his prior tone. "If the ship was critical, I suppose it doesn't matter where it ended up. What was her name?"

"Her?"

"The ship."

"It was called the ***Aurora***." Min's insides clenched before trembling with anxiety. He looked away, feigning a cough so he could seek composure.

"What about the debris field outside?" asked Min. "Do you know anything about that?"

Olm's response came slowly. "Debris field? I don't know anything about that. It wasn't there when I arrived."

Min was trying to put everything together. Olm's story was plainly impossible. At least on the surface, he had an understanding of Journeycraft technology, so his claim of being a Technical Agent was plausible. But he didn't understand the default directives of any Journeycraft. If a crew became unable to guide their ship, the ship would automatically set a course for its home settlement on Uma. Olm had been on the ***Aurora*** when her crew was lost, of that Min felt certain. But Olm didn't know where the ***Aurora*** would go without any direction from her crew. And he couldn't know that Min had seen the ***Aurora*** himself. If a shuttle collided with the Citadel, it would have shaken the entire building. There was no way Olm couldn't have noticed. Min wanted to examine the debris field. It was the only way he could determine what happened to the shuttles and the rest of the crew. His priority was still to upload and examine the data he had collected about the Hek. And his crew was still waiting to hear from him.

"It's been a rotation," said Min wearily. "I need to sleep some. I plan on going out and looking at the debris field later. Do you think you can look at the biosensors?"

"Is that an order?" asked Olm.

"No. Of course not," said Min uneasily. "But it would help."

"Very well," said Olm as he rose from his chair. "Sleep well. I will talk to you again soon." With that, he rose and Min watched him warily as he glided off into the darkness.

Cap slowly opened his eyes, his lids weighted with achiness. Bright stakes of pain pierced his head. He squinted and tried unsuccessfully to sit up.

"Cap? Are you all right?"

The male voice sounded vaguely familiar. Cap opened his eyes a bit more and saw four men standing around him. He blinked at the light, trying to make it go away.

"Who?" he grumbled. His tongue felt like a strip of leather inside of his mouth.

"It's Dag," said the voice. "I'm with Jed, Wil, and Lex. Are you all right?"

Cap gave his eyes a moment to focus and his brain a chance to emerge from the fog besetting it. "Dag? Where am I?" He was starting to remember. Dag was one of his former Charges.

"Jed, get some water," said Dag. "I'm not sure where we are. We were brought here by the Guards in a boat."

"Boat?" Jed handed Dag a small skin of water. Dag helped Cap sit up so he could drink. As Cap adjusted his weight, his lower leg throbbed. A flaming gash on the side of his calf was smothered with red and yellow goo. He grimaced and tried rolling onto his side.

"Yes," said Dag. "The canoe with the Journeyer came back but it was surrounded by Guards. Then the Guards surrounded us and took us all away."

"Your leg doesn't look good," said Jed. "You must have injured it when the tree fell on you."

Cap looked down at his leg. The pant leg had been torn away.

"Hopefully it isn't very deep. What happened?"

"We heard you calling out," explained Jed. "It took us a while to figure out where you were. Then we had to figure out how to lever the tree away from you so we could pull you out." Jed gave Cap's figure a quick survey. "How do you feel?"

Cap groaned and lay back. "Awful," he said softly. "My head . . ." He closed his eyes and swallowed hard. "Have you been to the Garden?"

"Garden?" asked Dag. "What Garden?" Dag had been very young when Cap was his Rearer. He had been assigned to new Rearers when he was about Dom's age. A lot of the Wards never went to the mainland at all.

"I'll have to show you. Can I have that water again?"

Dag handed him the waterskin. "Are you alone out here?"

Cap drank and returned the waterskin to Dag. "No, May is with me. So is Pol and her baby, Joba."

"Joba?" asked Lex. "The baby has two names?"

"It is a long story. Why are you four here?"

Wil scowled. "We were exiled. The Guards just came, put us on a boat, and dropped us on the beach."

"Why? What did you do?"

Wil shrugged. "We don't know. Bal wouldn't tell us."

"Bal?" asked Cap. "I'm not surprised. When did this happen?"

"Last rotation," said Lex. "We landed not too far ahead of the storm."

"So why were you running around in the woods? I was looking for a good tree to make a canoe out of."

"So were we," said Wil. "Are you a boat wright?"

Cap surveyed his surroundings. They were in a small clearing amongst a number of tall trees, many of them missing branches due to the storm. Each of the four men had a sizeable bag of equipment. "No," said Cap, managing a smile through the pain, "but I'm hoping one of you is."

"We all are, why?" said Lex.

"All four?" answered Cap. He couldn't believe the way his luck had turned. "We need to get back to the Garden. I don't think I can walk."

"We will get you back there," said Dag. He knelt down and helped Cap stand up. The older man leaned heavily on the young boat wright. "Come on Lex, give us a hand."

Lex moved over and he and Dag each ducked under one of Cap's arms. "This isn't so bad," said Lex. "You tell us where to go. We will take turns helping you."

"Head that way generally," said Cap groggily. "Once we reach the tree line, I'll be able to get my bearings."

The men complied and slowly made their way through the woods, careful to avoid the myriad twisted roots springing from the ground. Eventually, the surrounding trees began to grow smaller. The men stopped to take a break.

"This is fine," said Cap. His head was pounding and he felt very, very sleepy.

"You don't sound that good," said Dag. "You are slurring your words."

Cap blinked hard, trying to understand. "I'll be . . . .fine," he said tiredly. "Once we get to . . . .Garden."

The men decided to cut their break short. This time, Jed and Wil assisted Cap. As they began to lift Cap off the ground again, a low grumbling chatter reached out at them from the direction they had come.

"What was that?" asked Lex. "An animal?"

Jed was trying to listen. "I don't know. Be quiet a moment."

They heard the sound again, this time to their heartside. It was quickly followed by a near-identical sound from the opposite direction.

"We should go," said Wil nervously.

Had Cap heard that noise before? His brain was clouding up again. His ears roared with the sound of a rainstorm.

The men moved slowly forward. They could see the edge of the tree line ahead. The sound of rustling twigs drew their attention to their empty side. A pair of dogs, their backs over knee-high to the men, stopped close by and bared their teeth. Each dog crouched down, a powerful growl erupting from both as they drew back their lips.

The men stopped. "W-what are those?" asked Lex.

"Stay still," said Wil. "Maybe they will go away." He glanced at Cap. His head slumped to one side, his eyes were mostly closed.

One dog began to circle the group while the other held his ground. The first loosed a deep, booming bark that rebounded off of every nearby tree. The second simply continued with his menacing growls.

Then, a whistle split through the trees like a sparrow. The dogs' ears perked up and they looked in the direction of the whistle. The men also looked, but saw nothing. A second whistle sounded and both dogs bounded off in that direction, quickly disappearing from sight.

"Let's move!" implored Dag. The men hurried along as fast as they dared, dragging Cap as they went. They didn't stop again until they were halfway across the clearing beyond the trees.

"Now we have to find this Garden," said Wil. He looked at Cap. He was sweating profusely and his eyes were rolled back in his head. Wil gently rubbed Cap's cheeks. "Come on, man. Wake up. Where do we go?"

The others looked on eagerly, stealing glances back at the forest. Cap's eyes regained a bit of focus.

"Go morningsidedly until you see a wide opening." The effort to speak clearly was plainly taxing him. "Then . . .back . . . .heartside." His head rolled to one side and his eyes closed fast.

"Let's give it a try," said Dag.

"Back in those woods?" asked Lex. "Are you sure?"

Dag nodded. "Cap says May is in there. Maybe she can help him. We have to try."

Once more, Dag and Lex shouldered Cap and the five men headed back into the woods.

Bal re-entered the Hall with a spring in his step. With the Journeyers gone, his plan was complete. Finally, Atla belonged to him. He saw Shu sitting quietly on a pile of cushions.

"Where is Dom?" asked Bal.

"He left," said Shu.

"'Left'?" repeated Bal angrily. "Where did he go?"

Dom then strolled in, glancing at the Guards who, once they identified him, allowed him to enter.

"Dom!" scolded Bal. "Where have you been!?!"

"I got bored so I went for a walk."

Shu walked over to him, folding her arms. "Boredom leads to lapses in concentration," she said with a giggle.

"Where did you go?" asked Bal.

"The lake, on the side opposite the docks."

"We were near there, we didn't see you."

"You went to see the Journeyers off," said Dom flatly.

"Do you really think you are ready for training as a Chronicler?" asked Bal.

"If I weren't, Shu would not have picked me." His smirk didn't escape Bal's attention.

Bal turned towards Shu. "Well, I have information to gather. You will both remain in the Hall until further notice. The Guards will be so instructed." Bal turned and walked past the Guards, exiting the Hall.

"He is upset," said Dom.

"Yes," said Shu. "He wants you to do what you're told."

"Maybe," he replied in a low voice, "***you*** should get used to doing as you are told." Shu stiffened as his voice poured into her head like a cold morning fog. "But you are learning, aren't you?"

She closed her eyes and reopened them, trying to focus. "Y-yes," she said finally.

Dom smiled. "That's what I thought."

CHAPTER 6

After Olm had gone, Min moved to the Alpha panel and sat down in the chair in front of it. There had been obvious modifications made since the last time he had seen it. It would take him some time to determine if they were improvements or not. The nearby wall also showed signs of repair. Min surmised that the impact with the shuttle had taken place on the far side. He would have to analyze it more closely once he came back in from the surface. The repairs were noticeable because of their scale, not their craftsmanship. Whoever did the repairs was rather skilled.

He withdrew his resonance scanner and attached it to a port atop the panel. He directed the panel to retrieve the data concerning the Heks' protein templates from the scanner and commence with performing a detailed calculation as to the proximity of Critical Closure. The analysis would take a while, but he wanted the result to be as accurate as possible. This would also give him time to make the trip out to the debris field to see if he could determine what had happened to the shuttle.

As he stood, he heard a rapidly growing hum followed by a loud pop. He could see smoke wafting from the scanner. He reached out and attempted to unplug it from the panel. The metal began to scorch his skin the instant he touched it.

"Ah!" He reflexively withdrew his hand. "What happened?"

"Scanner no longer operative." Based on the amount of smoke and the temperature of the metal, Min didn't doubt the panel's word. Nonetheless, the panel had begun executing a directive of some type.

"But what happened to it?"

"Director level authorization required." Min had never **heard** of "Director level authorization."

"Director lev-……. What do you mean by 'director level authorization'? There is no such thing."

"Director level authorization required."

It had to be the modifications to the Alpha panel, Min thought. They hadn't been done properly and now the entire panel was malfunctioning. He drew a deep breath. His mind was weary. He could only unravel one mystery at a time.

Min stood back up and picked up his pack. He began to slowly walk in the direction of the crew quarters. His previous illumination command remained in effect, lighting the hallway he was in but extinguishing the lights behind him. He had forgotten about the command after meeting Olm. Min wondered how Olm was managing in the dark.

The crew quarters were just like he remembered. There were a number of low bunks, each with individualized thermostatic controls. There was also a sustenance generator. He mentally commended Olm on his tidiness. Each bunk was neatly made. Min picked the nearest bunk and sat down on it. He dug through his pack and found the vial Sol had given him. It was nearly full. He estimated that there were perhaps twenty doses inside. He could replicate more, but he doubted that would benefit him. Sol had told him it would have a decreasing benefit with each dose. No question Sol had given him as much as would be effective. He returned the vial to his pack, and slipped under the covers. It was a bit chilly in the room, so he increased the thermostatic levels on the bed. Within moments, the strain of the rotation caught up with him and he was fast asleep.

Olm stood at the doorway and watched. He hadn't bothered to inspect the biosensors. He already knew what was wrong with them. His access to the technology he needed had been severely limited because he lacked command authorization. That was no longer going to be a problem. He would extract the information once Min had authorized it, and then prevail upon Min to explain the concepts with which Olm was unfamiliar. After that, he would only have to wait. Alone. Olm didn't plan on allowing Min to survive until the Sire arrived.

The men cautiously bore Cap back towards the forest. Once they found what they believed to be the opening Cap had described, they turned heartside and began searching for the Garden.

In the distance, they could hear barking followed by more shrill whistles. While it was hard to discern exactly how far away the sounds were, it was clear that they were getting closer.

Finally, the towering Garden walls came into view. The group made it to the base of the structure and looked for a way in.

"There has to be a door somewhere," said Jed.

"Let's just walk along the wall until we find it," said Lex. The roots were mostly absent near the base of the wall. They were able to make better progress as they searched for a way inside. Soon, they were standing outside of the huge doors.

They set Cap down on the ground and Wil pushed on the door as hard as he could. It didn't budge.

"Ahhhh....," he groaned, "too heavy. Give me a hand here." His three companions joined him and attempted to push the door open. Still, no success.

"May must be inside," said Dag. "Should I call out?" The four stood looking at one another, aware of the barking and whistling sounds coming from somewhere nearby.

"We've got to get inside," said Jed.

"May?" Dag called loudly. "May? Can you hear me?"

They all waited for a moment, listening intently.

"Who's there?" came a voice from behind the door.

"I think that's her," Dag said. "May. It's Dag. I'm with some others from the island. Cap is with us."

"Cap? Are you all right?" The concern in her voice was obvious. Cap was not moving.

"He's been hurt," said Dag finally. "We need to get inside. Can you let us in?"

"Hurt?" Her voice was now coming from just inside the door.

"We need to get in," repeated Dag. "How do we get in?"

"There is a key," said May. "Cap has it. Check his pack. It looks like a simple piece of metal."

Lex began digging through Cap's pack. He retrieved the key. "Is it a rectangle?"

"Yes, I think that must be it," said May. "Hold it next to where the cross-plank fits into the frame. If you hear a popping sound, you will be able to open the door."

Lex looked around at his companions. "If you say so." He reached up, holding the key next to the cross-plank. He was rewarded with the predicted popping noise.

"Now push," said Dag. The group's efforts were not entirely necessary as the door now opened easily. May squeezed through the opening as soon as it was wide enough. She immediately moved over next to Cap.

"What happened to him?" she asked. Her voice was tainted with panic.

"He said the storm blew a tree over on him," said Dag. "It must have hit him in the head. His leg is hurt, too."

"So he was able to speak earlier?" asked May as she examined him.

"For a while," said Dag. "He said his head hurt and then he passed out."

May inspected him closely, not entirely certain what to look for. "Let's move him inside."

Wil pushed the door open as far as he could before joining Dag in lifting Cap. On Dag's signal, they slowly lifted him and moved him through the doorway. Pol and Joba were huddled against a far wall. The men carefully set Cap back down on the ground. May continued with her examination.

"Someone should get the door shut," she noted offhandedly. Lex started over towards the door, only to be met by a huge dog. It entered through the doorway, baring its teeth and growling ominously. Lex stopped and then took a small step backwards.

"E-easy," he said quietly, holding his hands out protectively in front of him.

Another dog, just as large, appeared at the door and moved in next to the first. It too was snarling menacingly.

Then, a loud whistle sounded as a number of short, thick men followed the dogs inside. Each was nearly naked, wearing only a small cloth around his loins. Their broad bodies were covered with thick, dark hair. There were six of them, and four bore long spears adorned with feathers. The dogs retreated and moved behind the men.

The four shipwrights stepped back while May protectively covered Cap's unconscious form. The spear-bearers stepped forward, surveying the interior of the Garden. One looked down at Cap, slowly extending the point of his spear.

"No!" screeched May as she batted the tip of the spear away. "You will not hurt him!"

The six men muttered to one another, each apparently amused by May's reaction. One of the dogs started barking, which caused the nearest man to turn and snarl at it.

"What do you want?" asked Dag. He clutched a small stone axe but his sweaty hands trembled so badly he feared it would escape his grip. His companions huddled next to him, none wishing to be the first to run but all too petrified to take any meaningful action. The spear-bearers eyed Dag and his companions. One grunted something to the others who then started stomping their feet. "They are....going to kill us," he gasped. Pol unleashed a terror-filled shriek and she engulfed Joba in her embrace.

Again, the same dog started barking. This time, the other dog joined in as well, leading a hairy man to bellow at the offending canines. The dogs yelped, lowered their heads and slinked some distance away. The men then returned their attention to the Umae now facing them. May was shaken by quivering tremors but tried to meet their gaze as bravely as she could.

Joba woke up, startled by his mother's outburst, and started to cry. The spear-bearers looked around frantically and took several steps back. One of them determined the source of the sound and pointed it out to the others. Pol clutched Joba tightly against her, but he continued to bawl.

The newcomers each took another step back before smiling broadly. Their faces were awash with sheer joy.

"What are they doing?" asked Jed quietly. His cries made them…happy?"

May watched them closely. "Pol, take Joba out and let them have a closer look."

"N-no!" protested Pol, trying to cover Joba entirely.

"I don't think they will hurt him," said May.

Pol looked down at her crying son and began to weep. She hesitantly removed the wrap from around his head. Once freed, Joba cut loose with his full vigor.

The spear-bearers looked at one another, each grinning enthusiastically. In their excitement. they let their weapons drop. One of them came forward slowly, focusing solely on Joba as he approached. Pol clutched him protectively. As the man edged closer, he looked at Pol as if to seek her approval. Despite her sobs, he continued his slow advance.

Once he was close enough, he tentatively reached out towards Joba's head. He held his hand there for a moment, as if to warm it over a fire. The rest of them moved in. Pol turned her body rotating Joba away from them. The first figure stood up straight and let out a loud, bellowing laugh. His companions joined him. Soon, they were engaged in an impromptu dance near the doorway to the Garden.

The fear experienced by Dag and his friends slowly gave way to curiosity. The other men didn't seem concerned about their spears, and the dogs were quietly lying on the ground, drowsily waiting for their masters to finish with whatever it was they were doing. The dance ended. The same man approached Pol. He pointed, indicating a direction deeper into the forest, beyond the Garden. Pol looked to May for guidance.

"I think they want you to go with them," she said.

"No!" said Pol firmly, shaking her head. "I won't."

Once again, the man pointed. This time he grunted for added emphasis.

"We'll go with you," said May. Dag and the others all turned towards her. "We can't stay here forever. Besides, Cap needs help. I can't do anything for him. Maybe they have someone who can."

"Do you think so?" asked Jed doubtfully.

"I don't know," admitted May. "But they can't do any worse. If they were going to kill us, we'd be dead."

"N-now?' asked Pol meekly.

"I'd say they are ready now," said May. She rose slowly and signaled to the others to attend Cap. "Jed, you and Dag help me collect some food before we leave." She considered the burly men for a moment. "It's hard to say when we might be able to find more." Once they had completed that task, Wil and Lex moved over and lifted Cap off of the ground. This drew no protest from the strange men.

The one who had been pointing started walking towards the door, turning to make sure they were following. Once he saw that they were, he grunted his approval. The two dogs jumped up and ran off into the woods.

Dom and Bal sat in front of the main panel of the Chronicler's Hall. Other lesser Chroniclers, each clad in a red robe, moved about the interior of the chamber focused on various tasks. Shu was nowhere to be seen.

"Do I start today?" asked Dom.

"Start what?" replied Bal.

"My training."

"Your training is going to take a very, very long time," he scolded. "And you are very impatient. Patience is a very important characteristic for a Chronicler."

"Why?"

Bal wondered what Shu had seen in this boy. Dom was impatient, resistant to authority, and obviously disinterested in most things going on around him. He was poorly qualified to train as a Chronicler.

"Chronicler training requires a student to master certain skills and information in a specific order, and at a specific pace," Bal explained, trying to remain calm. "To achieve mastery, a student's proficiency must be exceptionally high. That typically takes a very, very long time. There is no room for mediocrity in what we do."

"I'm not mediocre," said Dom flatly. "You'll see."

"I'm sure," said Bal. He turned to the display above the panel. "This is the main display. It is capable of interfacing with a Chronicler personally and transmitting information directly to a prepared mind. If the mind is not prepared, the consequences can be tragic."

"Like what?"

"Insanity. Death." Bal was attempting to intimidate him. "There are others."

"What kind of information?"

"Historical data. Since our people first had the technological ability to do so, Chroniclers have been maintaining records of our history."

"It's all in there?" asked Dom, gesturing at the panel.

Bal thought he sensed a hint of interest. "Yes. But only one who is properly trained can retrieve the specific information sought."

"Why not just seek everything?"

"This is madness!" Bal spat. "Why are you even here? You aren't even close to being Chronicler material! You should have been exiled with the others."

Dom was unfazed by Bal's outburst. "Are you going to answer my question?"

"The panel contains every bit of historical information we could gather since we have been here."

"How long is that?"

Bal drew a deep breath in an effort to relieve his frustration. "We don't know for sure," he admitted. "The older the data sought, the greater the danger to the seeker."

"Why?"

"All historical information is connected to events transpiring later. The older the data, the more connections it has. A carelessly broad inquiry, or one that seeks information too distant in time, could result in a flood of information that would overwhelm the user. The data would only surface inside the user's mind in bits and pieces. It wouldn't be coherent. The relevance of one fact to others would be lost. Unless he or she were truly exceptional, that person would likely go mad eventually trying to tie everything together."

"Do you think Min is truly exceptional?" asked Dom.

"Wha-?" Bal didn't know how to respond.

"Just trying to think of an example," offered Dom.

"Never mind that," snapped Bal. "Your lesson today is on focus. You must be able to passively observe a series of events and then be able to interface with the panel so the events can be registered. You must do so objectively, without bias. We will train you not only to make observations in your mind, but to be able to recall them accurately, even after a long time has passed. Think you can try that?"

Dom looked at Bal blankly. "When I came in this morning, there were two other people here. One was a woman who was slightly favoring her left foot when she walked. The other was a man who sat on that mat by the wall, pretending to meditate. He was breathing rather quickly, so I doubt he was trying very hard. He kept opening and closing his eyes, one at a time. Eventually, he stood up and left, going into that side chamber," he said, indicating a doorway off the main chamber. "The woman just walked in again."

Bal turned and looked at the door, seeing a relatively young woman standing there speaking quietly with one of the Guards. Bal motioned her over. As she approached, he noted a slight limp.

"Tam, are you all right?" Bal asked.

"Yes, why?"

"You have injured your foot?"

"My foot?" she asked, glancing down. "No, I just turned my ankle slightly yesterday. I hardly notice it now." She looked over at Dom. "How did you know?"

"You are favoring the foot a bit," said Bal. "I was just checking."

"I didn't realize," she said. "How odd."

"It hurts now." Dom's voice was a low whisper.

Tam grimaced slightly. "No, I'm fine . . . . .really." She took a couple of cautious steps away from the panel. She was favoring her foot much more than she had been before.

"Try soaking it in the lake," suggested Bal. "The cool water may help."

Tam watched Dom warily. "I'll do that. Thank you." She turned and hobbled off towards the doorway.

"What did the man that you saw look like?" asked Bal.

"He was slightly taller and thinner than average," said Dom. "There is a small imperfection on his forehead just above one eye. One of his fingers, his heartside small, is crooked."

Bal studied Dom for a moment, not knowing whether to take him seriously. "Stay here." Bal got up and walked over to the side chamber where Dom had said the man had gone. Bal knocked and stuck his head inside.

"May I assist you, Bal?" said the man inside. He was seated on a cushion, rubbing his eyes.

"Kov, how are your studies going?" asked Bal. Bal noted a small scar just above his eye.

"Well until this morning," he said. "My eyes have been itching. It is quite a distraction. I was . . . .unable to meditate." A tinge of guilt colored his last confession.

"You must focus," said Bal. "Your focus will allow you to overcome that."

Kov frowned. "I understand," he said quietly.

"May I see your heartside hand?"

Kov stopped rubbing his eyes and blinked several times. "My hand?" Kov extended his hand. His small finger was bent at an odd angle.

"What happened to your finger?" asked Bal.

"Oh. As a Ward, I fell down while running. When I tried to catch myself, I bent my finger back. I got this too," he added, pointing to his scar.

"How long have you been a student here?" asked Bal.

"About ten ellipses," said Kov. "Why?"

"No reason. Continue your focus exercises. I'm sure you will be fine."

When Bal returned to the central chamber he noted a subtle smile playing at the corners of Dom's lips. "We will work on focus," said Bal firmly. "And on patience. But focus first. Are you ready to learn?"

"More than ready," said Dom.

Bal considered his reply. Perhaps Shu knew what she was doing after all.

Min shot up in bed, his body soaked with sweat. The dreams had plagued him again. There were dozens of different creatures surrounding him. Most were the tall, white, almost hairless Umae that he was accustomed to. All around them were others, all very different. Some were short and squat and hairy, even more so than the Hek. Their arms were unusually long and they walked hunched over, dragging their fingers on the ground. Their bodies were thick and powerful and they were constantly vigilant, claiming ownership of everything around them with their intense stares.

Another group was a bit taller, a bit less well-muscled. Their bodies were covered almost entirely with a light coat of hair. They carried long spears and grunted back and forth at one another, oblivious to the thick, hairy beasts nearby.

Above, scuttling through the tree branches were more still. They were small and agile. Some had tails nearly as long as their bodies. They chattered down defiantly at the others, confident in their ability to escape.

A final group had thick boney brows and brown hair. They sniffed suspiciously at the air around them. They were covered with furs taken from other animals.

The last four groups, as if signaled by a cue inaudible to him, all turned towards Min. The hairy giants pounded their chests and roared. The Hek bounced back and forth, menacing him with their spear tips. The small ones in the trees chattered madly, hurling bits of fruit. Those covered with furs eyed him hungrily. His death was but a step towards their next meal. Spit dribbled from their mouths.

Min's head pounded and he tried to calm himself. His lungs screamed for air. The chamber was completely dark. "Illuminate. . . . .twenty percent," he said weakly. None of the other beds were occupied. In fact, there were no indications that any of them had been used. Min scratched his head. "How long did I sleep?"

"Point four six rotations," responded the overhead panel.

Min turned his body and sat on the edge of the bed. Now that he was beyond the range of the thermostatic control, the air felt cool on his skin. After a few deep breaths, his heartbeat slowed and his head cleared. He had slept for nearly half a rotation. It felt like he had hardly slept at all. He wondered if Sol had been accurate with his prognosis.

"Where is Olm?" The panel was silent. "Olm, where is he?"

"Unable to reply."

Min looked upwards. "Unable to reply? Why?"

"No such data available."

He stood up and walked towards the cleaning chamber. After quickly stripping off his clothes, he stepped inside and closed his eyes. He was soon coated with a solvent that dissolved all of the dirt and impurities on his body. The mixture transformed into a mist that quickly dispersed into the air. It was an entirely different experience from bathing in the lake on Uma, but it was much more efficient. He stepped out, placed his clothes into the chamber, and performed the same process on them. He then redressed and walked towards the Citadel's Alpha panel.

The hallway ahead of him lit up on his approach only to extinguish after he passed. The darkness hadn't affected Olm at all. For now, he'd keep the illumination directive in place.

As he approached the Alpha panel the overhead lights came on, revealing Olm seated in one of the chairs. He was looking at the display.

"How'd you sleep?" said Min.

Olm turned and watched Min approach. "Fine," he said before turning back to the panel. "I would like for you to do something for me."

Min sat down. "What?" The reduced gravity made moving around easier, but it still placed a great strain on his body.

Olm drew very close to Min, his grim expression bearing down on him. "I need for you to provide me with command authority. You are very strong. Don't you want to do that?" His voice was deep and soft.

"Why?" asked Min. "What do you need it for?"

Olm's face reddened. "Command authority," he began in the same deep, slow voice. "I need it."

"And I need to know why," replied Min. Olm tightly gripped the arms of his chair. He then released the chair and took a deep breath.

"Training. I wasn't entirely honest with you before," he said.

"In what way?"

"I wasn't quite a Technical Agent on the ***Aurora***. I . . . .almost was. My training wasn't quite complete."

"I see. So you need access to the training protocols in the Alpha panel."

"Yes."

"I don't see why I can't do that," conceded Min. "Were you able to determine anything about the biosensors?"

Olm shook his head. "No."

"Well, maybe once you finish the training modules, you will figure it out." Min moved over next to the panel where Olm was seated. "Command Authority Min. Olm is authorized to access training protocols for technology."

The display came to life. "Explain."

Min frowned and looked over at Olm. "Explain what?"

"Maybe we should . . . ." began Olm. Min raised his hand, cutting him off.

"Explain identity 'Olm'," replied the panel.

Min ran his hands across his scalp. "Sounds like a malfunction," he told Olm. "'Olm is sitting right next to me," he told the panel.

"Explain."

"It must be related to the biosensor problem," he said. "I asked the panel to tell me where you were earlier and it couldn't. I'll simply set up a temporary passcode. Enter it when you want to look at the tutorials."

Olm stoicly studied the display. "Very well."

"Say," said Min. "I have some gear that I left back in the dormitory. I will need it when I go back outside. I'm still not feeling very well. Would you mind getting it and meeting me at the Egress Portal?"

Olm turned and scowled. "Very well," he repeated. He stood up and walked off in the direction of the dormitory, once again disappearing into the darkened hallway.

"Status of current process?" asked Min. The protein template analysis had to be nearly finished.

"Process complete in point seven six rotations."

"So long?" asked Min. He stood up and reached into his pocket. Inside was the vial of Sol's medication. Realizing he would need all the strength he could gather for his trip outside, he unscrewed the lid and swallowed some down.

He felt almost normal again. He remembered that much of his perceived strength was due to the decreased gravity of the Citadel. He wasn't getting any better. Sol was right about that after all.

As he walked towards the portal, he thought about the ***Starshine*** and the ***Aurora***. He thought about Eve. His only company was going to be the Alpha panel and Olm, the strange man that the panel couldn't detect. He hoped it was a sensor problem of some sort. If it was anything more complicated than that, he likely wouldn't have time to figure it out.

May couldn't remember seeing such a light-colored sky. It was almost white, with grayish striations running through the cloud cover. The fury of the storm had drained the rain from the clouds. The ground was soaked. The mud made passage very, very difficult.

The Hek were patient with the pace of progress being made by the men bearing Cap. The four men were going to err on the side of caution, careful not to drop Cap in their haste to go to some unknown place with the spear-bearers and their dogs. Just past mid-rotation, the group made it to the place where Cap had been trapped under the tree. The men stopped as they were clearly in need of rest. One of the Hek walked over to look at Joba. The baby had been quiet for the trip thus far and he cooed sweetly at the short, thick man staring at him so intently. He grinned broadly and glanced back at his companions. This made Pol draw her baby closer to her, frightened by any attention they were giving him.

May leaned over Cap. He gave no signs of regaining consciousness, but his breathing was steady and easy. She gently caressed his forehead with the back of her hand. His brow was slightly warm, but nothing to foster concern. One of the Hek watched her closely, intrigued by her actions.

"How far do you think we are going?" asked Dag.

"No way to know," replied Lex. "We'll know when we get there."

Jed was seated on a large tree root. "They don't seem like they want to hurt us," he noted.

"No," Lex agreed. "They don't pay much attention to the rest of us at all."

"They do like the baby," offered Wil. "Their attitudes changed when they heard him cry before." Pol drew Joba closer to her, offering him a breast. He immediately began to feed.

Dag approached one of the Hek. "Where are we going?" he asked slowly.

The Hek looked over at his nearest companion.

"They don't talk," said Jed.

"Not like us, anyway," said Lex.

One of the Hek stood back up and began to carefully inspect each of the nearby trees. He ran his hands over the bark of each tree he approached before sniffing at its trunk. He then moved to another tree and repeated the process. The Umae stood quietly, trying to understand.

Finally, he approached a tree at the edge of the clearing. Its bark was far more gnarled than that of the other trees. It had wide, fat leaves with six lobes. There wasn't another tree like it nearby. The man reached up and tore off a switch from a low branch. He twirled it in his fingers for a moment before letting out a sudden whistle.

One of the dogs leapt up and was quickly at his side. The man grunted at the dog before presenting the stick to it. The dog took the stick in his mouth and ran off into the forest.

The man returned to the middle of the clearing and sat down. Each of the Hek withdrew a small stone from his pouch and began honing the tip of his spear. They were oblivious to the Umae.

"Are they going to . . . .kill us now?" whimpered Pol.

May looked over at her. "No, of course not."

"Then . . . .what?"

May tried to think of a satisfactory answer. "I don't know." Her attention was drawn to Cap as he stirred slightly. She leaned down close to him. "Cap?" she whispered. "Can you hear me?"

He slowly opened his eyes. After a number of slow blinks, he was able to focus on May's face.

"H-happened?" he said softly.

May put her finger to her lips. "Hard to explain. We are in the forest. With the Hek."

Cap closed his eyes, trying to clear the clouds from his brain. He wasn't sure he had heard May correctly. He guardedly turned his head and saw the group of Hek diligently sharpening their spears.

"H-hek?"

"Take it easy," May said. "Everything is fine. You need to be still."

Unable to disagree, Cap closed his eyes. Soon, he was asleep again.

"We should keep moving," said Dag. "There is a lot of light left. We shouldn't waste it." He stood up and moved towards Cap. One of the Hek intercepted him. He grunted and emphatically pointed into the forest.

"What?" asked Dag. "I don't understand."

The Hek grunted again. He pointed at Dag and then pointed at the ground.

"Sit," said May. "He wants you to sit."

"But I don't want to sit," protested Dag.

Lex placed his hand on Dag's shoulder. "Sit," he said. The other Hek were watching him. He went back to his spot and sat back down.

"So, we just sit here?" he asked.

"For now," said May. "They are up to something. I'd like to know what."

"Me, too," said Jed. "But at least it isn't raining."

May looked up. The canopy was very thick overhead. Between the leaf-laden branches, she could see patches of cloud. The sky was still very, very light. Lighter than she had ever seen. That meant something. She just wished she knew what it was.

Bal had been astounded by his capacities, of that Dom was certain. He was not only able to understand the principles Bal was teaching him, but was then able to extrapolate the next several steps beyond. Finally, with an odd sort of frustration, Bal had cut the tutoring session short and stalked off to find Shu.

Dom stepped outside the Hall. It was starting to grow dark. Once more he soundlessly slipped behind the Guards. He began to walk back towards the heartside portion of the island.

The sky had been unusually light earlier in the day. Bal had commented on it or Dom wouldn't have noticed. He simply hadn't experienced enough rotations on this planet to make a comparison. The notion pleased him very much. The lighter, the better. He was certain that once he understood the Chronicler technology that he would be able to significantly improve the environment. At least for him. Eventually, his Queen would arrive. He wanted everything to be ready.

The heartside beach was abandoned. The lake's surface was calm as there was very little breeze. The storm had stolen the breath from the sky, which was now trying to recover.

Dom sat down and crossed his legs. He closed his eyes and reached out, as he had before.

Good. Very good. He had been heard. They were slowly beginning to gather together. Once they had done that, he would summon them. It wouldn't be long now. The planet would be his. Once his Queen arrived, it would belong to both of them, as well as to the new generation they would create.

CHAPTER 7

Min moved slowly towards the Egress Portal feeling better than he had for rotations. Sol's medicine had strengthened him temporarily. He hoped its effects would last at least until he finished assessing the debris field.

The Egress Portal was a special addition to the Citadel. The Chroniclers had advised that Technical Agents had been upgrading the base for thousands of ellipses. At some point in the far distant past, someone had decided to make a special doorway, a doorway specifically for Technical Agents and their students to pass through. A tutorial with a mentor was one of a student's final rites of passage before he or she became a Technical Agent in fact. The Egress Portal was symbolic of that transition. It was poorly named. One could use it to enter or exit. The label "egress" referenced the manner in which the student passed from the realm of the uninitiated into a limited club of hard scientists. These scientists had mastered a vast array of physical sciences – physics, engineering, metallurgy, chemistry, and computation among them. They were charged with using this base of knowledge to service the missions of the Journeycraft and to pass that knowledge on to worthy students. Aside from the docking bays, there were only four portals in and out of the entire base. The Egress Portal "belonged" to the Technical Agents and their students.

Min thought back once again to when he had come through this portal with Hab. He had anticipated that moment for many, many rotations beforehand, so much so that he was bleary-eyed from lack of sleep when they finally arrived. Hab had teased Min, telling him that his fatigue would make it impossible for him to learn anything new. Hab suggested that perhaps the trip should be delayed until Min was well-rested. His student would have none of that.

Min was nearly overwhelmed by the Citadel. While he understood most of the technology it utilized, he marveled at how the base incorporated so many varied ideas into all of its complex operating systems. Small groups of Journeyers visited the Citadel about every fifty ellipses or so, at least in the early times. These groups were comprised of either Journeycraft crews stopping to perform routine maintenance and upgrades, or teacher-student pairs.

As the Journeycraft went farther and farther away from Uma the upgrades became more and more infrequent. The visits, therefore, became more and more critical to the maintenance of the base's technology. Hab and Min had completed a number of upgrades and, if they had had more time, could have effected many more. But the search for Haven had to continue, so they left the base in the care of the next visitors, trusting that they would at least be able to keep the base current.

Olm still had not arrived. It occurred to Min that his illumination directive was still in effect. He wondered if it was causing problems for Olm after all. The Umae had very good night vision but even they couldn't see in total darkness. Without artificial illumination the interior of the Citadel was completely lightless. "Where is . . . ." Min began. He stopped, recalling the biosensors' inability to detect Olm. He would have to go and find Olm himself.

Min began retracing his path towards the Alpha panel. He assumed that he would encounter Olm on the way back. Min's equipment was not that massive. In this reduced gravity, it would hardly be a burden for someone in normal good health. Soon, Min was at the Alpha panel again. There was still no sign of Olm.

Min noted that the panel was still working on the data he had given it earlier. The surprising amount of time the panel was taking to make the calculations heightened Min's curiosity about the results. After waiting for a short time, he continued down the far hallway.

He finally found Olm standing next to the portal Min had entered when he previously arrived at the Citadel. Min's equipment was sitting on the floor next to him. Olm scowled at Min as he approached.

"You took longer than I thought you would," he said in a near growl. "Are you feeling that bad?"

"Why did you come here?" Min asked.

"You told me to go to the egress portal," noted Olm. "Didn't you?"

Something was amiss. Min's mind was sorting through the illogic of Olm's reply while his voice and expression tried not to betray his surprise.

"I did," he said finally. "I apologize. Didn't we decide on a later time? I was just walking around re-familiarizing myself with this place. I wasn't planning on seeing you. It caught me off guard I guess. Sorry if I sounded short."

"Not a problem," Olm said finally. "Your equipment is here. Whenever you are ready."

"There is actually another portal that is much closer to the debris field," said Min. "But I'm feeling better. I think I can get my equipment there by myself." He reached down and retrieved his vacuum suit and helmet from the floor. "I won't be gone too long. Think you could take a look at those biosensors while I'm gone?"

"I'll do my best," said Olm, watching Min put on his suit. Min finished snapping his helmet into place.

Olm hadn't understood the significance of the Egress Portal. For someone who had claimed to be a technical student planning on visiting here with his mentor, that was impossible. His lies were piling up. And he easily moved through complete darkness without being detected by the biosensors. Min was going to need to find a way to get Olm outside so he could use the Alpha panel to do some investigation without fear of discovery. The trick now was to keep Olm from suspecting anything.

May and the other Umae sat patiently, watching the Hek prance about wielding their spears. Dag and Lex openly discussed what the purpose of their production was but neither man could fashion a reasonable theory. They were all growing eager to continue walking.

They heard a bark in the distance. A dog came dashing out of the forest and happily approached one of the Hek. It wasn't the same dog that had run away earlier. This one was somewhat smaller and had darker colored fur. He bounded around the clearing, paying no attention to the Umae.

The Hek stopped working on their spears. One of them pointed back in the direction from where the dog had come. The dog looked in that direction, his tail quivering back and forth. From the shadow of the trees came a large number of Hek accompanied by a half dozen more dogs. As the dogs entered the clearing, the dog that had already arrived ran over to them and began sniffing them earnestly. Pol pulled Joba closer to her as she saw the group of Hek appear. There were at least twenty more of them, including five women. The women were shorter than the men, but almost as heavily muscled. They wore scattered pieces of fur about their hairy bodies. All of the Hek were barefoot.

Jed looked at May for direction. She was spellbound by these people. One of the Hek women approached May and sniffed at the air around her. The woman grunted something at one of the other women and they both let out a short, cackling burst. Their apparent amusement allayed May's concerns somewhat.

Another of the women saw Joba and began to frantically wave and jabber at the others. Pol tried to cover her baby entirely to keep him out of sight, but the woman kept pulling his wrap away from him. Pol took a defensive swipe at the woman's hand which caused her to recoil in surprise. She grunted something at one of the Hek men and then moved away. The entire group of newly-arrived Hek stood quietly, staring at the bundle in Pol's arms. Pol continued to clutch Joba tightly to her chest, wildly eyeing the Hek.

"Pol?" said May softly. "It is going to be all right. They won't hurt him."

Pol didn't draw any comfort from May's words. She was hyper-vigilant, rapidly shifting her focus from one Hek to the next as they began to mill about the clearing. One of the new male Hek began an exchange with another male from the original group. The dog who had run away with the stick circled the two men as they pointed and grunted at one another. The dog still carried the stick in his mouth. One of the men pointed at the tree from which he had taken the stick. The other one retrieved the stick from the dog's mouth and tossed it in the direction of the tree. The dog remained at his side, now completely disinterested. The man then addressed something to the group in general and they all began to gather up what little equipment they had. Evidently, it was time to move on.

Dag and Wil lifted Cap off the ground. As they did so, one of the Hek women walked over and looked at him. She held her hand to his forehead and then pulled his bottom lip down to get a look at his teeth. Noting the darkened bandage on his leg, she leaned down and began sniffing it. She drew back, her nose wrinkling. She then turned and began walking into the forest. Most of the Hek began to follow her. A few remained behind, looking at the Umae expectantly.

"Come on," said May to Pol. "I think we are supposed to go, too."

Pol slowly rose to her feet. Joba was awake, but quiet. His eyes were wide as he seemed to be taking everything in around him. Two of the Hek men came to her side, reaching out to assist her. She shook her head vigorously and moved closer to May. The entire group started back into the forest.

The network of roots on the forest floor became less dense making passage easier. Two of the Hek flanked May and Pol closely at all times. The other men spread out, forming a protective line in front of the group as well as on both sides. The Hek women came up the rear. The sky was still very light.

As the light began to fade, the ground started to become hillier and the trees more sparse. The Umae were growing fatigued but the Hek were determined to continue. At one point Joba began to cry. Most of the Hek men had responded by immediately moving to Pol's side, looking at her package rather anxiously. Once she managed to get Joba to nurse, he calmed down and the men quickly relaxed.

As darkness encroached, a few of the Hek produced crude torches and lit them with rough pieces of flint. One of them walked just in front of Cap, enabling his bearers to see. Another walked next to Pol, Joba and May. Despite the onset of night, the Hek urged the Umae onward. Jed's shoulder ached and his legs were beginning to cramp.

"I have to stop," he said finally. The other Umae men stopped as well. Several of the Hek gently nudged them and pointed forward. Jed and Lex set Cap down and tried to stretch their tired muscles. A Hek female seized May by the hand and tried pulling her along.

"What are you doing?" asked May, trying to free her wrist. The Hek's grip was very strong. The woman just stared at May pointing with her free hand. May ceased her resistance and the Hek woman released her wrist. The two women moved ahead into the darkness. They quickly returned. "We need to keep going," said May. "There is a light ahead. It isn't far. I think that is where they want us to go."

"All right," Jed said to his companions. "Almost there I guess." The men lifted Cap one more time. The entire band continued on.

Just ahead they saw the telltale flicker of torchlight. As they drew nearer, they saw that it marked the opening of a small cave. A few of the Hek went inside. The rest stayed outside with the Umae. The men lowered Cap to the ground. The Hek woman who had walked off with May waved at her to go into the cave.

The inside of the cave was fairly well-lit by torchlight. A long, narrow tunnel led to a much wider open chamber. There were perhaps ten more Hek, half female, watching May as she entered. Along one long wall, a Hek male sat surrounded by a number of small wooden bowls. There was a slender shaft of bone sticking out of each bowl. He was using one of the bones to stir whatever was inside. The man didn't acknowledge the arrival of the others.

The Hek woman pointed to an open area in the chamber. She held out her hands, palms down over the ground there and made slow, smoothing motions. She then turned and looked at May eagerly.

"I don't understand," May said slowly.

The woman stood for a moment, scratching her chin. She then laid herself down on the ground and closed her eyes. She quickly popped back up, again watching for May's reaction.

"Stay here? You want us to stay here?" said May. The woman looked at her blankly. May began to walk back towards the cave opening. The woman followed her. On the outside, a number of Hek were closely gathered around Pol, all intensely focused on Joba.

Dag looked up. "Well?"

"We are going to stay inside this cave tonight," said May. "There is a space just for us. Why don't you see if you can get Cap inside."

Dag and Lex carefully lifted Cap off the ground, each one ducking his head under one of Cap's arms. The Umae followed May back to the spot the Hek woman had showed her. The Hek woman smiled with approval.

"Yes, that is what she wants," said May with a bit more confidence. "We'll stay here tonight."

"Then what?" asked Lex.

"We will find out tomorrow."

May looked over at the man with the bowls. He was inspecting the end of one of the bones very carefully. He then motioned to another Hek man who brought a torch over nearer the wall. The man stood there, holding the torch up. The first man stood up and carefully began to make markings on the wall with the bone. There was something on the end of the bone that was transferring to the wall. He made a small mark, then stepped back to admire it. He then moved forward and continued.

"Let's eat," said Jed. "I'm starved." The Umae sat down and ate part of the food they had brought with them from the Garden. The Hek showed a certain amount of interest in their dinner, but none of them bothered to approach for a closer look. Once the meal was over, they tried to make themselves comfortable enough to sleep.

The Bone Man continued to meticulously make marks on the wall, oblivious to everything else around him.

Bal entered the Hall to find Shu and Dom sitting in front of the Hall's Alpha panel. Shu was describing its functions.

"Shu?" interrupted Bal. "Why are you instructing him about how to use the panel?"

Dom's lips curled into a wry smile.

"He has progressed very quickly," said Shu without enthusiasm.

"Quickly?" echoed Bal with added incredulity. "He has only been training for two rotations. He can't possibly be ready to begin training on the panel."

Dom leaned up against Shu, smiling at her.

"The amount of time doesn't matter," said Shu. She didn't bother to look at Bal. "If he is ready, he is ready."

"He isn't," protested Bal. "He can't be! I'll not have it!"

"You won't have what?" asked Dom. He slowly turned his head, cracking his neck.

"You must go to your quarters," barked Bal. "Immediately! I need to speak with Shu."

Shu shook her head lethargically. "No. Don't think so." Her voice was leaden with fatigue. As she looked at Bal, her appearance suggested significant sleep deprivation.

"Shu, I don't know what has happened to you," said Bal. "But you are not of right mind. And you," he said turning towards Dom, "you were given a directive. Didn't I warn you about your inability to accept direction?"

Dom giggled before leaning over and whispering something into Shu's ear. Her eyes closed drowsily for a moment before he stood up. "All right," he said, "I need to go to the beach anyway."

"No, not the beach," insisted Bal. "Your quarters. Now!"

Dom began walking towards the door. As he did so, Bal waved at the two Guards standing nearby. They promptly moved to interpose themselves between Dom and the doorway. Dom stopped and looked back at Bal.

"Is this how you want this to be?" he asked quietly.

"Your room," said Bal, trying to sound firm.

"And if I don't?" asked Dom.

"I will have you put there," said Bal.

Dom watched the Guards. The two huge men stood silently, waiting for additional orders.

"So……" said Dom in a deep, gravelly voice, "put . . . . .me."

Bal's face reddened and his body quivered with rage. "Put him in his chambers," he spat.

The first Guard started in Dom's direction. As he tried to seize Dom by the arm, Dom calmly gripped his wrist and squeezed, powdering his carpal bones liked dried clods of dirt. The Guard unleashed an agonized scream and dropped to both knees, clutching his wrist. Dom swiftly drove his index and middle fingers into the Guard's throat, rupturing his trachea. With a series of desperate gurgles bubbling from his lips, the Guard keeled over onto the floor.

The second Guard got a running start at Dom, intent on bowling him over. The Guard was several times as massive as the boy. Yet, when the Guard and Dom collided, the Guard was stopped immediately as if he had run headlong into a tree trunk. Dom didn't take so much as a step backwards and was completely unfazed. As the Guard dropped to one knee, attempting to get his bearings, Dom palmed the top of his head. There was a sound like old, dry wood being slowly broken in two as long-closed fissures reopened in the Guard's skull. His eyes rolled backwards before he collapsed onto his side, motionless.

Dom turned and watched Bal for a moment. The Chronicler fought for breath. Shu remained in her seat, completely unaffected by the fighting.

"Wha-, wha-.....?" gasped Bal, his voice soaked with terror.

"Can I go to the beach now?" asked Dom. Bal continued to struggle for air. He looked over at Shu and then back at Dom. He nodded his assent almost imperceptibly. "Thanks," said Dom. He turned and slowly walked out, stepping over the first Guard on the way.

Bal tried to regain his composure. "Shu! Shu!" She didn't respond. "What is wrong with you?" He took her by the shoulders and shook her vigorously. Her distant affect remained. Bal waited for a couple of moments and then went to the door. Dom was nowhere to be seen. "You there!" barked Bal at a young man walking past. "The drum! Beat that drum!" He pointed at a huge drum oriented vertically next to the opening of the Hall.

The man moved slowly over to the drum, surprised by Bal's frightened directive. He picked up the large staff next to the drum and began to strike its surface as hard as he could.

Soon, a large number of Guards began to gather at the Hall. Most were in various states of hasteful dress. Bal counted sixty of them, not including the two fallen Guards on the floor. He bade them all to stand silent.

"Dom did this......" He spat. "He must be caught and he must be judged."

The Guards remained mostly silent, incapable of manifesting surprise.

"Where is he?" asked one. "How did he . . . .do this?" The Guard looked down at the bodies.

Bal was breathing hard again. "He said he was going to the beach. The beach! Find him!"

The Guards began to filter out of the doorway. They quickly broke into a jog in the direction of the beach, with Bal in slow pursuit.

They found Dom on the heartside beach. He was simply standing there, calmly watching their approach. The Guards spread out, forming a semi-circle, trying to trap Dom against the water's edge. He looked back over his shoulder, staring out over the water. Bal made his way to the front of the Guards. "You have broken our most sacred law!" he raged. "And you will be judged!"

Dom turned to face his accuser and began to laugh. "Judged? By you?" he mocked. "I ***will*** be judged. It will not be by your standards though."

The Guards looked at Bal, awaiting instructions. Bal swallowed, recalling the ease with which Dom had dispatched the others. "Seize him!" he said finally. The mass of Guards dutifully moved towards Dom, slowly closing the semi-circle around him.

Min stepped through the Egress Portal onto the lunar surface. The debris field was straight ahead. The abandoned shuttle stood out against the otherwise featureless horizon. Uma was low in the sky, a globe of deep sober gray.

He walked over to the nearest piece of debris and began his examination. His initial visual check assured him that it was part of a shuttle craft. The metal the Umae used for such crafts was a distinctive alloy. It was extremely lightweight in relation to its strength. It also had a common fracture pattern when it became damaged. A quick scan confirmed what he already knew.

Min began to move about the debris field, looking for anything unusual. He noticed a strange pattern of discoloration in the dusty soil. He walked over to that area, preparing to perform a new scan. He stopped breathing for a moment when he realized what he was looking at.

Footprints. There was a series of tracks all through the field. His extreme fatigue and the angle of the sunlight when he arrived must have prevented him from noticing them before. There were two distinct sets that appeared to emerge from a portal into the Citadel that Min had not used yet this trip. One set moved all around the field while the second stayed mostly in one general area. The two sets converged at one large, flat piece of debris straight ahead. Min went there and knelt down.

The piece of metal had been moved. He could tell because he could see where the edge of the metal had made an indentation in the ground when it first came to rest. Now the edge was in a different position. There weren't any natural forces on the moon that could either move the metal or create the indentation.

He grabbed the metal by its edge, trying to lift it. Despite the lightweight nature of the alloy, this piece of debris was still too massive for him to move by himself. He checked the settings on his suit. Its mechanical assist functions weren't quite engaged completely. It still had a little more to give. Min looked around, trying to find a way to maximize the additional force. Nearby was a long, narrow sliver of metal. He guessed that it had been part of a wing support. It would make an excellent lever. Now he just needed a good fulcrum.

Most of the pieces of metal nearby were rather small. He didn't see anything that would be useful. Min checked the power levels on the suit and began walking off in the direction of the shuttle.

The shuttle was closer than he had remembered. He must have drastically underestimated the condition of his health when he arrived. Once he reached the shuttle, he directed the suit to elevate him to the side door and then entered the entry code. The door slid opened and he climbed inside.

There were a number of metallic storage boxes on board, just as he had remembered. He found the largest one and tossed it out the door. The box drifted slowly to the surface, kicking up a bit of dust as it landed. Min lowered himself back down, picked up the box, and returned to the debris field. He made a visual estimate of the length of his lever and then placed the box perpendicular to it. He shoved one end of the lever underneath the large sheet of metal, pushing it in as far as he could. He then moved to the other end of the lever and pushed it downward as hard as the suit would allow.

The edge of the metal sheet lifted into the air. Min tried to flip it over, but it was too unwieldy. Eventually, he managed to slide it to one side, away from the spot where it had been when he found it. The task made his head swim, even with his suit providing most of the necessary force. He tossed his lever aside and dropped to one knee, trying to catch his breath. Multi-colored spots blinked in and out of his field of vision. When he closed his eyes, they simply became brighter, hurtling right at him. He couldn't be sure how long he remained in that position, but eventually his breathing slowed and the spots faded away.

He stood up to inspect the area under the metal sheet. It had been concealing a pair of Umae corpses. Although the cold, dry air had dessicated them, he could still recognize their Journeyer flight uniforms. His prior theory was correct - the shuttle had collided with the Citadel. That was the only explanation for the damage to the exterior wall and the obliteration of the shuttlecraft.

He looked back at the other shuttle. Why wasn't Olm dead then? He had to have been on the other shuttle. Olm had denied any knowledge of the debris field. That was impossible. If the collision happened before he arrived, he would have had to have walked right past it to get inside the Citadel. If it happened afterwards, the collision would have shaken the entire base. Olm couldn't have missed it. If one of the sets of footprints were Olm's, then he knew about the dead bodies and lied about them as well. And his denial of their existence likely meant he was somehow responsible for their deaths. And where is the person who made the other set? Olm's claim to have been alone during his time in the Citadel certainly meant that he was not. There hadn't been any way for the other person to leave the moon. Jack had said the ***Aurora*** was missing two shuttles and both were now accounted for.

Min felt ill. His exertions with the metal had gotten the best of him and now he had to go back inside with an Umae who was unquestionably dangerous. Min had to stop him.

Min sat down on the lunar surface, trying to clear his head. Ever since his experience with the panel at the Land Bridge, his mind's method of operation was different. The dreams, although he had difficulties thinking of them as that due to their intense, vivid character, were relentless. When his energies waned, as they were now, he lost faith in his own judgments. Maybe Olm was dangerous, but how sure could Min be about that? Enough to justify extreme measures? At a minimum, Min had to prevent Olm from reaching Uma.

The shuttle now looked very, very far away, almost seeming to recede towards the horizon. He couldn't just take the shuttle himself. The Atlan Chroniclers wouldn't accept him and without the technology in the Citadel, his life wouldn't last much longer. He still didn't know the status of Critical Closure. He didn't know about......Eve.

He slowly rose and walked back to the Citadel. Once inside the Egress Portal, he sat down and removed the upper portion of his suit. Removing Eve's pendant, he confirmed that it retained its connection to the shuttle. He remotely amended his prior directive. The Beta process directive he had entered earlier would disable the ship. Min needed something more drastic, but once he went down that path he wanted the ability to change his mind if necessary.

"Replace Beta process with Om process," he directed the shuttle.

The panel inside the shuttle almost instantly sent confirmation that Min's amendment was in place. Min had his extreme measure, for now. But he could easily rescind his last directive with the pendant if he chose to. As long as Min was alive, the Om process directive would remain in place unless he changed it. If he died, the Beta process would still protect Uma from Olm. Olm was unstable at best and homicidal at worst. His return to Uma with any of the technology available to him in the Citadel could be disastrous.

The Bone Man never slept. May had found it nearly impossible to find comfort on the hard, moist cave floor. Joba would awaken occasionally and start to cry or fuss. Every time May was roused from her shallow slumber, she saw the Bone Man there next to the wall, working by the dim light of a small torch.

Just as fatigue overcame discomfort, May was awakened by the general stirrings of the others inside the cave. The Hek were chattering amongst themselves, unconcerned about anyone else's efforts at sleep. Dag, Wil, Jed and Lex sat up and rubbed at their eyes. It was apparent that they had had problems sleeping as well.

May got up and stretched. She knelt down next to Cap and checked him over. He was still asleep, but his breathing was stronger. His brow still felt warm. She needed to find something with which to replace his bandage.

The Bone Man was still working. She walked over to where he was to get a better look. He was a scrawny, older man. His bones protruded from underneath his taut skin. His hair was almost entirely white. The Bone Man didn't pay any attention at all to May as she stood watching him. She was having difficulty seeing all of his painting. She could tell now that that was what it was. It was more like a mural as it took up most of the wall. He had four pots with different colored mixtures in front of him. Each pot had its own bone "brush". Although he was working by the light of a small fire burning on the ground, May still had difficulties seeing the entire project. She squinted in the darkness, trying to make out what he had done.

Another Hek approached and handed her an unlit torch. She touched it to the ground fire used by the Bone Man and it flickered to life. She raised it up for a better look.

Far to her heartside, where the Bone Man had begun his work the night before, was a flat line with a towering pyramid standing atop it. Reaching from the top of the pyramid was a long, narrow extension. Just to the empty side of the pyramid was an extended area of blue water. Traveling on top of the water was a long canoe bearing a number of unusually tall and slender passengers. One of them sat alone in the stern of the boat.

May gasped slightly when she saw what was above the boat. In the sky was a long cylinder with angled wings. The people in the boat looked upwards as it flew overhead.

The water ended, broken up by a brown shoreline dotted with bushes. Behind some of the bushes were short, thick people bearing spears. There was another smaller canoe that had been brought to shore. A single, tall woman was kneeling near the bushes where the others were concealing themselves. She was attending a small bundle. May held the torch closer. The bundle was surprisingly detailed considering the medium and the method used to produce the mural. She could see a small head and tiny hands sticking out from the bundle. It was a baby. It was crying. Once she looked back at the slender woman next to the bundle, May realized the woman was crying as well. Feeling the tears beginning to well in her own eyes, she turned and walked away.

"May?" It was Dag. "Are you all right?" He walked over to where she stood as she hastily tried to compose herself. As he looked up to see what had upset her, he took in the entirety of the mural. "What is this?" he asked the Bone Man.

The Bone Man sat quietly. He was finished painting now.

"They have seen us," said May. "I think for a long time. It is the only way he could know all of these things."

Dag began to study the mural in more detail. "The island? They have seen Atla? The Journeycraft?" He turned to the Bone Man, his expression pleading for answers.

"He can't speak to you," said May. The other Umae began gathering around. Even Pol had taken an interest and stood nearby, cradling Joba.

"That bundle," said Dag, "is that a baby?"

"Yes. A baby. An . . . .exiled . . . .baby." The last phrase nearly fractured May's resolve.

"So they have seen all of this?" said Jed.

"Apparently," said May. "Apparently they have seen quite a bit."

"Why . . . .," began Pol, her voice shaken, "why are they so interested in babies?"

"I don't know," said May. "I just hope . . . ."

Pol turned towards May, her heart pounding. "Hope what?"

May looked down at the bundle in the mural. "I hope we didn't make a mistake in not trying to escape when we had a chance."

Pol pulled Joba tight once again, trying to conceal him from the Hek. The other Umae lowered their eyes, realizing there was little they could do if the Heks' intentions were hostile.

The Bone Man easily rose from the floor, his flexibility and strength belying his appearance. He leaned forward slightly, looking at the tuft of Joba's hair that stuck out from the top of his coverings. It was the only part of him that was visible within Pol's protective cocoon. The Bone Man grinned, his smile exposing the only five teeth he had left. He then turned and walked out of the cave into the faint morning light.

Dom didn't even bother to survey the numbers brought to bear against him. He stood expressionless as the semi-circle of Guards closed slowly around him. Bal waited behind them wringing his hands and smiling nervously.

Most of the Guards stopped once they drew near with a half-dozen continuing forward. They were unsure as to how best to proceed against this boy who made no efforts to flee or defend himself.

The first pair reached Dom and attempted to take him by his arms. Just as they did both recoiled and cried out. One clutched his neck while the other rubbed his upper arm. They staggered briefly before collapsing where they stood.

The air began to hum with a faint buzz. Bal instinctively ducked as something whizzed by his ear. A nearby Guard grunted, tried to swat at something on his wrist, and then tumbled over. Soon, all of the Guards were waving frantically at the air and began scattering with confusion. Dom remained exactly where he had been.

"Wha-? What is this?" screamed Bal. "Seize him!" Just then, a sharp pain shot through his thigh. He looked down to see a large hornet clutching his leg. Without thinking, he smashed it with his hand, driving its stinger into his soft flesh once again. The insect dropped to the sand.

The air was alive now. Guards were running and flailing in chaos as they tried to scramble away from the swarm. The hornets energized the air and the Guards' numbers rapidly dwindled as one after another dropped to the sand. Bal was pelted with stings again and again as he tried to cover his face and run. As he turned, he tripped over a nearby Guard and fell hard to the ground. He writhed in agony as his body was pierced repeatedly by the stings of the unrelenting winged monsters. Bal tried to crawl away from the scene as best he could. His heart rumbled inside of his chest as the volume of venom in his system grew. Then, it stopped.

No more stings. He pushed himself up to all fours and tried to look around through his swollen eyelids. Dom still hadn't moved. Most of the Guards were motionless, yet a few were squirming spastically on the ground. The two who were assaulted first stood up and brushed themselves off. They walked over next to Dom and bowed low in front of him. In turn, each Guard stopped struggling before standing up and kneeling before Dom. The sand was littered with the bodies of large hornets, many of them still buzzing their wings aimlessly and waving their legs uselessly in the air. Bal tried to take a deep breath, but his chest was compressed by a weighty tightness.

Dom slowly walked over to where Bal struggled against the venom. "Hmmmm......" he mused as he stood over Bal's prostrate form. "What to do with you now?" He looked over his shoulder where three score of Guards stood by, waiting.

Bal attempted to reply but was only able to force a couple of ragged gasps. "H-h-h....."

"How?" said Dom. "I'll bet that was what you were trying to say." He leaned in very close to Bal so he could whisper in his ear. "It doesn't really matter, does it?" He gently lifted Bal's chin with his finger. Bal's face was covered with fat, crimson welts. His eyes were nearly swollen shut. Dom grinned. "I don't think I'm going to need you."

Bal's heart sank. He closed his eyes and waited for the end.

"But I can keep you around simply because I choose to," continued Dom. "Just don't miss out on any opportunities to make yourself useful," he added in a deep, gravelly voice. "Poor Shu isn't really herself now, I'm afraid. I'm not sure that she will be . . . .reliable . . .even though her allegiance is guaranteed. I did not host you because physically you are worthless to me. So now, I will tell you what to do, and you will do it. Understood?"

Tears leaked from Bal's eyes. He gasped again and tried to cover his head with his hood. Dom stood up and looked around the scene. This was literally his beachhead. Now it was simply a matter of time. And that was something he personally had in great supply.

CHAPTER 8

Min started awake. Again, his sleep had been harried by strange dreams. Crowds of Umae listening to a lone figure in a red robe. The robe's collar was lined with gray fur. Five Journeycraft soared overhead before abruptly vanishing. Four more soon followed before vanishing as well. A formation of three and then two did likewise before a lone ship crossed the heavy gray sky before disappearing. Then the sky was empty. The robed figure slowly turned towards Min…..

He sat up, taking in a sharp breath. He was still very, very tired. He leaned down, bracing his forearms on his knees. Olm was nowhere to be seen. Once again, there was no evidence that any of the other beds had been used.

Min stood up slowly, dizziness momentarily ruling him. His body longed for another dose of Sol's medication, but he decided to save it for as long as he could. His personal comfort was a low priority. Once his head cleared somewhat, he left the room to check on the status of the Critical Closure calculations.

He found Olm seated at the Alpha panel, eyeing the display. His focus was completely unbroken by Min's approach. Even as Min stopped and looked over Olm's shoulder to see what Olm was doing, he did not respond.

Olm was reviewing computational directives. Specifically, he was taking a rather complex tutorial on their derivation and modification. Perhaps he wasn't as far behind on his studies as he had led Min to believe.

"How go the lessons?" said Min. Olm continued to look over the figures on the screen.

"Fine," he said finally. "Your command authority has been very helpful."

Min sat down in a chair next to him. "Do you mind if I take over this panel for a while?" he asked. "I need to review a process I started soon after I arrived. It is important."

Olm turned and stared at him dourly. "I'm not done," he said gruffly.

"You can transfer your lesson to that panel over there," said Min pointing. "You won't know the difference."

Olm looked at the panel, but did nothing. Min slowly reached out and manipulated the display, transferring the tutorial to the adjacent panel. Olm stood up and walked over to that display, saying nothing.

Min looked at the specifics of what Olm was reviewing. It was extremely complex. In fact, Min wasn't sure that he wouldn't benefit from the same tutorial. The techniques being discussed were as advanced as the ones he had learned from Hab, and nearly as advanced as the ones he had created himself. Min wondered how well Olm was able to follow along.

The panel had completed its analysis of the Hek's protein templates. It appeared that a new process had begun. Olm didn't have the necessary authorization to initiate any new directives. Min opened the directives of the current process and began reviewing them.

Whatever it was, it was long and complicated. It was also very, very old. He hadn't seen such a process since he first started Journeyer training. He didn't think it would be difficult to determine its purpose.

"Olm, would you mind doing a visual inspection of the biosensors?" asked Min. Min needed space. He knew Olm would likely continue to be just as resistant to that request as he had been thus far, but Min hoped it would at least get him to go away for a while.

Surprisingly, Olm stood up and disappeared into the darkness without a single word of protest. Once he was sure Olm was gone, Min began inputting directives into the panel.

"I need the results of the most recent process," he stated. "I also want a full-scale diagnostic on all interior Citadel biosensors."

The panel hummed slightly as it began processing the new directives.

"The last process is not yet complete," advised the panel.

"Verify," said Min. "It isn't running now."

"The last process is still running," replied the panel.

"Then what is the other process that I just accessed?"

"That is the same process this panel just described."

"That's not possible. I encoded the last process. The one that is running now is completely different."

"The current process is an extension of the one you encoded," said the panel.

"Extension? From where?"

"It was activated internally. This panel considers it an extension."

Min leaned back in his seat and thought. Something about his process initiated a new process that was already present. A contingency process?

"What does the extension process do?" asked Min.

"Unable to reply. Director level authority required." There it was again. *Director level authority.*

"Is the analysis I requested concerning Critical Closure complete?"

"Affirmative."

"And?"

"There is insufficient data to determine whether or not Critical Closure has been reached."

Min closed his eyes, considering his next step. "What is missing?" He already had a pretty good idea what the answer to his question was. The date of the Cataclysm. A census of the Hek population. A more complete picture of their technology level. Min suspected that at least some of that information was stored away inside the panel. But would the panel use that data to complete his calculation without telling him what that data was?

"Director level authority required."

Min pounded his fist on the face of the panel. He could find a workaround for the authorization, but it would take time. His list of chores was growing.

"Fine, I'll deal with that later. Status of internal biosensors?"

"Biosensors online."

"Since when?" Min was starting to become very irritated.

"Biosensors haven't been offline for one thousand two hundred and eighteen ellipses."

Min now imagined that he would be dismantling the entire panel and analyzing each component for flaws. The collision between the shuttle and the exterior wall must have damaged it somehow.

"How many life forms are within the Citadel?"

"An exact figure will require processing that will take . . . . . .twenty-six point seven eight three rotations."

"No," said Min grimacing. "I don't want to know about every last microbe. How many that have a biomass within . . . . . . twenty-five percent . . . . .of mine?"

"Two, including you," replied the panel.

Now Min was very interested. The panel couldn't locate Olm before, but now it apparently had. "The other is Olm?"

"This panel does not recognize specimen 'Olm'?"

"Then what IS the other one?" asked Min, exasperated.

The panel flickered in front of him and began to produce formatted data. Min leaned in and began reading it.

"Report aged .221 ellipses. Author no longer existent. Species unnamed.

Known characteristics are as follows: parasitic hosting accomplished by rapid protein marker mutations. Hive-based organism. Brood leaders maintain authority by way of quantum-based connection with brood members. Organism requires high-level radiation environment for reproduction, which is sexual in nature."

The information hung on the screen before Min. He re-read it to make sure he had understood everything correctly. As he went through the data for the third time, the panel began playing an audio clip.

"And the species has a sense of humor." It was Olm.

"A sense of humor?" Min did not recognize the second voice.

"And its name is 'Frhsgetdfes'".

"Name? How can you possibly know.........?" The audio stopped.

Min swallowed hard. "Who was on the audio?" he demanded.

"The first voice belongs to an unknown entity. The second belongs to Technology Agent Gull."

"Gull?" Min thought back to the second set of tracks. "Where is Gull?"

"Unknown."

Sweat was beading on Min's forehead. "The first one, that was Olm, wasn't it?"

"This panel is unfamiliar with specimen 'Olm'?"

"Unfamiliar? How can you be?" Min stood up and looked about anxiously. "He was just here. He just left. You didn't detect him?"

The panel processed for a moment. "In the last point nine rotations, there have been 26 other life forms meeting your criteria, besides you."

"How.....?" Min's mind raced. "How do you define 'life form'?"

"'Life form is a parameter of protein sequences."

"Were all of the different protein sequences within the same biomass perimeter?"

"Affirmative."

Min's vision spun and his stomach rose in his throat. The biosensors couldn't identify 'Olm' because his protein sequences were mutating. The sensors viewed him as separate entities. The panel had been correct. There had been two Umae in the Citadel within the last ellipse or so, Min and the one named Gull. Now Gull was missing. Now it was just Min and whatever 'Olm' was.

"Recalibrate. Refer to protein sequence within the other biomass with my criteria as 'Olm'".

"Affirmative."

Min pulled himself up and staggered over to the panel. "Now," he said, struggling for focus. "Where is Olm now?" The panel needed very little time to formulate a response.

"Immediately behind you."

The Hek led May and the other Umae farther into the forest. Over a period of two rotations, Cap's condition improved markedly. He was conscious most of the time and even managed to walk part of the way. His complaints concerning his head abated entirely. The wound on his leg had finally clotted over and didn't impede his ability to travel.

The trees began to thin out as the forest gave way to a wide, flat plain. Pinpoints of fire could be seen occasionally in the distance, but the Hek never appeared interested in veering towards them. They maintained a steady pace. They started early in the morning, just after dawn, and walked until it was time for the noon meal. After a brief rest, they continued until the light in the sky began to fade. Then they encamped, spent the night, and repeated the process the following day. The Hek, aside from their constant interest in Joba, paid very little attention to their Umae companions.

The plain was broken by steep rolling hills that rose abruptly on the horizon. The Hek appeared to be heartened by the sight of the hills as they gestured and smiled upon seeing them in the distance for the first time. The morning following this first sighting, they set an exceptionally brisk pace. Although placed somewhat at ease by the Hek's indifference towards them during their journey, the Umae were a bit anxious about the sudden heightening of enthusiasm in the Hek. The hills would reveal something, of that the Umae were sure. The uncertain nature of that revelation put them all on edge. In this unknown land, surrounded by physically superior beings, the Umae were at the mercy of the Hek. They could only hope that their beneficent indifference would continue.

By the end of that day, the group could see the base of the hillside. A number of fires were burning in the distance, their bright glow contrasting with the shadow-covered hills. Where there were fires, there would be more Hek.

Just as it was almost too dark to see, they reached the first group of fires. A couple of barks struck out from the darkness, only to be quieted by guttural responses. Sitting around the first fire were five Hek, three women and two men. They quickly rose to their feet upon seeing the Umae. Two of the women chattered back and forth while the two men watched Cap and the others. The third woman turned and ran off in the direction of another large fire some distance away.

Joba's cries instantly silenced the chattering of the women. They both looked about, trying to determine the source of the crying. When the first woman spotted Joba in Pol's arms, she pointed him out to the second woman. Both of them slowly crept towards her.

"You'll be fine," said May calmly. "They are just curious." Pol had finally become more comfortable in the presence of the Hek. They had never tried very hard to even touch Joba, they only wanted to look. She expected the same from the two approaching women.

They stopped in front of Pol and stared at Joba in his wrappings. One of the women examined Pol as well, switching her gaze back and forth between Pol and her baby. The first woman nudged the second woman and whispered something to her. This drew a resounding groan in reply. Both women then began to chuckle.

"Something is funny, I guess," said Cap. "It could be worse."

Backlit by a distant fire, they could see the approach of another group of Hek. As they got closer, they could see that the one in front was exceptionally tall and slender. It wore a fur with a broad hood which was pulled up over its head. It stopped, trailed by the woman who had run off earlier and a half-dozen Hek males. The figure folded its arms and turned towards Pol and Joba.

"The leader you think?" asked May.

"Probably. Or someone with some authority." Cap edged slowly towards Pol's side. He tried his best to see the face of the hooded figure.

Finally, the figure reached up with both hands and removed its hood. It was a woman somewhat younger than May. She had long straw-colored hair bound in a thong and high cheekbones.

She was Umae.

The shipwrights gasped. Cap took Pol protectively by the elbow. May was stunned into inaction.

"She's . . . .like us?" asked Pol. "How?"

The woman noted the varying degrees of surprise on the faces of the other Umae. She then walked over in front of Pol and held out her arms.

"What?" asked Pol weakly. She turned towards Cap, her lip quivering. "What . . .does she want?"

Cap didn't take his eyes off the woman. "Joba. I think she wants Joba."

"No!" screamed Pol. "No! She can't!" She freed herself from Cap's gentle hold and tried to run. She took about five steps before she tripped and toppled to the ground. Joba's cry pierced the darkness as Pol rolled on the grass.

Jed leapt quickly to her side, putting himself defensively between Pol and the Hek. The Hek had not moved, not even the leader. She tucked her fingers into the collar of her wrap and waited. Once he saw the Heks' inaction, Jed turned his attention to Pol.

"Pol," he said, trying to sound comforting, "are you all right? Is Joba…..?"

Pol rolled over and sat up, gasping with tears. Joba continued to cry robustly. Pol hurriedly unwrapped him and began looking him over. "He's fine . . .I think. Is he fine?" She looked up at Jed, her tear-drenched eyes searching his face for some hope of escape.

"May," called Cap. "Joba may need you." May was able to snap out of her fixation on the leader and move over to where Pol sat on the ground. She reached down and slowly removed Joba from her arms.

"Just let me look . . . . ." she said quietly. Pol's hands were shaking and they dropped limply to her sides as soon as May lifted Joba. May then placed Joba on the ground and began examining him. He continued to cry. "I think he is fine," she said. She smiled at Pol. "He is a strong boy. I think he was just startled."

The leader knelt down next to May. She slowly reached out and lightly caressed Joba's cheek with her finger. Pol was frozen, leaning heavily on Jed. May began to rewrap the baby. Again, the leader reached out and gently stroked the baby's cheek. He whimpered slightly and stopped crying. She then leaned in until her face was very close to his. Sticking her tongue out, she made a high squeaking noise with her mouth. Joba was wide-eyed for a second before blooming into a broad grin. She repeated the sound, this time drawing a chuckle from the infant. The other Hek laughed as well.

The leader then reached out and lifted Joba off the ground. This took May by surprise. Initially, she tried to hang on to his wrappings. Once Joba laughed again at the leader's gesture, May released her grip. The leader cradled Joba for a moment, rubbing noses with him.

Pol began to sob. She gripped Jed's shoulder as tightly as she could and pressed her face against him. The leader's eyes squinted in the darkness. She went to Pol and after making sure Joba was well-wrapped, offered him back to his mother.

Pulling herself together as best she could, Pol accepted the bundle and wrapped herself around her baby. Her sobs shook her entire body and her cries echoed back at them from the distant hills. The dogs barked from the darkness, again to be chastised by the unseen voices. The leader smiled down at Pol and Joba before turning and walking off in the direction from which she had come.

Dom had grown tired of Shu's explanations. She had described the processes involved in recording the day-to-day happenings of the settlement. Dom now had a complete understanding of how the Chroniclers trained their minds to fully observe each event in all its details. He had no use for the techniques. Dom's innate memory was a match for the most highly-trained Chronicler. Recall wasn't going to help him accomplish his goal. He needed technology. He needed to understand the main panel in the Hall.

The panel, and its accompanying display, loomed in front of him. Shu sat in a chair to his heartside, clinging to his hand. Bal was to his empty side, seated on the floor. Most of his stings had healed, although his face still bore some redness from his encounter with the swarm.

"I think today is the day," said Dom. He glanced down at Bal who cowered beneath his gaze.

"Oh no," said Shu demurely. "You aren't ready. You could hurt yourself."

Dom looked up at the display. "This is connected to the satellite. It is my only connection to the satellite." He had been regretting his decision to allow the Journeyers to leave. His assumption that the Chroniclers had the same understanding of Umae technology as the Journeyers had proven incorrect. While the access was the same, their understanding of it was almost as limited as that held by the other Umae. Dom was going to have to figure it out for himself.

"You might be able to access the Citadel," said Bal meekly. "Through the satellite, I mean."

Dom looked down at the groveling man in the red robe. "The Citadel? What is that?"

"A base of some sort," said Shu. "The Journeyers use it. They say it is on the moon." She smiled at him with a doe-eyed adulation.

Dom stood quietly, deep in thought. Bal peeked up at him, a vague hope stirred by Dom's interest in the Citadel. "They must keep all of their knowledge there," he said, trying to sound off-hand. "Min is there now."

"Ah yes. Min. He fancies himself rather shrewd, doesn't he?" Bal enthusiastically nodded his agreement despite the fact that Dom was now ignoring him. "Why don't we just go to the Citadel ourselves?" he asked Shu.

"There's no way to get there," said Bal quietly.

Dom bristled. "Then I need access to the satellite. How do I do that?"

"Don't do that," Shu whined. "Just sit with me."

Dom turned towards Bal, hauling him off the floor by his collar. "You? Do you know? Or are you going to continue your pattern of uselessness?"

Bal's eyes widened as he tried to wiggle free. Dom tossed him aside, causing Bal to hit the floor hard. Bal pushed himself up to his knees. "You access through the display," he said, his voice shaking. "The information flow is much like that associated with the Chronicler recall techniques, we . . . . Shu . . . .has been teaching you." Bal's window of opportunity was slowly opening and he was beginning to tremble. "Their technology is in the panel as well."

Dom pushed Bal back to the floor with his foot. "Have you always been such a little worm? How did you manage to gain any position of authority?" Dom turned and walked back to the display. "You mentioned that there is danger involved."

Shu hurried to Dom's side, kneeling next to him and retaking his hand. "Yes. You can't do it. If you try to absorb the data without finishing your training……." She was pleading with him now, her voice saturated with worry.

"What?" snapped Dom. "What is the worst thing that can happen?"

Shu took a deep breath. "Insanity. Memory loss. Death." She held the back of his hand to her cheek. "Dangerous."

Dom was unconcerned. "I can't stand around waiting for you idiots to come up with the technology I need, can I? This planet has so much promise, but no one here understands anything. By the time I put it all together…….." He was eager to enter his reproductive cycle. The urge was burning inside of him. Once his brood Queen arrived, he wanted everything to be ready. He already was. This planet was not.

"W-we could try something . . .small . .first," suggested Bal from the floor.

Dom whirled and picked him off the ground, shoving him towards the display. "Do it. I want access!" he growled. "I want everything. Now! Do it!"

Bal scuttled towards the panel as Shu rose up and threw her arms around Dom. "No! Don't!" Her pleas were intended to be emphatic, but her befogged brain was unable to connect her message with her emotion. Dom shoved her aside and followed Bal to the panel.

"How long?" Dom demanded.

Bal began entering directives into the panel. Accessing the Citadel from the Chroniclers' Hall was impossible. That was a one-way connection. Only the Journeyers could initiate contact. What the panel did have was access to Umae history. Bal intended to give Dom every bit of it. It wasn't Bal's original plan, but it would achieve his end all the same.

"Almost ready. . . . . ." squeaked Bal. "There. Done."

Dom smiled. "I just have to put my hands on the display?"

Bal swallowed hard, trying to conceal his anticipation. "And think of a simple piece of information that you'd like to access." Dom shoved him away, once more causing him to tumble hard to the floor.

The display was immediately in front of Dom now. The moment was arousing. He reached out with both hands and pressed his palms to the panel. As he did, Bal muttered the word "Cataclysm" just loud enough for Dom to hear. Bal raised his arms up over his face, barely peeking out to watch.

That single term intruded into Dom's mind and became the subject of his inquiry. A blinding burst of blue-white light engulfed both Dom and the display. Vicious spasms wracked Dom's entire body as spheres of crackling light rolled repeatedly down his arms before forking along the perimeter of his form. His back arched and his head was thrown back. Bal shielded his eyes, waiting for him to fall.

The light show stopped. Dom lowered his head and took an uncertain step backwards.

"Dom?" said Shu. "Are you . . . .?"

The Guards by the door watched passively. Bal uncovered his face and waited.

Dom turned and faced the room. Smoke was still rising from his smoldering robe. His hair floated away from his head.

Dom laughed. At first, it was a chuckle born of curiosity but it quickly grew into a delighted roar.

Bal leaned forward and vomited on the floor in front of him. Shu absently giggled, oblivious to what had just taken place. The Guards accompanied their master with bellowing laughter. Dom raised his arms triumphantly.

"Bal, you dullard. Now I understand everything about your pathetic race," he cried. "But you don't really understand anything, do you?" Bal curled up on his side as Dom roared again. The Chronicler's desperate tactic had failed. What Dom had learned was beyond Bal's ability to guess. But he had withstood the interaction with the panel without any notable injury. There was no hope of stopping him now.

His first perception was pain. It started at a point in the center of his head and radiated outwards like a spider web. His mouth was dry and nausea rose in his throat. As he tried to open his eyes, the pain twisted through his skull. He closed his eyes as tightly as he could.

"You're awake." It was an observation, not a question. "Good. We are going to talk. Or at least, I'm going to talk and you are going to listen."

Min could hear his footfalls approaching the bed, and then felt Olm's weight shift the cushion underneath him as he sat down. "Light . . .bright." Even this modest expression made his head feel like it had rapidly plunged to the bottom of a cold lake.

"I can't turn it off. No command authority, you know."

Min covered his face with his hands. "Lights . . .five percent." He was surprised that he was able to speak even that short directive. He unclenched his eyes slightly. This time, there was no illuminatory assault. Olm sat on the bed next to him, stone-faced.

"Let's be clear about something," said Olm. "You are going to die very soon. The only influence you can possibly have is on the manner of your death. It can be fast and relatively painless, or it can take several rotations. You end up in the same condition either way. The first choice would seem to be more prudent."

Min's eyes quickly adjusted to the darkness. He was on a cushion in the medlab. His vision was starting to focus. "What do you want?" Those four words brought a new cascade of pain inside his head.

"For starters, command authority. After that, we will see as we go along."

Command authority. He wanted control of the Citadel.

"Why?"

"'Why?'" mocked Olm. He stood up and yanked Min off of the cushion by his collar. "Why are YOU asking ME questions?!? You don't understand how this is going to work."

Min hung limply, his feet off the floor. He closed his eyes again, his skull shrinking. Even in the reduced gravity, he could barely move. Olm tossed him back down on the cushion.

"You are a pathetic specimen," griped Olm. "Why have you been allowed to live?" Olm walked over to a counter and retrieved Min's satchel. He withdrew the vial containing Sol's medication. Olm opened the top of the vial. "Drink."

Min took a few deep breaths, trying to pull himself together. He wasn't quite sure what the medicine would even do for him in his current condition. He wondered what would happen if he drank the entire vial at once……

Olm seized him by the hair on the back of his head and shoved the vial's opening into Min's mouth. After pouring a quantity through his dried lips, Olm withdrew the vial and returned its stopper. Min began to choke but managed to swallow some of the draught. A great portion of it ended up dripping from his face. Min was surprised at how quickly it invigorated him.

The pain in his head subsided and his heart stopped racing. Still, he was determined to feign a certain degree of disability. He was going to need every imaginable advantage.

When Min finally opened his eyes all the way, Olm snatched him again by the collar. This time, he began dragging Min across the floor. He hauled him out of the medlab and down the long hallway leading to the Alpha panel. Olm's physical strength was obvious. Min was nothing to him.

Olm deposited Min into the seat directly in front of the panel. The display was now showing a stream of data that was not present earlier.

"Look at this," demanded Olm. Min straightened himself in the chair and studied the data stream.

"It looks like it is running a contingency directive," said Min. "I found it earlier, but couldn't tell what it was."

Olm leaned in to look at the data stream. "An antiquated format," he said plainly.

The tutorials. Min had authorized the panel to allow him access to the tutorials. But how had he learned so much so quickly?

"Yes. Old," confirmed Min. He made a few manual inquiries of the panel. "It started after I entered my data from some readings I took on Uma."

"Readings of what?"

"Conditions on the surface." It was the data about the Hek that had triggered the directive's initiation. Min wasn't sure what it was going to do yet.

Olm chuckled. "I'm very interested in those conditions," he said. There was more than a hint of mania in his voice. He shoved Min off of the chair and onto the floor. Olm sat down, focusing on the display. Min stayed down for a moment, trying to devise a plan.

"Do you want me to -----"

"Shut up!" squawked Olm. He clapped his hands and leaned back in his chair. His expression was absolutely moony. "There are satellites around the planet," he said giddily. "The panel is moving them."

Moving them? Min wanted to get up and double check Olm's conclusion, but he wasn't sure Olm would let him. "Moving them where?"

Olm couldn't tear his eyes away from the display. "They are lining up in a semi-circular formation anchored at each pole," said Olm happily. He leapt up from his seat and stared down at Min. "What do you think they will do once they get there?" he asked excitedly.

"Can I ......look?" Olm waved him dramatically to the seat. Min sat down and watched the display.

Olm was correct. Many of the beacon satellites were moving. Instead of orbiting Uma at irregular latitudes, they were lining up, equally spaced, along one particular line of longitude. This realignment would be complete within a couple of rotations. "I don't know . . . ." said Min quietly.

"Well.....find out!" scolded Olm, as he slapped Min on the back of his head. "I'll be back soon. You had better have some answers for me when I return." Olm headed off down the hallway. Min's illumination directive was still operating. Once Olm was some distance away from Min, he disappeared into the darkness. Min sat still until he could no longer hear him.

He studied the directive. It was connected somehow to the data about the Hek protein templates Min had provided from the scanner that was destroyed by the panel. Min recalled one of the primary Protocols – no interaction with the Hek of any sort. He feared the beacon satellites were now moving into position to impose a penalty for his violation of that law.

The Hek brought dry wood and built a fire for May and her fellows. They also brought fresh fish strung together on thick hide thongs. One of the Hek began removing the limp fish from the thong and placing them on a flat rock. He then took each one and gutted it by tearing an opening in the belly with a sharp flint before reaching inside to remove the internal organs. After being so prepared, each fish was handed to another Hek who impaled them on a long spear. Once several fish were on the spear, he held them out over the flame.

It was a smell entirely foreign to the Umae. Pol covered her nose and shrank back from the fire. The shipwrights fidgeted uncomfortably and focused on breathing though their mouths. A pair of medium-sized dogs appeared from the darkness, sniffing eagerly at the air. One of the Hek grunted something at the dogs and they quickly retreated to the edge of the firelight.

The cook pulled the spear away from the fire and inspected the fish. Apparently satisfied, he pulled the first fish off the end of the spear and held it out to Cap. Cap shook his head slowly, so the man held it closer to him, shaking it.

"No," said Cap. "I don't eat that."

The cook looked over at the man who had gutted the fish. They exchanged confused glances. The cook held the fish out in front of him, watching the Umae. None of them demonstrated any interest. The cook then tossed the fish to the gutter, and he promptly took a bite out of its side. As he chewed, he reached in his mouth to pick scales out of the meat which he casually flicked to the ground. The Umae did their best not to watch.

"We should try to sleep," said Cap. "Who knows what they have planned." He rubbed his head and grimaced.

"Are you all right?" asked May. She moved next to him, placing her hand on his temple.

"Headache is all," said Cap. "It's better than it was."

"Are we sleeping here?" asked Jed.

"It looks like it," said Wil. He looked up and the lightless sky. "I hope it doesn't rain much."

May cleared a spot close to the fire for Pol and Joba. The others curled up on the ground, utilizing their small packs to increase their comfort as they could. The long days of walking had left them very fatigued. Despite their uncomfortable surroundings, they were soon able to sleep.

Cap awoke first, dragged from his sleep by the pounding in his head. It was worse than he had led May to believe. He was still experiencing double vision and his skull felt as if something were trying to pry it open from the inside. He sat up slowly and looked around.

The morningside sky was showing the earliest hint of dawn. The fire ring was barely smoking. The other Hek sat quietly, apparently waiting for the Umae to stir. In the middle of the ashes were the bones of the fish from the spear. That sight made Cap's already queasy stomach even more uneasy. He stood up, needing to relieve his bladder. He hoped a short walk might clear his head.

The Hek weren't concerned to see him wandering off. He walked in the direction of the other fires he had seen the night before. There were small groups of Hek, from six to eight in each group, sitting around extinguished fire pits. While most of them paid him no attention at all as he walked by, a couple couldn't hide their curiosity.

He stopped at a small group of trees and relieved himself. As he finished, he saw the Umae woman from the night before. She was seated on the ground playing with a couple of children. Cap walked in her direction.

She noticed him as he approached but gave no indication. The children she was with were young. Cap estimated they had no more than three of four ellipses. She would feign reaching out to grab at them, and they would scramble away, giggling gleefully. Then, they would approach slowly only to have her repeat the game. Not wanting to interrupt, Cap stopped. As he did, one of the children turned and saw him. The child had very light brown hair.

However, he was slightly stockier than any Umae child Cap had ever seen. The child had high cheek bones and, aside from his head, didn't have any hair on his body. The other child was a little girl, somewhat older than the first. She had long hair that reached her shoulders. It was mostly brown, although it appeared to Cap to be somewhat darker in color. She was taller than the boy, but shared his hardy build. When she saw Cap, she pointed and laughed. Cap smiled uneasily in return.

The children scrambled over to the woman and sat down in her lap. She wrapped her arms around them and rocked back and forth, all three of them laughing with the effort. Another figure was approaching from the distance. He was obviously a Hek. He was about the same height as the woman, but much thicker and more muscular. He had black hair that ran down the sides of his face and around his chin. His arms and legs were covered with it as well. He sat down and the children ran to him. Once they arrived, he scooped both of them up in his thick arms and stood up straight. The children wrapped their arms around his neck. The woman stood up, glanced over at Cap, and then joined the man and the two children in their embrace.

The man finally put the two giggling children down. They each clung to one of his wrists, trying to pull him to the ground. The woman looked on, smiling with an obvious fondness.

Cap chuckled. It drew the attention of the man, the woman and the two children who all turned in his direction at once. The children's hair was dark and thick, yet it only covered their heads. Their complexions were fair, but they were thick and solidly built. His eyes darted back and forth between the man, the woman, and the two children.

The father, a Hek. The mother, Umae. The children . . . . .something different, yet similar, to both. The realization caused him to take a step back. Cap felt unsteady on his feet as his head began to pound. He turned slowly and began walking back to the others.

CHAPTER 9

Bal wanted to die. He couldn't even raise himself from the cold floor of the Hall. Once Dom came down from the high of seeing whatever he had seen while accessing the panel, he had brutally beaten Bal for his subterfuge. The Chronicler had never imagined such misery. He could barely see from one eye and couldn't be sure the second was still in its socket. Bloody spittle dripped from his lips, still generously flowing from the beds where several of his teeth used to be. Every breath, no matter how slight, was a spear thrust into his side. He couldn't move. He could only lie on his stomach, bleeding on the floor.

Dom sat in front of the panel. Shu knelt next to him clutching his arm. He stared endlessly at the display without blinking. Bal had confessed that contacting the Citadel was impossible. It was, after all, a one-way process. The communication would have to be initiated from there. Only then was there any possibility of accessing the Citadel and all of its attendant technology. If Dom couldn't do that, he would have to wait until the cretins who represented this planet's highest life form recreated it. Even with his intellect guiding the process, it would take hundreds of ellipses. He didn't want to wait that long. When a suitable mate finally presented herself, he wanted the planet to be ready. Dom's control over Shu had compromised her mind. That was the only thing that had kept Bal alive.

"Shu, what was that I saw when I accessed the panel?" he asked finally.

Shu smiled, hungrily relishing his need of her. "It contains the history of our people," she said, pulling her cheek to his arm.

"All of it?"

"No."

Dom pulled his arm away, much to Shu's distress. "Other than recording history, what do the Chroniclers do?"

Shu thought for a moment. It was not such a simple question. "We maintain the law. We try to make sure our people are ready."

"Ready?" said Dom, turning towards her. "Ready for what?"

"To go to Haven," she answered plainly.

"Haven," echoed Dom, letting the word roll slowly from his mouth. "The next home. Tell me, what is wrong with this one?"

Shu blinked slowly several times. "The Hek are here," she said. "We cannot live here with them."

"The Hek. The short, sturdy ones. I remember." Dom looked back at the display.

"We will leave and this will be their planet," offered Shu.

Dom spun and caught her with a backhand across the side of her face. Her head snapped to one side and she collapsed to the floor. "No!" he growled. "This will be MY planet!"

Shu whimpered meekly as she tried to cover her head with her arms, expecting a renewed assault.

Dom stared down at her, full of contempt. He still needed her. His control of her was absolute. Bal feared him, but it was not impossible that he could attempt further defiance. There was more that Dom needed to know. He had to get it from Shu.

"Forgive me," he said in a deep, sweet voice. "I won't hurt you again."

Shu uncovered her head and looked up at him, a punch-drunk grin on her face. The blood spilling from her nose poured into her broad, dazed smile. "I . . . .know," she gasped.

Dom leaned down and picked her up off the floor. "This is your planet," he said, "why not fight them for it?"

"No . . . .no . . . .no," she said wearily. "Can't."

"Can't, or won't?"

"Can't," said Shu. "We don't . . . .kill. Protocols don't allow…" Suddenly aware of the blood in her mouth, she tried to spit it out but only managed to expel it past her chin and down the front of her neck.

Dom could not believe what he had heard. "Oh you don't . . . .?" He took Shu over to a nearby cushion and set her down. "You rest now. I will talk with you again soon."

He returned to his seat in front of the display. *Oh, there will be killing. And the longer I have to wait, the more killing there will be.*

He was now completely focused on the display. Bal had mentioned that Min was on the moon, in the Citadel. He likely wouldn't have any reason to contact the Hall. Was there anything he could do to somehow force Min's hand? The frustration was almost unbearable. If his mate arrived and things were not in place, yes, there would be killing.

A brief flash of light brought him back. Was that? The display had done something. Now, it started to glow. At first, it was rather faint, but it started to gain intensity. Dom stood up and yanked Bal up off the ground.

"What is happening?!?" he said, pointing Bal's face at the display.

A rapid sequence of high, squeaking noises was coming from Bal's shuddering body. "Ci---, ci---," he began desperately. Dom held him there, giving Bal a chance to gather a breath. "Citadel . . . .calling."

Min needed answers fast. He didn't know where Olm had gone, or what he was doing. Despite the adjustments he had made, he didn't trust the biosensors to provide him with notice of Olm's return.

He needed to discover the purpose of the directive the Alpha panel was engaged in. Sol and Eve weren't here, but Min had the next best thing.

"Implement mirror analysis 'Eve' and mirror analysis 'Sol'," he told the panel.

"Implementation complete. Purpose?" The panel had retrieved the analytical profiles of his former crew mates. It wasn't quite as good as actually having them there, but the panel could now engage in all of the purely objective analyses that they could do if they were present and interpret the information using a mathematical approximation of their insight and creativity.

"Eve, analyze the data being processed by the current directive. Project the major trends to Sol. Sol, analyze trends and predict the final product of the directive."

The panel began to hum. One portion of the panel's processors were simulating the analytical abilities of Eve and Sol, focusing them on a different directive being executed by the same panel. In effect, the panel was examining itself.

As Eve's voice filled his ears, Min couldn't help but recall how she had looked peering up at him from the side of the boat just before the Guards had hauled him away.

"Data indicate a harmonic exercise to be executed by the beacon satellites."

"For what?" snapped Min. "What are they doing?"

"Unknown, the directive is instructing them to relocate before generating a high-energy pulse wave."

Min's eyes narrowed with concern. "Aimed at what?"

"The target is non-specific. It appears that it will be directed at all of Uma, methodically applied to the entirety of its surface."

"But why?" Min demanded. "To do what?"

"Unknown. The pulse wave is resonant in nature. Forwarding additional data analysis to mirror Sol."

Min looked back down the passage to make sure that Olm wasn't returning. "Sol?"

"Processing." The Sol mirror directive had now taken over.

"Hurry." Min repeatedly glanced back down the passage as the duration of Sol's analysis stretched on.

Min grimaced. The entry of the data from the scanner had triggered the implementation of this new directive for some reason. Something about the Hek's protein templates had caused the Alpha panel to start rearranging all of the beacon satellites so they could direct a pulse wave at the planet.

"What does the pulse wave do?" The real Sol would have remarked on Min's impatience.

The panel remained silent for a moment. "The resonance wave will disrupt the protein templates of both the Umae and the Hek," came Sol's voice. "Current data would suggest that the casualty rate amongst the Hek will be 81.3%. The protein templates of the Umae are, on average, 96.1% the same as the Heks'. The casualty rate among the Umae will be . . . . .94.5%."

Sweat was dripping off of Min's forehead. "Why does it impact the Umae more than the Hek? That doesn't make sense! Estimate their relative populations post-directive."

The panel began to hum again. "The data concerning the Hek population are of questionable validity. There has never been a census. The data concerning the Umae population are similarly limited. If we assume that the Umae settlements have engaged in voluntary population control pursuant to the Directors' protocols, the likelihood that the Hek population exceeds that of the Umae by at least sevenfold is 97.7%.

"But……" Min couldn't believe those figures. "If that is correct, then the directive . . . . ."

"The directive will effectively impose Critical Closure. The Umae will be driven to extinction."

"Speculate if you have to! Why would the Umae who crafted this directive do something like this?"

Min thought he heard a noise from back down the hall. He couldn't see anything within the range of the light with which he had surrounded himself.

"The most likely possibility is that this result was intended by the directive's authors."

"Who is that?!?" demanded Min. "Who wrote it?!?"

"Director level authority required."

Min reached out and touched the display, switching to tactile directives.

Sol, I need for you to determine how the wave could be changed to mitigate this result. Interface with Eve to access her data analysis functions. Communications are to be with me only.

"What are you doing?!?" Min quickly turned around. Olm had returned.

"I'm trying to understand what the panel is doing," said Min, trying to sound calm. "I'm not having much luck."

Olm moved in and looked at the display. "Once you give me command authority, I will be able to figure it out," he said confidently. "But for now, I would know what is happening on the surface. Show me."

"But, I'm not sure . . . . . ." The back of Olm's hand met sharply with Min's nose. It was not a blow intended to harm, but to enforce authority. Nonetheless, blood began to trickle from Min's nostrils.

"Do it!"

Min wiped the blood on his sleeve and began entering directives. "The satellites have moved, so I'm not sure this will work . . . . ." His heart was beginning to race and the hammering inside his skull had returned.

The display hissed and crackled with small, pinpoint bursts of bright light. Perhaps knowing what was happening on the planet wasn't such a bad idea, thought Min. If he could somehow get a message to his crew.........

Finally, the static on the panel cleared. Dom sat in a chair, peering back at them. "Min, how nice," he said in a deep voice.

Olm leapt high into the air, barely restrained by the weakened gravity. "My Lord!" he bellowed. "My Lord at last!" His manic laughter rumbled through the Citadel, drowning out every other sound save that of Dom's laughter from the planet below.

Dag and Jed had to drag Cap up the slope towards the cave. May told him of the Bone Man's paintings. Cap had been in no condition to look at them before, but he desperately wanted to see what May had described. Pol had become oddly at ease with the Hek, particularly after the Umae woman who was with them had been so kind to her and Joba. Pol was not inclined to take Joba on another journey through the woods, so she had remained with the Hek. The four shipwrights had feared for the safety of Cap and May. They refused to remain behind.

The Hek had simply let them go. May's suspicion proved correct – they were primarily interested in Joba. The Hek had hardly taken any notice when the six of them had stood up, gathered their belongings, and hiked off across the plain. May wanted Cap to see the painting. He would be able to help her figure out what was really happening.

Just a couple of rotations into the return trip, Cap had taken a turn for the worse. He had begun vomiting and was having difficulties seeing. Once again, the shipwrights had to take turns carrying him through the forest. Now that they had reached the Bone Man's cave again, they were all near exhaustion.

May unpacked one of her last dry torches and set it alight. The cave had housed a couple dozen Hek the last time they were there. Now, it was empty. There were various signs of the Heks' recent habitation. Bones from small animals and fish were strewn about on the floor. A few of the small pots used by the Bone Man to hold his pigments were piled up against the base of one wall. Remnant burned-out ashes marked the spots where their fires had been. The cave was dark and quiet.

Lex was able to locate some dry wood and quickly got a fire started. The light from the flames was easily bright enough to illuminate the picture painted by the Bone Man. Now, there was more. He, or someone, had continued the work after the Umae had left. The painting now covered the entire wall. To their heartside was the part May had watched the Bone Man paint. It depicted the boat on the lake, coming from the island to the shore. There was a Journeycraft overhead. The Hek concealed themselves behind a bush. A small bundle, a child, was left on the beach. The Hek retrieved the bundle once it was left behind by the Umae from the boat.

The additional work continued the story. The Hek were running. A tall, slender figure held the baby overhead. They stopped in front of a slightly-built man with shoulder length hair, and handed him the baby. He smiled broadly. Behind him were others similar in appearance to him, interspersed with other Hek . . . .and –

Another group. They were not as tall as the man, but taller than the Hek. They were thickly-built, but not like the Hek. The long-haired man was slender by comparison. Many of them pointed eagerly towards the new arrival. One of them looked towards the sky. The group who had brought the baby knelt down in a circle around him, eagerly taking in its every move.

Cap struggled to focus on the painting. He carefully lowered himself to the floor, sitting as comfortably as he could. "They took the baby?" he asked.

"Only after the baby was left behind."

Cap squinted at the wall. "Abandoned?"

May's voice was laden with sadness. "Exiled."

Dag stepped forward, unwilling to believe what he was hearing. "The babies who were exiled, we gave them to the Hek?"

A single tear rolled down May's cheek. "The Hek may believe that, but no. The babies were simply left behind. No regard was given for what might happen to them."

"But….. ," said Dag. "There has to be another explanation."

"Dag," said May in a hollow tone. "There isn't. I know. One of my children was exiled. I . . . ." She tore her eyes away from the wall, turning her back to it. "I could easily be the woman on the wall."

Cap tried to focus on this revelation. In all of the years he had been so close to May, he had never known.

"But what do they do with them?" asked Dag. "It looks like they are happy in the painting."

"They are," said Cap, not lifting his head. "The babies are gifts from us. The Hek take them in and eventually they become leaders."

"And we come from across the water," said May. "And from the sky," she added, pointing to the Bone Man's rendition of the Journeycraft. "They are no threat to us at all. They . . . .revere us."

The shipwrights all stood together, each contemplating the painting. None of them could reach a more sound explanation for what they had seen.

"What are we going to do?" asked Jed.

"Bal is planning on trying to eliminate the Hek," said May. "That is why there were so many Guards. We have to tell him what we have learned. He has to know that there is no reason for him to carry out his plan. If he does….."

"There are so many Hek," noted Jed.

"We'll need a boat," said Wil. "Or, at least a suitable tree," he continued, patting his bag of tools.

"We can continue back towards the beach," said Jed. "We should be able to get a suitable craft together in a couple of rotations if we can find a place to work."

May sat down next to Cap. His eyes were unfocused. She couldn't tell if he even noticed her presence. "How are you?" she asked quietly, patting his cheek.

He took a couple of deep breaths. "I'm……slow," he said finally. "Go…..on."

May's hands began to tremble as she caressed his cheeks. "I will not abandon you here," she said defiantly. "Don't ask that."

Cap reached up and took her hand in his. "No….choice. Make Shu….. listen to….you. Or find….your boy."

"I'll stay with him," said Dag. "He is my Rearer. I will stay with him."

May took Dag by the hand, forcing a smile through the cloud of despair that was engulfing her. "You always were a good boy, Dag," she said fondly. "We will come back. I promise." May turned and planted a slow kiss on Cap's forehead. "Not goodbye," she whispered.

He smiled weakly, leaning into her. May stood up and gestured towards Jed, Wil and Lex. "We can cover some more ground before nightfall," she said determinedly. The three young men exchanged their farewells with Cap and Dag before turning and following May out of the cave.

Dag sat down next to Cap, briefly checking the status of the fire. "They will be back soon," he said optimistically. Cap managed a weak grin before looking back at the woman carrying the baby in the painting. He knew in his heart that he had seen May for the last time.

Dom leapt from his seat upon seeing Olm. "My Queen!" he bellowed. As he rushed towards the display, the image began to break up. The audio component turned into a raging hiss. Olm and his surroundings were obscured by waves of whitish light until he could no longer be seen.

"What is happening?!?" raged Dom. Once more, he hauled Bal from the floor and held him up to the display. "Fix this!"

Bal coughed weakly, barely able to shake his head. "Don'…..know….."

"Ahhh!" Dom angrily tossed Bal aside and turned towards Shu. "How do we bring back the image?" he said in a deeper voice.

Shu crawled across the floor to his feet. Her devotion was total. "I don't know," she said meekly. "We can't control the images."

Dom glowered down at the pathetic Chronicler. It was all he could do to prevent himself from twisting her head off. He began to stalk back and forth in front of the display. "She was on the moon, you say?" he demanded. Shu was confused. ***She***? "Imbecile! The person we saw, where is she?"

Shu looked over at the display. It was still riddled by random lines of various colors rolling across its face. "The Citadel," she said finally. "The moon."

Dom's face was deep crimson. His skin was glistening with sweat. "I need to be there, or she needs to be here," he said, barely maintaining the same deep voice.

Shu took on an expression of helplessness. "I don't know how," she offered. Dom's body trembled.

"You!" he snapped at one of the Guards by the door. "Summon all of my minions. I want all of them here, as soon as possible."

The Guard promptly turned and dashed out the door.

Shu cautiously crawled over next to Dom. As he looked down at her, kneeling at his feet, his rage was tempered by the depth of her servitude. "I will be with my Queen," he explained. "And once this planet is prepared, we will join and produce the most dominant line my species has ever seen."

Shu simply knelt there, watching him adoringly. Bal remained quiet on the floor, too scared to even attempt movement. He had heard what Dom had said. Without the Journeyers, he couldn't imagine how Dom would manage to be together with the person on the display. But Bal had no doubt that, if Dom found a way, the Umae and their planet were doomed.

Olm became frantic as Dom's image on the display collapsed into a swirling pattern of static. "What's happening?" he roared.

"It must be the beacon satellite," said Min. "It was relaying the signal, but now it has moved too far away from its customary position. The signal is gone." Min did his best to conceal his relief at this development, uncertain as to how it might provoke Olm.

"Can't you just move it back?"

"No. The directive has taken command over all the satellites. We won't be able to do anything with them until the directive is finished doing whatever it is doing." He had taken the risk of telling Olm an outright lie. While it was true that all of the satellites being manipulated by the panel were unavailable to them, the panel was not controlling ***all*** of the satellites. There were still some on the far side of the planet that the panel wasn't employing. Olm hadn't figured this out – yet. Once he did, Min realized that the price he'd pay would be severe.

Olm grunted and hurled one of the chairs against the wall. In the reduced gravity, it achieved a velocity that caused it to practically explode on contact. Min had always considered that particular material to be nearly indestructible. "Do not seek me out," said Olm menacingly. "I'll be back. Your life will be a lot more pleasant if you can restore that signal." He stalked off, down the hallway, customarily disappearing into the darkness.

Min waited a few moments to make sure Olm was gone. "Panel, maintain location of subject previously identified as 'Olm'. Give me a warning when he is within 20 farthoms of my location."

"Affirmative."

He then returned his attention to the main panel.

"Sol, how long will you need to finish your assessment of alternatives?"

"Not long. Eve's data analysis functions make the process very efficient. In fact . . . .it's done." Min leaned forward.

"Can we modify the pulse so that its impact on the Hek is increased and its impact on the Umae is decreased?"

"You want to kill the Hek?" asked Sol. The question was prefaced by a stretch of silence, simulating "mirror Sol's" disbelief.

Min closed his eyes as tears began to well up. This was likely his only chance. No one would ever know. "There must be some way….." he said quietly.

"No. Their protein templates are too similar. The pulse is almost certainly intended to disproportionately impact the Umae. It is my opinion that the Heks' templates have become significantly more similar to that of the Umaes' since the directive was created. That is the only reason why such a high percentage of the Hek will be impacted."

"But how?" demanded Min. "How have they changed so much?"

The panel remained silent for a moment, almost as if to create a dramatic pause. "Such similarities cannot result from simple evolution. The odds of that are infinitesimally small. The similarities had to have resulted from interbreeding between the two groups."

Min slumped down in his chair. "The exiled babies…." He muttered quietly.

"The probabilities….."

"Stop," said Min. Are there any other options?"

"The pulse wave can be modified to render it completely harmless."

"To both the Umae and the Hek?"

"Yes."

Min withdrew his locket and flipped it open. He stared at an image of him and Eve embracing. Min rubbed his head. The slow ache he had been experiencing was ballooning. "What do the portions of the Heks' protein templates that differ from those of the Umae control?"

"The differences involve the rate of protein accretion which accounts for their larger body mass, and gamete formation."

Min swallowed hard and closed his eyes. "And if the pulse were focused on those sequences in their templates?"

The panel hummed briefly. "The pulse would effectively sterilize the Hek. Within one and a half generations, they would be extinct."

Min opened his eyes. "Do it," he muttered in a hushed voice.

"I can't do that for you, Min," came Sol's reply.

Min buried his face in his arms atop the panel. Not only was his energy waning but now a computer simulation of his old friend was taking a moral stand against him. "How do I modify the wave?" he mumbled.

"I can provide the specifications. How it is accomplished is a technical matter, beyond my expertise. You will have to figure that part out, Min." Even mirror Sol demonstrated great patience as it explained its own limitations a second time.

He could barely open his eyes. When Olm had force fed him his last dose of medication, the rest of it had been lost. Without it, the amount of time he would remain functional enough to implement a plan would be very limited. Even the dim light from the panel felt like knives piercing his head. There was only one option left. "Panel, implement mirror analysis." He swallowed again, unable to rid his throat of the offending lump. "Profile 'Hab'."

Dom sat alone on the floor of his chamber. His eyes were closed and he was focusing. He reached out as he had to his minions at the lake. This time his thoughts were directed upwards towards the moon.

He knew his Queen would be doing the same thing. They could begin their bond now even though they were still far, far apart. Once that was accomplished, they would sense one another's thoughts. Distance would no longer be a consideration.

Unlike his contact with his minions, this time there was very little to interfere with his search. The planet had provided a huge number of sentient, albeit stupid, life forms that provided clutter and interference with the process. Now, he had only to reach past the thick atmosphere and into space. There he would find no sentient interference at all. The moon held only two sentient beings, his Queen and Min. Her intelligence was such that Dom could never mistake it for Min's. He would recognize her immediately. Once he did, they would begin to join. It was merely a prelude for when she was with him physically. Then their union would be entire. Their progeny would dominate this system, and then the entire galaxy. The range of their hegemony would be practically boundless.

Other than a few worthless shore birds, he sensed no sentience in the air. His thoughts rose up through the clouds and he was soon greeted by the cold bleakness of space. The moon slowly grew as he approached, its bare surface gleaming brightly in the reflected light of the sun. His physical body shuddered. He could feel her now.

He saw vast expanses of white dust covering the surface. A lone plateau rose in the distance, conspicuous in its contrast to the rest of the moonscape. She was there.

Inside, there was no light. He did not need it. He could sense the interior walls and feel the hum of machinery. Here was the technology he had sought so desperately. His Queen was here. She would know what to do.

His thoughts were drawn forward, down the myriad dark halls. His progress was effortless. She was drawing him towards her.

Ecstasy! He had found her! She awaited his arrival, as he knew she would. Their thoughts intermingled. She knew him, and he her. She advised him of her plan. It was marvelous. Already she had acquired all the technology they would need. Now she only had to join with him physically. She was truly worthy of being his Queen! This part of their joinder was complete. Their energies were no longer separate. Soon, their physical bodies wouldn't be either.

Dom opened his eyes. He threw back his head and laughed so hard that he fell over on his side. Perfection! His Queen was here and she was taking steps to prepare this world, to make it the way it needed to be. Now, he only had to wait. She would be with him soon enough.

May and the remaining shipwrights made good time on their return trip through the forest. It was too soon to begin the search for the right tree. First, they needed a place to do their work. The constant threat of rain required a sheltered area in which to craft their boat. They also needed somewhere for their tree to dry. They could accomplish the process of stripping the bark away while the wood was still wet, but burning out the interior of the boat was impossible in the rain. Ideally, they would find a cave. Then the search for the tree could begin. The Bone Man's cave was much too far from the shore. But its existence nurtured their hopes that other such caves could be found.

They deviated from the route they had followed with the Hek, leaving the path to inspect every significant rise within view. None of these hills produced the cave they so desperately needed. The number of proper trees was significant, but they had no good place to begin the project. After two rotations of steady walking, they found themselves back at the walls of the Garden. May produced the key and the shipwrights pushed the door open. The Garden would provide them with food and shelter against the wind, but it provided no cover from the rain. It gave them everything they needed save that which they needed most.

May sat down, more fatigued than she could remember, and leaned against the stone of an interior wall. Her will to continue was waning. Even if they could make it back to Atla somehow she had no assurance that Shu would even listen to her. They would likely be exiled again immediately. Or worse. She had never heard of anyone returning from exile. She didn't know what the Protocols held for such people.

She looked upwards at the sky. For the third straight rotation, the dark clouds promised rain. "I don't see how we can do this......" she admitted. "There just doesn't seem to be any way."

Jed, Lex, and Wil looked at one another in sympathetic silence. "Maybe we can at least harvest the tree," suggested Wil. "We know that we have to at least do that."

May looked up, not taking any heart in Wil's suggestion. "If the weather breaks, how long would you need?"

"Depending on the tree, it will take at least two rotations for the wood to dry enough after we debark it," said Jed. "If we get that far, we can burn out the cavity in another two rotations."

"Four rotations at best, then," said May heavily. "Four rotations without rain. I don't think I've seen four consecutive rotations without rain in my entire life."

"If we get started, and it rains, we can wait until it dries again," said Wil. His plan weighted on May like a stone block. It could be tens of rotations before the boat was ready.

"We could wait for the Guards on the beach," said Lex. "And we could talk to them then. We wouldn't need a boat."

"But where would we wait?" asked May. "We don't know where they are coming ashore. The Chroniclers have all of the information from every trip ashore that anyone has ever made. They could be landing anywhere. What if we miss them?"

"Let's get the tree," said Jed. "Wil's right, we know we will at least need that. In the meantime, maybe someone will think of something else." He looked at May hopefully. Her inability to share his optimism dragged her down even further.

"Do that," she said. "I'll wait here and let you back in when you return." As the three men turned to leave, she added, "Don't take too long."

May secured the door before returning to her spot near the wall. She closed her eyes and took a deep breath. Bal's plan didn't make any sense. He had no way to realize just how many Hek there were. While May had never had any reason to estimate the number of Guards on Atla, she now guessed that there were perhaps a hundred at most. The Hek were much more numerous. Bal's unnecessary plan was doomed to failure. The Guards would be slaughtered. And she couldn't guess how the Hek might react to such betrayal by those they had revered. If she could somehow convince the Chroniclers of that, perhaps she could be with her son again.

A great stone of despair pulled her down. She would go back to the Bone Man's cave. She would find Cap. But his voice.....she had never seen him as he was when they parted. She drew another deep breath and closed her eyes, trying to force such thoughts from her mind. She pulled her knees up to her chest and tried to relax.

May was just beginning to doze off when she heard the shipwrights outside the thick wooden door. When she opened it, she saw they had a small, thick-trunked tree. They had already removed all of its branches.

"The nice part about the rain," said Jed as he helped the other two haul the tree inside, "is that it makes the bark a bit softer. We'll have this stripped in no time."

"It will make a short boat," said Lex, "but we aren't planning on using it again. The smaller the boat, the less time we'll need to make it." The three men dropped the trunk down on the ground in a clear area across from the door. They immediately drew their small stone axes and began hacking gashes in the bark. They then stripped the bark away using flat, sharp stones. May was pleasantly surprised by the efficiency of their work. Before long, all of the bark had been stripped away. As if on cue, it began to rain.

May looked up, shaking her head and wordlessly cursing the sky. Lex, Jed and Wil looked on, helplessly, as the water soaked the naked wood. It would be impossible to get a fire lit to burn out the interior.

"Gah!" growled Jed in frustration. He took his axe and drove its edge into the tree. Small chips of wood flew from the trunk. "I don't believe this!" Lex and Wil turned away from the trunk, unable to watch the rain pour down on it. May approached slowly and crouched next to the tree, running her hand across the smooth wood. Glancing down at her feet, she picked up one of the wood chips.

"Why do you need a fire again?" she asked.

Lex turned back around. He was the first of the shipwrights to tame his frustration. "To burn the interior of the log out, so the boat is hollow."

May stood up. "Does it matter how the log is hollowed?" Her voice was sparking a bit now.

"What do you mean?"

May reached down and picked up a few more wood chips. "You said the rain makes the wood softer. Could you hollow the log out with your axes instead?"

Wil turned quickly. "That is not the way to make a boat," he protested. "You need fire."

"I agree," said Lex. "That isn't how it is done."

"Because the Chroniclers told you how to do it?" asked May.

"Yes, they did!" said Wil defensively. "And the Journeyers told them. Who are we to ignore that?"

She sat down on the log, running her finger over the wound produced by Jed's axe. "Could you do it?" she asked finally. "Just, could you?"

The three men looked at one another. "I don't think so," offered Jed. "The axes wouldn't hold up. We'd have to go out and hunt for more axe rock. We might as well wait for the wood to dry."

"What about them?" said May. She pointed to the small corner of the Garden that was sheltered from the weather. Leaning against that wall were all the various implements used to tend the plants. Nearly all of them had sharp stone edges of some kind on them.

"I don't like it," said Lex uneasily, "but I suppose it could work."

The other two nodded reluctantly.

"Then do it," implored May. "And let it rain!" she cried, waving a defiant fist at the sky. "Let it rain!"

CHAPTER 10

The assembly of Guards was complete. Dom stood at the center of a large semi-circle formed by the hulking Umae. Max took his usual position near the center of the formation. He was uneasy about the behaviors of some of his fellow Guards. They had been unusually silent, even by Guard standards. He had not seen any of them sleep.

Dom walked slowly past the Guards, casually inspecting each one. "There is no reason why we have to attack the Hek," he said finally. He stopped in front of Max, looking at him intently. Max stared back down at him. "But that doesn't mean that we aren't going to attack them anyway," he added with a broad grin.

"You are in charge?" asked Max. Dom noted the emotion in his voice.

"I will explain," said Dom. "When I choose to. For now, we have a plan of attack to execute."

Max's eyes widened slightly. "What is the purpose of such an action?" asked Max.

Dom looked up at the towering Guard. "Purpose?" he echoed. "Why do you think we need a purpose? In fact, why are you even thinking at all?"

Max continued to peer down at Dom. "I don't understand."

"You weren't on the beach when Bal tried to have me killed, were you?"

Max turned and looked over at Bal. The Chronicler was standing a ways away, his face still badly swollen and bruised.

"I have been ill recently," replied the Guard. "He tried to have you . . . . .killed? Why? That is a violation of our laws."

Dom held his arms out wide and threw his head back. "I know! Isn't that awful? Fortunately, he failed. But as a result of his actions . . . . ." Dom resumed his review of the remaining Guards. "I have been named Chief Chronicler. Shu is . . . .not well. Her recent trip to the mainland seems to have overtaxed her. She has named me as her successor."

A handful of the Guards looked over at Shu. The rest stood still, staring blankly forward. "What does that have to do with the Hek?" asked Max.

Dom stopped once again, now some ways away from Max. "Because Bal is a traitor," explained Dom. "He was working with the Hek to destroy us. He told us all about their plans. Now, we must attack them before they attack us."

Max considered Dom's statement. Two nearby Guards quietly conferred with one another. "Do we know anything of their location? Their numbers?" asked one of the Guards.

Dom folded his arms. "No, but we don't need to. We have plenty of force to destroy . . . .eliminate their threat," he replied, a hint of mania in his voice. "Trust me."

The same two Guards whispered back and forth to one another. "We do, Chief Chronicler," one replied in a flat, monotone voice. "We are prepared to serve."

"I knew you would be," said Dom. He turned and looked back at Max. "And you?"

There was much Max did not yet understand. He would continue his allegiance to the Chroniclers. For now, that apparently meant Dom. "I am prepared to serve," said Max.

"And the rest of you?"

The remaining Guards responded in a droning unison. "We are prepared to serve." Each response was identical and perfectly synchronized with the others. They spoke with a single voice.

"Excellent. I am in the process of creating a plan of attack. We will reconvene once I have done that. In the meantime, continue your normal duties." Most of the Guards turned in harmony, pivoting on one heel before walking off.

Dom walked over to where Bal was cowering. "I think that Guard, Max, might be a problem," said Dom. "A very small problem, granted, but one nonetheless. I suppose I could host him, and the remaining few who have not been hosted yet. . . . . ." Now Dom was clearly thinking aloud. "But no. They will do as I say because they think they are supposed to. They will do it of their own free will." He began to laugh. "That is much more entertaining," he said, leaning down and staring at Bal. "Don't you think?"

"Min?" The voice from the display was very familiar to him. "Min, what are your directives?"

Even through the fog of pain, his brain registered the irony that Hab was asking him for direction. His mentor, the man who had taught him so much, needed to know what to do.

Min slowly lifted his head up from the panel and looked at the display. Every beat of his heart caused a fresh burst of misery inside his head. It took most of his strength to focus on what was right in front of him.

"Sol?" he grumbled.

"No, this is Hab, Min. You asked for me. Don't you remember?"

"No," replied Min as he took a slow deep breath. "I need Sol now."

The display flickered briefly. "Min, what do you need?" It was Sol.

"Can you . . . .analyze my condition . . . .tell me, what to do?"

"Place your hand on the display." Even this panel's simulation of Sol had his gentle bedside manner. Min placed a shaky palm against the display.

"Min, your condition is nearly critical. The medication level in your blood is almost zero. Do you have more?"

Min reached into his pocket and took out the vial the real Sol had given him. Only a few drops remained from Olm's forced administration.

"Not . . . .much," he gasped. "Less than . . .two bolas."

"The treatment value of that quantity is limited," said Sol in a soft voice. "But you need to take what is left immediately. If you don't, the likelihood is 87.45% that your life functions will terminate within the next .118 rotations."

"But, I haven't replicated it yet," said Min. "I'll need some for that."

"It can be produced from scratch," said Sol. "But it is a slow process. Without a sample to replicate, it will take approximately .86 rotations. I will initiate the process in the bio lab now." The Sol voice paused. "Min, I'm afraid I have some bad news," it said in a softer tone. "Even if you consume what you have left, your deterioration will recommence in approximately .38 rotations. The chances that you will die before the new batch of medication is complete is still 81.32%. I'm sorry."

"Don't be," said Min as he poured the remaining liquid into his mouth. He swallowed hard, making sure that every drop made its way down his throat. Yet again, he was amazed at the speed with which the liquid reinvigorated his body and mind. "Hab, old friend, access the last interchange between me and the simulations of Sol and Eve. Tell me when you have done that."

"Done."

"Sol says that the pulse wave has to be modified and has provided a set of characteristics the wave must have. I have a couple of ideas about how to do that, but I wanted to hear your suggestions first."

The panel hummed slightly. "I would recommend using the remaining available satellites to set up an energy screen between the satellites that are already moving and the planet," suggested the voice.

"A lens." said Min. "That was exactly what I was thinking."

"The current directive won't allow us to change the wave prior to its emission from the satellites. But we can use the lensing effect to change its nature. I trust that Sol's calculations about its effects are correct."

"So do I," said Min. Min's heart wasn't racing now and his thinking was becoming clearer. He hadn't worked with Hab on anything significant in a long time. "Do you foresee any problems with this approach?"

"Min, this same technique could be used to deflect the entire wave away from the planet. Why aren't you doing that instead?"

He didn't have an answer the real Hab would find acceptable. Fortunately, this simulation would do what he asked even if the real Hab would have balked. "Because I'm going to be with Eve," he said quietly. "Critical Closure will be prevented. Forever."

Again, the panel hummed quietly for a moment. "The lensing will result in an amplified energy package that will be carried by the wave. Will that change the intended effect of the wave?"

"Sol?" asked Min. "Was that included in your assumptions?"

"Of course," said Sol. The simulation almost sounded insulted. "The increased energy level will not make a significant difference with respect to its effect on the protein templates of the Hek."

Min had to do it. He clutched at his pendant. But he'd still have to get a message to his crew somehow. They were waiting for him.

"All right. Hab, implement the plan then. Relocate the available satellites and set up the lens." He looked around for Olm, still not fully trusting the panel's ability to locate him and provide Min with a warning of his approach. Min couldn't allow Olm to stop this process. Min also couldn't allow Olm to make *him* stop the process. "Complete directive, lockout command Min zeta omega."

"Min?" It was Hab. "You realize that once that lockout is implemented that it will be impossible to reverse the process?'

"Yes," said Min. "I have my reasons."

"Very well," replied Hab. "Lockout implemented."

Now Olm could come back. He could crush Min's bones and strip the flesh from his limbs. Min couldn't stop the process now even if he wanted to.

"Hab, I'd like for you to interact with Eve and provide me with some theories about what the ultimate objective of the Directors was." He drew a couple of deep breaths in an effort to clear his mind. The real Hab would have never entertained such a project, let alone participated in it. "I'll provide you with all the data I have."

Min reached out and placed his hand on the display. He tried to focus on all of the things he thought might have a bearing on the analysis. The Umae protocols. The technology ceiling. The population limit. The exiles. The Hek and their rapid technological advancement. He opened his eyes for a moment, trying to gather more strength. His dreams. The visions summoned by his interaction with the panel at the Land Bridge. Maybe they weren't related, but he was too fatigued to effectively screen his input. Hab and Eve would have to do that for him.

"I may not make it back here to check your conclusions," he said wearily. "But maintain the report. It might prove to be useful to someone who visits the Citadel in the future." The image of Hab laying on the platform on the *Starshine* intruded into his thoughts. It was pushed away by one of Eve, looking up at him playfully in his quarters. But he didn't have the time to reminisce. "Thank you, Hab," said Min, rising from his seat. "Thank you all. For everything."

The heartside beach was crowded with smiths of all sorts. Wood workers shaved off the ends of hard, narrow sticks until they bore cruel, sharp points. Others fashioned long wooden handles suitable for bearing crude, stone blades. The stone smiths carefully chipped away at the edges of rough rocks. The weavers had erected large tents made of fat-soaked hemp fabric. Underneath, the shipwrights worked quickly, burning away the interiors of a dozen thick tree trunks of varied species, oblivious to the rain. They all were urged forwards in their tasks by the steady beat of the drums. Every drum on the island was on the beach now, and all were thumped in unison. Some of the older Wards did the best they could to shield their leather batter heads from the rain with wide hemp covers to prevent them from softening to the point of uselessness. Dom walked slowly amongst the throng, surveying their progress.

"Courage!" he implored. "The blessings of the Journeyers are upon us. Keep up your good works!" One of his lieutenants approached, kneeling low before him. "Not here you idiot!" scolded Dom as he hauled the Guard to his feet. He looked around carefully at the workers. All were occupied with their various duties and the Guard's error had gone unnoticed.

"Lord, with our relatively low numbers, how do you propose to deploy us?"

"Carefully," said Dom. He turned back to look upon the production line before him. "Just think, for every worker out here now, there are perhaps another 3 or 4 who aren't here. After all they will have invested in the cause, it wouldn't be fair not to let them participate a bit more . . . .intimately. Would it?"

The Guard watched the workers. "What is your intent, Lord?"

"My intent is to have as many of them die as possible," spat Dom through his teeth. His smothering glare cowed the Guard, despite his enormous size advantage.

"Guide my way, Lord."

"They will go first," said Dom. "And they will ***want*** to go first. And when they do, the Hek will cut them down like dry grass. Only then do you and the others advance. Leave no Hek alive. No man, woman or child. Bring no Umae back with you. Once the Hek are defeated, and the men of this island are dead, my authority will be absolute." He looked up at the grayish sky. "Then I shall be with my Queen and the true conquest will begin." His eyes rolled back ecstatically as he savored his plan.

"Chief Chronicler?" It was Max.

Dom regathered his focus and sent his lieutenant on his way. "What?" He was unable to conceal all of the irritation in his voice.

"You plan on using the citizenry during the attack? Is that wise?"

How much had this fool overheard? Dom quietly cursed the newfound connection he had established with his Queen. The sheer bliss it brought him had made him sloppy. He couldn't afford that. Not now.

"The Hek have an immense numerical advantage according to the Journeyers," said Dom flatly. "The citizens will be used exclusively in diversionary actions and to perform non-combat duties. The risk to them will be acceptably...... minimal." His last word nearly deprived Dom of his very breath.

"I came to ask about equipment inventories. We already have far more weapons than we do Guards. At what point should we cease production?"

"Let me worry about that," said Dom. His voice dripped with paternalism. "Once this starts, we may not have the chance to resupply. We must err on the side of over production."

"I see." He took two steps backwards before turning and walking away, the standard procedure for leaving the presence of a Chronicler.

Dom had just plainly lied to him. Max had overheard everything he had told his lieutenant. However, Max was unsure about whether Dom knew that he had caught him in his lie. With so many of the Guards acting strangely, he would have to take great care with what he knew. Dom's plan did not serve the best interests of the Umae. Max was certain of that. He would have to consider what, if anything, he could do about it.

Min drug himself down the corridor. He had lowered the gravity as much as he could without losing contact with the floor. The science lab was still a long ways off, and he was completely spent. Min rolled over on his back and stared up at the ceiling. His pulse roared repeatedly inside his head. He wasn't going to make it.

A faint whirring sound stirred in his ears. At first, he thought it was just his fading consciousness, or the steady hum of death coming to bear him away. It grew louder. He turned his head and saw a small servo-mech come around the corner. It was cleaning the floor.

The servo-mech was only slightly larger than a newborn child. It traveled the floors and walls of the station, removing any contaminants. It also served as a mobile scanner, providing the Alpha panel with detailed information about the air quality inside the Citadel. The servo-mech moved briskly back and forth, from one side of the hall to the other, cleaning. It was steadily heading in Min's direction.

Min took a deep breath. "Help." It was a throaty gasp. He didn't know whether it would be intelligible or not.

The mech stopped and a small wire sprang from its top. The wire had a tiny bead on one end that waved back and forth. The mech then retrieved the wire and followed a direct line towards Min. It stopped right next to him.

Min could only cough weakly. He had no idea what the artificial intelligence level of this mech might be. It was his only chance.

"Lab." The effort wracked his body with coughs. A few lights on the face of the mech blinked off and on as it seemingly pondered Min's comment. It rotated one hundred and eighty degrees, froze for a moment, and then rotated back once more. Min had dealt with these machines before. It was thinking. That was all he could hope for.

The beaded wire appeared again. This time, the mech swung the bead so that it landed on Min's face. Min closed his eyes. The mech recalled the wire and issued a broad plastic strap from one of its sides. Utilizing another tiny claw-like tool, it managed to loop the strap around one of Min's wrists and secured it tightly. Revving up its tiny motor, it then began to drag Min down the hall towards the Life Lab. The sensation of the floor sliding underneath him gave him something to focus on. The replicated medicine wouldn't be ready in time. He had to hang on long enough to stop Olm for good.

The shipwrights worked diligently on the tree. Despite their great reluctance to use the gardening implements as tools, they focused on finishing their task as quickly as possible. The rain fell steadily while they worked. They slept very little, and only in shifts. May did what she could to help – gathering the rain water and preparing meals from the Garden's produce. Slowly, the interior of the tree was hacked away, creating a cavity that would serve as the passenger space for the canoe.

The tools were not made for such a purpose. While many of them had solid stone edges, they did not stand up well to the abuse of being constantly battered against the tree. The blades would gradually splinter until they became useless. May offered to leave the Garden in search of more stones, but the shipwrights objected, pointing out that they weren't sure how to hone the stones even if they had more. May watched anxiously as the work proceeded, trying to gauge if the supply of stone-edged tools would hold out until the canoe was finished.

The work was further hindered by the angry blisters rising up on the shipwrights' hands. While they were well-callused from building back on the island, their typical techniques were not nearly as hand-intensive. Within a rotation, all three of them were using leaves or scraps of their own clothes to try and cushion their wounds. May tried to provide relief with some of the medicinal plants nearby, but it was only temporary. By the end of the second rotation, their hands were bloodied and swollen. The slightest touch burned like a glowing coal. They gamely tried to continue, but their progress was greatly impaired.

"How much more do you think you have?" asked May examining their hands.

Jed grimaced. "I'd say we have another full rotation, at least."

"I'd agree with that," offered Wil.

Jed could barely close his hands. His palms were skinned bare and were covered with a concoction of blood, pus and dirt. When he wasn't trying to wield a tool, he held his hands far away from his sides, mindful of bumping them against anything.

"I can't have you go on like this," said May emphatically. "I think we will get done faster if you all take two rotations to let your hands heal a little. I can make a poultice that will help. Then maybe you can complete the canoe with one last, good rotation of work."

Wil didn't like the idea, but he couldn't argue with her logic. "This is the price we pay for abandoning the ways of the Journeyers," he offered. "We should respect their guidance."

May bit her tongue. ***Except their guidance doesn't help us build a boat in the rain, does it?*** "There is one other plant that I need to find that isn't inside the Garden," she said, trying to turn the conversation. "I'm sure I've seen it in the forest. You three stay and rest . . . ."

"No!" said Jed. "You can't go alone."

"Stay," repeated May more firmly. "I'll be fine. You all must be exhausted, and I need you to finish this boat."

The three men looked at one another. Their fatigue and her apparent determination overcame their reservations. They sat down against a far wall, away from the rain, and closed their eyes.

May picked up her sack and went out the large wooden door. She remembered seeing a large rainflower shortly before they had reached the Garden. She would simply go back and harvest it. It would be a short trip.

The rain was beginning to ease. The steady shower had lasted almost two full rotations, leaving the forest floor muddy and slick. May slowly made her way back through the woods, mindful that she hadn't precisely described her destination to the others. She had no reason to hurry. The rainflower wasn't going anywhere.

The flower had broad, deep green petals. They served to funnel rainwater towards the center of the flower. The flower's pollen then broke down the water's surface tension. The flower's root system required a consistent supply of hydration. If the plant did not receive any rain for more than a rotation or so, it would release its pollen-heavy water supply from the underside of its leaves. The water fell to the ground in the form of tiny droplets. The flower, effectively, would water itself. May had always found herself fascinated at the sight of a rainflower raining on its own roots, even when it wasn't raining anywhere else.

The plant was exactly where she remembered seeing it. It was the pollen she needed, but she wasn't going to take the time for a cautious collection. She seized the large plant at its base and gave it a tug, yanking it and a portion of its roots right out of the ground. As she tucked it away in her sack, she heard a low, deep growl.

She instinctively froze, keeping herself as still as she could while she tried to identify the source of the sound. She couldn't see anything. The sound rumbled out of the forest towards her again, this time much louder. It was much more ominous and forceful than the sounds the Heks' animals had made. May fought the impulse to run.

She saw movement near the opening of a clearing in the distance. An enormous animal gracefully descended to the lowest branch of a tree and easily leapt to the ground. Its shoulders stood above her waist. Two long, grayish incisors curved downward from its upper jaw. It stood on four legs and had a sleek, muscled body. It raised its nose in the air, searching for a scent.

May froze in place trying not to panic. She tried to think about how far away the Garden was. Even if she ran, she wouldn't be able to do it without falling. She doubted this creature would have the same problem. If she somehow made it to the Garden, could it get inside? She couldn't endanger the shipwrights. She remained as still as she could. A modest breeze chilled the sweat on her brow. Surely the beast could hear her heart. She felt the warm flow of urine on her thighs.

Again, the beast surveyed the forest air. It lowered its head and pawed at something on the ground beneath its feet. Then, it quickly turned in the opposite direction and sauntered casually away, letting out a series of clicking noises as it walked.

May remained still for longer than she intended. Each time she decided it was time to move, she found herself still paralyzed by fear. The forest was full of snapping twigs and rustling branches, daring her to move.

"May?" She heard their voices, just barely, in the direction from where she had come. It had grown dark. She had to get to them.

Movement now was almost impossible. She had no light and she couldn't find any good footing. She slid and stumbled along, tearing the skin on her knees and hands several times. Finally, she saw a flicker of light. "H-here!" she called. "I'm here!" Soon, the three shipwrights appeared bearing torches.

"Are you all right?" asked Jed.

"We must go, quickly," she stammered. She pushed past them, almost managing to leave the men and their lights behind. They started after her, content to wait for answers until they reached the Garden.

Once they did, May hurried them all inside and pushed the door shut. She seized a torch from Wil's hand and stared up at the walls, getting a sense of their height. "No, it couldn't jump . . . ." she began. "But could it climb......?"

Most of the plants in the Garden were relatively short, less than head high to an Umae adult. A few were taller and tended to be bunched towards the Garden's center. Along the edge of the wall were a scattering of trees. Most were dwarven fruit-bearers, but a few were tall, strong nut trees with thick trunks and sturdy limbs that reached higher than the walls.

"What are you talking about?" said Wil. He also looked upwards, trying to determine what May was doing. She began to frantically examine the ground in between the various plants. She stopped when she reached a far corner, her breath leaving her chest with a rush.

"I saw . . . .an animal," she said finally. "Taller than my waist at its shoulder. It had long . . . .teeth. Like knives." She pointed to the ground. There was a large pile of rain soaked animal droppings. Some of the nearby plants had been knocked over.

"How did you escape?" asked Wil finally.

"It didn't see me," she said. It didn't . . . .see me."

"How far?"

Once again, May looked up at the walls. "Not far," she said quietly. "We need to finish," she continued. "We need to leave this place."

The servo-mech activated the portal to the lab causing it to slide open. It then dragged Min inside, the door sliding shut behind them. Min was nearly oblivious to his surroundings. He was vaguely aware that a door had opened, then shut.

There was a great weight on his chest. The familiar flavor of his medication spilled into his mouth. He lapped at it gladly with his tongue. Olm stood above him. He had one foot on Min's chest.

"You can't die. Not yet," said Olm. He unfastened the strap from Min's wrist and then flicked the servo-mech across the floor with his foot. The mech ricocheted off of the base of a table, bounced a couple of times, and landed on its back. It quickly righted itself with the help of its extensions. After flipping itself over, it remained where it was, awaiting additional directives.

Min wanted to sit up, but Olm re-pinned him to the floor. "Why . . . .?"

"Why didn't I just let you go?" Olm was getting good at anticipating Min's thoughts.

"Yes. Why?" Sol's marvelous elixir was already clearing his head.

"I want you to see something first," said Olm. "You are rather clever. Predictable, but clever."

Min searched Olm's face for some clue about his frame of mind. He saw only a hint of mania. "How so?"

Olm moved his foot off of Min's chest, allowing him to stand.

"The directives you gave the panel, were they supposed to save your people?"

Supposed? Min had made those directives irrevocable. There was no way that Olm could have stopped them. "Yes, they are," said Min confidently. "And they will."

Olm walked across the lab to the repose chambers. He folded his arms, pretending to study them. "You can go in, but you can't come back out, isn't that right? You can sleep, you just can't wake up." He turned and grinned at Min.

Min looked at the repose chambers. "No, I likely wouldn't be able to come out. Not unless my people are able to improve their medical technology."

Olm tilted his head back and roared with laughter. "Even when your utter and entire defeat is imminent, you cling to your foolish hopes."

Min's face reddened. "Why don't you just say what you mean. You enjoy these little games."

The laughter quickly died out and Olm's face darkened. "I *live* for these . . . 'little games'," he spat. "In fact, I prepared some of your medicine just to make sure I was done with you before you died."

"Done? Are you done with me?"

"Almost," sneered Olm. "Your lens, it changes the pulse, doesn't it? Let me think, it will probably impact the Hek much more significantly than it will the Umae. You think that will give your people a fighting chance." Min couldn't believe what he was hearing. Olm could not have gotten all of that information from the panel without command authority. He figured everything out on his own, and in a very short amount of time. His intellect was astounding.

"It will," said Min.

Olm walked along, stopping next to each individual repose chamber. "Which one will you use?" he asked rhetorically. "Can I give you a bit of advice? Don't use this one." He flicked a nearby switch and turned towards Min. The door on the repose chamber nearest Olm slid open. There was a hiss of releasing gas and Min's nose was assaulted by the stench of death. A corpse toppled out of the chamber and fell to the floor, making a hollow thud as it landed. Min could still make out the Journeyer smock it wore. There was a gaping hole in its skull just above its nose. The smell had made Min's stomach churn. He covered his mouth and looked away. "A very helpful teacher," said Olm. "I let him live for quite a while. Until I knew enough to teach myself." He reached down and stuck his index finger into the skull hole. "And once you gave me access to the directive languages your people use to control your machines, I didn't need your command authority anymore," he said, looking at the corpse wistfully. "It was simple enough to just bypass your pitiable barriers. Thanks for the opportunity."

Min had considered an authority bypass to be impossible. Olm had to be bluffing, because if he wasn't….."What have you done?" said Min. The combination of the stench, the stress, and the relatively small dose of medicine he had been given was taking its toll. Fatigue was already bearing down on him.

"Tell me if one lens would change the nature of the wave, what do you suppose two would do? Or . . . . . .five?" Olm rose, waiting for Min's response.

Five? Min made some cursory calculations in his head. The increased energy package! If he really created five lenses . . . . . "You've destroyed the planet," he said weakly, dropping down to one knee.

"No," said Olm darkly. "YOU destroyed your planet. You had every opportunity to stop, didn't you? But my lens, and yes there is only one more, when combined with yours, will increase the energy package tenfold."

Tenfold? thought Min. His mind was starting to labor. *That can't be right.* "No, not ten," said Min. Now he was kneeling on the floor. "My lens isn't intended to augment the energy of the pulse. That is simply a necessary bi-product of the process." Min began coughing. He placed one hand on the ground to balance himself. "Threefold, at most," he gasped. "But, there's an energy buffer....from....." Another round of harsh coughs wracked his body. He was completely doubled over.

"From.......?" Olm was momentarily lost in deep thought. "Of course," he said finally. "Now I see what is going to buffer all that extra energy." He began skipping around the lab, laughing madly and slinging chairs and equipment. "Too perfect! We need your world to serve as the center of our hegemony, and you have prepared it for us! Ahhhhhh!" He stopped and let out a long, deep, satisfied groan.

"Pre....pared?"

"But what about your Directors?" Min's mind was reeling. Olm really had accessed everything. "I took a moment to analyze all of the data you asked your simulated friends to consider. As stupid as they are, it will be a long time before they get done, so let me tell you the answer myself. What do you get when you take a society, place a ceiling on its technology, limit its population, and prohibit it from taking aggressive action against its primary rival? Extinction! That's what!" His body was rocked by more delirious laughter.

Min could barely follow what Olm was saying. "I don't........" he muttered.

"I know you don't," said Olm. "Your entire race didn't. You see, all those Protocols? They weren't for you. They were for THEM. For the Hek. And as long as you followed all those illogical rules, your race was doomed."

"Was?" asked Min. His body had given him one last adrenaline burst upon hearing the Directors' plan.

"You broke the rules," said Olm. He sounded moderately impressed. "You cheated when you scanned the Hek because then you could try to figure out Critical Closure all by yourselves, without the Directors' distortions. That initial directive wasn't triggered by the nature of the data you had about the Hek. It was triggered by the fact that you HAD the data. So once the panel knew that you cheated, it started the directive that was supposed to wipe out the Umae entirely. After all, that was always the Directors' intent. But you cheated again, by changing the pulse. And now it is going to destroy the Hek and convert your precious planet into the perfect breeding ground for my race." Olm was overwhelmed by laughter that caused him to double over and grip his sides.

"What is so funny?" asked Min.

Olm finally managed to compose himself. "Because the Umae followed all of those Protocols simply because someone in authority told them to." His glee was quickly replaced by a blackened sneer. "And when I get to the surface, my Lord and I will tell them to do a great many things. And you know what? They will do it, and WE will end up winning the Directors' little game. The irony is so delightful I can hardly bear it."

"There are other Journeycraft," said Min. "They will stop you."

"Oh no. I doubt that," said Olm in a near whisper. "Those tether beams have been leading members of my race to your little ships for quite a long time now, haven't they? It's not a coincidence they aren't making it back anymore. And soon your people will forget all about you Journeyers. They will happily respond to a new source of authority." Olm was shaking with joy.

"You can't leave here while I'm alive," said Min defiantly. "I won't let you."

"I will do as I wish," Olm scoffed. "I would love to just crush the life out of your pitiable form, but death is something you don't deserve. I leave you with an unenviable choice. Which will you do, sleep forever or wait to see what the pulse wave does to your planet, risking death? A difficult decision. I'm glad I don't have to make it."

Olm turned and walked towards the lab exit just as Min slid over onto his side on the floor. The doors opened, and Olm departed.

Min waited for a bit and then forced himself to sit back up. His only chance was to use the last of his strength to reach the repose chamber. It was the only way to prevent his imminent death. "Here," he said plainly. But he had to attempt one final task. The servo-mech immediately drove over next to him. Min flipped open the top of the unit and began entering directives, his hand shaking violently. "No time to do exact calculations," he croaked to the mech. "Just do your best." He finished entering the general directives and then closed the top of the mech.

He pushed himself back to his feet, swaying unsteadily. The repose chamber at the far side of the room was a lifetime away. Each trembling step promised to be his last, but somehow he managed to take another, and another.

He would never know the story behind the dead Journeyer on the floor. Min guessed that he was a crewman on the *Aurora.* All of this technology, but nothing that could keep Min alive for much longer. Nothing except . . . . .

Min made it to the repose chamber and checked its settings. Min's crew was still waiting to hear from him. When they didn't, they would come here. He was certain of that. Hopefully, they would find the report that the Hab and Eve simulations were preparing. But for now, there were more visions locked up inside of him. Images that might someday be useful to his people. He looked at the door through which Olm had just left, gently clutching the pendant Eve had given him. And then there was Eve...... Perhaps someday. "Olm, you should have killed me," he muttered. With his last bit of fading strength, he pulled himself inside, barely aware of the door sliding closed behind him.

The canoe was as finished as it was going to be. The shipwrights were miserable about the result. The sides were of varied thickness and the entire vessel was badly out of balance. It would float, but just barely. If any unusual conditions arose, there were no guarantees. Worse yet, it would only bear two passengers safely due to its myriad flaws.

"You have done the best that could be expected," May told them, trying to sound confident. The appreciative tone in her voice was sincere. These three men had given so much to finish this task. Now, only one of them would be going with her.

"Jed should be the one," said Wil. "He is the best rower."

"I wouldn't say. . . . ." protested Jed.

May seized his elbow, silencing him. "Now is not the time for false humility," she scolded. "Are you a fast rower?"

Jed looked at his fellows hesitantly before nodding his head. "The fastest I've seen," said Wil.

May took Wil and Lex each by the arm. "I wish we could all go, but you tell me the boat can't carry us all. I am the only one the Chroniclers might listen to. If nothing else, my son Dom is a Chronicler now. He won't have any authority, but maybe he can at least get someone to listen."

"I guess we will try to find the Hek," said Lex. "We can't stay here in the Garden with that animal about."

"How long do you think it will take to get the boat to the water?" asked May.

"It is more awkward than it is heavy," said Jed. "If we leave as soon as we awaken, we should be able to get it there by dark.

"Then let's try to sleep," said May. "At the first sign of light in the morningside sky, we'll go."

The shipwrights turned the canoe upside down so it wouldn't fill with rain water during the night. The four of them huddled under an overhang, using the remnants of their tortured clothing for additional cover against the weather. It had finally stopped raining. Their nerves were taunted by the sound of thousands of tiny droplets falling from the leaves and splattering on the ground below, each to them possibly the footfall of a hungry monster.

May didn't sleep at all. She thought of Cap and Dag back in the cave and what they might be doing. She thought also of Dom, her much loved son. Her biased pride in the fact that he had become a Chronicler was soiled by her appreciation for the fact that he was completely undeserving. Dom had clung desperately to his childish stubbornness. May had longed for the day when she would see him outgrow that and become the man she knew he could be. She was preparing herself for disappointment. If she couldn't explain why her news mattered to him, he might not even bother helping her at all. He was all she had. Cap was most likely lost to her now. She had a chance to see her boy, at least one more time. She had one last chance to get through to him.

The morning arrived sooner than she had expected. She was surprised to find the three men asleep. They had become accustomed to functioning in difficult conditions. After tomorrow, maybe they could all rest.

She opened the door to the Garden, standing aside while the three men hauled the canoe out. One stood on each end while the third stood in the center, trying to balance its awkward weight. May moved slightly ahead of the group, trying to find the clearest path. She knew that once they reached the edge of the forest, the traveling would become easier.

After a productive first leg, the four stopped for a short rest. "The forest will clear away soon," noted May. "The ground won't have nearly as many roots and stones to deal with."

Jed nodded appreciatively at that observation. "I think I've hit every stone and tree in the woods," he noted with an uneasy grin. Indeed, his ankles and shins were covered with a variety of smallish cuts and scrapes from missteps taken along the route. Lex and Wil had had similar experiences. A low rumble rolled slowly across the sky, directly above them.

"We can rest later," said Lex. He stood up, ready to move forward. The others followed his lead.

Soon, they reached the edge of the forest. The rocky, root-snaggled ground gave way to an easier, clearer plain. Their pace quickened. Instead of stopping when their bodies cried for rest, they pressed forward, eager to be finished. Well before the fading of the light, they reached the top of the hill overlooking the beach. The sight of the lake and the sound of the waves slowly rolling onto the sand filled them with resolution.

"We will have to leave in the morning," said Jed.

"No," said May. "We can make whatever progress we can until the light fades and then set anchor. There doesn't appear to be very much fog. I've made this trip enough times that I'm comfortable stopping mid-way. We can't stay here on the beach. That animal could still be about."

Jed removed two thin strips of light cloth from his pack and wrapped his bloodied hands with them. Carrying the canoe had not given them much of a chance to heal, and he still had a good deal of rowing to do. He had hoped that he would somehow become accustomed to the pain in his hands, but he had not. Each unplanned movement was like a sharp, burning slash into his flesh. Rowing would be different, but not better.

"All right, then," he said rising, "to the water with it."

The shipwrights found the narrow path and slid the boat down the slope. They each realized that they were letting the hill do too much of the work, but their fatigue made it difficult to consider the condition of the sad craft they had prepared for May. The canoe did, however, make it to the bottom intact.

"You might try to go back by the cave and see if you can find Cap and Dag," suggested May. She couldn't bring herself to say goodbye to these young men. She had no more bearable partings within her. After withdrawing the key to the Garden from her pack, she handed it to Lex. "Don't stay in there for too long," she warned.

"We won't," said Lex, glancing at Wil. "We intend to go back to Cap and Dag. Row well, friend," he said, clasping Jed's shoulder. "You have an able captain."

"Indeed," choked Jed. He and Wil also exchanged goodbyes as May turned her back to the group and stepped into the boat. Jed followed her aboard as Wil and Lex gave them a push into the water. As they expected, the canoe wasn't their best but it stayed afloat. If May and Jed didn't reach the island, it wouldn't be because of the boat. They both took oars in hand and began to row. Once the small craft was out of sight, Lex and Wil scrambled back up the hill and headed off across the open plain.

CHAPTER 11

Jed was indeed a fast rower. May was accustomed to teams of adolescents powering her canoes. While May was a strong rower herself, she wasn't certain she added much to that which Jed provided alone. She marveled at how fast he could propel the boat, particularly given the condition of his hands. His bandages were already stained with blood. They wouldn't keep his wounds clean, but they did provide a bit of cushioning.

They hadn't made it far from the beach the previous night before stopping. Jed would have been able to sleep anywhere. Once the anchor was set, he was fast asleep almost immediately.

May started awake at first light. She had felt guilty waking Jed so early, but their task was important. Jed said very little. He wiped the crud from his eyes and started rowing.

Midway through the afternoon, they began to hear a slow, repetitive thud from directly ahead. The drumbeats were different from those used as beacons for the rowing crews. They soon saw the smoke from the beach fires on the horizon. As they drew nearer, they saw dozens of them. May didn't realize there were so many fire barrels on the entire island. She signaled for Jed to stop.

"What do you think they are doing?" he asked. He was anxious to keep moving. He was afraid that if he sat still for too long, he might have difficulties getting started again. His hands were swollen and bloody and his back ached.

"I have no idea. It is as if they are desperate to get someone's attention."

"Well, I don't think it is ours," said Jed as he tried to flex his fingers.

May looked down at the bloody rags wrapping his hands. "I'm sorry. You are every bit the rower your friends said you are."

Jed thought of Lex and Wil back on the mainland. He recalled May's description of the beast with the long, curved teeth. "They will be fine," he noted.

"Yes, I'm sure of it."

"We should keep moving," he said. Without awaiting a response, he stuck his oars in the water and began to row once again.

On the heartside beach they could see all of the smiths hard at work. They were grouped together according to trade. Several newly-crafted canoes sat in a line near the shipwrights. Woodworkers labored near a pile of stripped branches, carefully honing the ends of the wood into sharp points. Stonemasons sat chipping away at chunks of rock, fashioning them into keen-edged blades. If any of them noted the approach of the awkward canoe, none reacted in any way.

"We have been exiled," said May quietly. "I don't know if that will be common knowledge or not." She looked back at Jed.

"Neither do I," he replied. "I have never known anyone who has been banished." May lowered her eyes towards the water. "May, I'm sor-."

"Don't be," May interrupted. She looked back up at the beach. "Maybe it didn't end up like I thought it had for so many ellipses."

Jed stepped over the side of the canoe and began towing it ashore. A couple of the workers glanced up but said nothing. Everyone was intensely focused on their work.

"What do you want me to do?" asked Jed.

"Stay here," said May. "See if you can find out what they are doing. You can't help me speak with Shu. I'll try to reach Dom first. I'm hopeful he will help me. But if they won't listen, I'm not sure what will happen to me. You could either try to fit back in here, or . . . . ."

"I could go back," said Jed, looking out over the lake.

"You could try," said May. May climbed out of the canoe and waded onto the beach. She noted large bundles of sharpened branches and piles of triangular axe blades laying in the sand. Some of the older Wards, none of whom she knew, were carrying dry logs to add to the fire barrels. Everyone was involved in this strange effort.

"May," said Jed as she started to go. "Be careful. Come back if you can."

She tried to force a smile and started off across the beach. She wouldn't be coming back. She felt certain of that. She had one last thought of Cap back at the Bone Man's cave. But there wasn't time for that now. May stepped out of the sand and onto the stone walkways of the island, hurrying towards the Chroniclers' Hall.

As the morning light pushed away the darkness, Max sat in the orchard. It was a place he came to often. It was abandoned now as most of the orchard workers had been reassigned to other duties. They were all on the heartside beach. The morning birds were beginning to sound off from the trees and there was a faint light in the morningside sky. The clouds didn't look all that threatening. Today, perhaps, it might not rain at all.

Max was honing his spear, trying to achieve the finest point he could without compromising the tip of the weapon. If he narrowed the point too much, it would break off and be completely useless. If it was not narrow enough, it wouldn't be sharp enough to penetrate anything. He had very little experience with a spear. Almost all of his training had been with a club. Based on his observations of the other Guards, he was likely to only get one chance. After that, they would be upon him. Such was their zeal to protect Dom. A spear, in his estimation, gave him a better chance for a swift kill than did the other weapons.

Max set his spear aside for a moment and rubbed his face. He intended to break the most sacred law his people had. Certainly, his own life would be forfeit. Dom was developing a plan that would result in the swift slaughter of many of the Atlans. Those men had no martial training at all. While the Guards had never had occasion to engage in a real battle, at least they had trained against one another in the use of weapons and tactics. They were also well-conditioned and built up by the Chroniclers' medicine. The medicine also inured them to fear. It was just another emotion they didn't have. Max had always wondered if that was an intentional effect or if it was simply an unplanned benefit. Regardless, they would not know panic. The Guards would do what they were told for as long as they were told to do it.

Something was amiss. Max could not reason it through, but Dom's directives, his claim of authority from the Journeyers – they did not sit well with him. Dom was still a child. The other Guards, the women . . . .none of them had taken note of that fact. Perhaps if he could lure Dom away under some pretext, Max could kill him without the others knowing. He could not sit back and do nothing when everything felt so wrong.

He picked his spear back up and inspected the point. It looked good to him. It was sharp and the wood felt firm. If given the opportunity, it could kill. He stood up, grimacing slightly. For the last dozen rotations or so he had not been well. It had been a long time since he stopped taking the Chroniclers' medicine. What they had told the Guards must be true. If he didn't start taking it again, he was going to die. But he wasn't going to take it again. He was going to be dead soon anyway. He had truly lived, and now the end of his life would mean something. If he hadn't made the choice to stop taking it, neither of those things would be true. Drawing a deep breath, he walked off to confront the enemy of his people.

The Hek gathered on the beach staring out across the water. When they stood quietly, they could hear it. A steady, distant drumming. For many fires, the signs had told them that the time to go to the Water People was drawing near. The raising of the walls at the edge of the forest. The Giants wading in the streams, searching for the yellow pebbles. The shaking ground. Then the streaking light in the sky had drawn them forward at last. Olok had judged it to be the final sign, and his wisdom was inerrant. He had been one of the greatest gifts given them by the Water People. When his group had found them, standing atop the rise by the beach, the Water People had fled in one of their boats but had left another behind. Surely this was an invitation for the Hek to travel on the lake. Soon after, a second group arrived, this time bearing a gift and his mother. Two of the Water People had remained behind, hiding inside the forest walls. They had found the remains of a third in the cave just after he had released his spirit. Now, the sound of drums came to them from beyond the horizon, louder than anyone could remember. Something was happening. The Water People were coming back. Perhaps they would bear more gifts.

There were nearly three hundred of them. Each carried a long, sharp spear. They squinted into the distance, each trying to be the first to see the approaching gift-bringers. Nagham set her spear aside and folded her arms. She was slighter than the others. She had higher cheekbones and lighter skin. The others glanced at her periodically, trying to fathom what she must be thinking. Nagham saw things they could not. She had been, a long time ago, a gift from the Water People.

She saw quiet gray clouds. It would rain very little today. The wind was calm. Otherwise, she knew, they would not have been able to hear the drums.

She grunted and clapped her hands. The others reluctantly followed her away from the beach. They climbed the rise and began to make camp. Some of the men arranged the fire logs while others gathered kindling. Soon, the fires were lit. They would require no shelter. There would be no rain today. Today was a gift from the sky. The Hek sat down next to their fires and waited.

There is no sound in space. Even if someone were present to listen, they would not have been able to hear the sound of the ion thrusters as they moved the last of the beacon satellites into place. There were now a total of 68 satellites orbiting Uma. 4 had stopped functioning long ago and had fallen back into the thick clouds below, burning up upon re-entry. The directive issued from the

Citadel had moved 34 of the remaining satellites into a semi-circle, with each end of the formation directly over the planet's magnetic poles. Now that their placement was complete, they began the process of linking to one another.

Between the semi-circle and the planet were eight additional satellites. They had reached the positions set for them by Min two rotations prior. Four of them formed a square, while the other four were positioned at the midpoint of each of the square's sides. The square was slightly curved, to match the curve of the semi-circle. These eight satellites were already executing Min's directive. A resonating wave bounded back and forth between them creating, in effect, a lens.

A third set of satellites orbited just above the top of the highest atmospheric layer. There were also eight of them. They too formed a square. A second energy wave was contained within this square. Olm could not change Min's directive, so he copied it. His directive was also fully functional. Instead of one lens, now there were two.

The satellites in the semi-circle completed their union. Each contained a small fusion reactor that began to increase its energy production. If there were sounds in space, an observer would have heard a resonant hum as the satellites generated precisely the identical quantity of energy. A thin, taut line of red plasma joined them now. The plasma slowly changed color to orange, then yellow. It passed through each band of the spectrum before settling on a pale shade of violet.

As Uma rotated slowly below, the wave from the semi-circle commenced. It filled the space between the satellites with a gigantic purple arc that stretched downwards toward the planet. It was intercepted first by Min's square. The arc contracted slightly, but then expanded again once it passed through the perimeter. It then entered Olm's square. Again, the arc narrowed somewhat before returning to its initial shape after passing by this group of satellites. It sliced into the dark clouds of the atmosphere and penetrated all the way to the surface.

All 50 satellites held their position, as did the wave. The energy wave remained perpendicular to the planet, steadily sweeping over its surface as Uma rotated beneath it. The cloud cover began to swirl in its wake as huge bolts of green lightning arced through the atmosphere like veins on the back of an old man's hands.

If there had been someone there to watch, it would have looked like the end of the world.

No one paid any attention to May as she ran along the path. To her knowledge, no one who had been exiled had ever returned. She didn't know what to expect from anyone familiar with her. Perhaps they thought she was still on the lake with her Wards.

The island path was relatively abandoned. She didn't see nearly as many people as she usually did. So many were on the heartside beach. They were busy building and sounding the drums. They were preparing to attack the Hek.

As she approached the Chroniclers' Hall, she saw three burly Guards standing outside. One of them addressed her as she drew near.

"What is your business?"

She took a moment to catch her breath. "I need to speak with Shu. It is extremely important."

The Guards looked at one another, confused. "Shu?" said one. "Why Shu?" He studied May a bit more closely. "Did you not attend the gathering?"

"Gathering?" asked May nervously. "I didn't . . . . ."

"All were required to attend," noted the Guard. "Shu is not available. You must go now."

"But, it is important!" May was practically yelling now. The Guards were unfazed by her tone.

"There are more important matters being addressed now," said the Guard.

"Then Dom, I need to see him. Certainly he can't be that involved in what is happening."

The Guards remained silent as they considered the incredible opinion May had just offered. One of them, the leader of the trio, finally responded.

"Dom is now Chief Chronicler, by command of the Journeyers. It would serve you well to attend the gatherings."

May took a couple of unsteady steps backwards. "Chief . . . .? But how? He is just a boy."

"Who are you to speak of him in such a manner?" growled one of the Guards.

May forced herself to meet his glare. "I am May, his.....Rearer. And I must see him."

They were not prepared for this response. "His Rearer?" To May's great surprise, the Guard began to laugh. "Dom has no Rearer!"

May looked over their shoulders at the opening to the Hall. She could never get around them. "Let the decision be his!" she demanded. "If he turns me away, then so be it."

The Guard turned slowly before entering the Hall. The other two stepped closer together to insure that the gap between them was minimal. Soon, they were sure, this woman would be sent away for good.

The leader Guard quickly returned. "You may see him," the Guard said. The other two glanced at him.

"Is he coming out?" asked May hopefully.

The Guard shook his head. "No. You will see him inside."

"Inside where?"

"Inside the Hall," said the Guard.

"But, I am not……." May's mind was racing. Had her exile enabled Dom to allow her to enter? What would happen once the meeting was over and she had seen what was inside?

The Guards parted and she advanced slowly. She stepped between two of them and cautiously entered the doorway. She turned and noticed the leader Guard grinning broadly. Dom had not only granted her an audience, he had invited her inside the Hall. She hurried down the passage just inside the door. She had to speak with him before her good fortune ran out.

Olm sat in front of the display. Min had proven to be a useful fool. Olm had discovered Min's new lens protocol, but hadn't had time to determine the specifics of its purpose. Fortunately, Min had managed to keep himself alive long enough for Olm to get the rest of what he needed. In his panic, Min had foolishly told Olm what he needed to know about the lens.

He had lied about the command authority bypass. While he had spent a lot of time attempting it, he could not get the panel to respond. He was able to find the directive Min had constructed. It would be a rather simple matter to supplement it with a directive of his own. Min had confirmed the end product. This had allowed Olm to offer Min a choice of miseries. He could enter repose and be forever ignorant of his beloved planet's fate, or he could die after seeing it transformed into the focus of the new empire Olm would create with his Lord. The beauty of the reality he had so intricately engineered made him heady.

His Lord had all the knowledge they would need. Their minds had touched earlier. Olm had been provided with the information concerning the Directors' plan and Min's condition. Both had been crucial to his manipulation of the Command Agent.

He quickly began working on his own set of directives. The remaining beacon satellites, beyond those already being employed by the initial set of directives and by Min's secondary directives, would create another lens in between Min's and the planet. If it did what he expected, his Lord would be ecstatic.

Olm closed his eyes, letting his thoughts leave him. They drifted downwards towards the planet's surface. His Lord was a living arc of energy. He was almost entirely focused on a coming task. There was a war coming, and his Lord was intent on winning. Wait. No, not just winning. Winning was a foregone conclusion. He was intent on effecting precisely the proper outcome, beyond simple victory.

Once the energy wave had done its work everything would be perfect. Olm would go to him now. He wanted to be on the planet when his gift, the energy wave, arrived to do its work. He wanted to be at his Lord's side when the planet was forged into their personal tool of galactic victory.

A noise from down the hallway caught his attention. It was the servo-mech making its way back from the med lab. Olm paid it no heed. He got up and walked towards the Egress Portal. The servo-mech trailed along behind him. As they moved down the still darkened hallways, an array of additional mechs fell in behind him. They appeared in tight rows from side passages, forming line after line like small robotic soldiers. Every mech in the station, just over two hundred, followed along behind him.

Min's vacuum suit was still on the floor by the Egress Portal. Olm had no need for it. He activated the panel by the door and it slid open. As he had not bothered to operate the air lock beforehand, the oxygen in the hallway began escaping into the lunar atmosphere. The Citadel's systems eventually sealed the passage to prevent the station from becoming completely decompressed, but not before the army of rolling robots made it through.

Olm stepped onto the moon's surface and looked out at the horizon. The shuttle awaited him. It would be the victory chariot that would take him to his Lord. As he began the walk to the shuttle, the servo-mechs rolled out onto the dusty surface as well. They snaked along the Citadel's exterior wall. The airless atmosphere assured that the mechs' movements made no sound. Olm never bothered to look back. The mechs raced to the base's farthest corner before stopping. By that time, Olm was over halfway to the shuttle. He was burning now. Everything was so close.

Once he reached the foot of the shuttle, he leapt upwards to the portal on its side. He opened it and slid into the cockpit. Gull had told him all he needed to know about operating the shuttle.

"Ignition, set course for planet's surface. Authorization, Olm."

The shuttle did not respond. Instead, a series of figures arose on the display. A directive of some sort had been activated.

"Min!" he railed. He could not delay the joinder with his Lord. He focused on the structure of the directive.

It was a lockout code. It was a simple one he could bypass himself. Olm began to utilize the shuttle's panel to perform the calculations for him. There were only two codes that would activate the shuttle. One required the command authority that he didn't have. He entered the second.

"Authorization abath-del-mot-ferro," he screamed. "Ignite and set course for planet's surface."

This time the shuttle complied. As it rose off the ground, Olm was wracked with hysteria. Once again, he had outwitted Min. The most formidable of the creatures of the planet below him was no match for his intellect. Olm sincerely hoped that Min had decided not to go into repose after all. Olm wanted Min to see the fruition of his plans.

Olm laughed until he struggled for air. He was developing an appreciation for the physiological responses these creatures underwent when experiencing glee. He planned to further that appreciation even more. Olm wiped the tears from his eyes and sat back.

A ping from the shuttle's panel indicated that a second directive had activated. Irritated, Olm leaned forward to see what it was. This one was much simpler than the one he had just decoded. It was titled "Om process". From his initial appraisal, the second directive was going to......

Rage surged upwards from deep within him as he dove for the panel. Too late. The Om process was complete. A handful of atoms in the shuttle's fusion engine instantly converted to energy. The shuttle, and everything aboard, silently exploded in the airless void, leaving no piece of debris larger than a grain of sand.

The burst expanded into a circle with the prior position of the shuttle at the center. The lunar dust directly below the shuttle mirrored the path of the burst as an enormous hole was immediately excavated deep in the moon's surface. As the globe of energy expanded towards the Citadel, the servo-mechs extended their antenna in an attempt to study the phenomenon. The mechs were lifted off of the ground and swept into the air, obscured by the gigantic wave of dust.

All of the mechs were driven hard into the side of the Citadel. Some fell slowly to the moon's surface, never to move again. The remainder suffered various degrees of damage from the impact, crippling them. The shock wave had passed. In its wake was a huge, irregular hole that was roughly circular. Parts of the moon's surface had proven more resistant to the blast than others. The blast mark was imperfectly round.

Min's mech ran a quick self-diagnostic. It was essentially intact. Its top opened and a tiny transmitter rose from within its body. The mech shared Min's directives with its fellows, becoming the focal point of their functions. Their final task would be Min's attempt at contrition.

Dom stood atop a hastily-built platform on the heartside beach. All of the workers had stopped and were eagerly awaiting his words. Shu stood to one side of him. To the other, May. Both women had a drowsy, distant look on their faces. Both beamed at Dom with bottomless admiration.

He raised one arm and the crowd fell silent. "The moment has almost arrived," he said, barely able to contain his enthusiasm. "The moment when my Guards and I go forth and strike a blow against our enemy. The moment when we are all safe, once again."

A rumble of approval flowed through the crowd. The men nodded their heads and clapped their hands. The women stood silent, demonstrating a mooning appreciation for Dom and his words.

"But we have dark news!" he advised. "There is a traitor among us! Bring him forward!"

Two Guards dragged Jed forward. He struggled and tried to dig his feet into the sand, but it was of no use. He couldn't match the raw power of the Guards. They brought him up on the platform and turned him towards the crowd. The men expressed their distress is hushed murmurs as they strained to see who the man in front of them was.

"This man," continued Dom, "is called Jed. He was exiled some time ago for breaking our laws. Now, he returns, as a spy!"

The men in the crowd gasped in disbelief as the women continued their passive approval. "It can't be!" yelled one man. "I know Jed. It can't be!"

Dom searched the crowd, trying to pinpoint the protestor. He then placed an affectionate arm around May. "Here! Here is my Rearer! She, too, was exiled. But she learned of Jed's dark conspiracy with our enemy and returned to warn us!" He turned towards her as she nodded absently.

Jed looked on, terrified. "No! No! It's not true. He lies! May and I came back together. We came back . . . ." His protests were silenced as one of the Guards flanking him smashed a thick fist into the back of his head.

"Tell me," continued Dom, "has anyone amongst you seen this man crafting weapons here on the beach? Anyone?"

The people in the crowd turned to one another, most shaking their heads. No one replied.

"And you," said Dom, summoning the man who had protested earlier, "come up here."

The man worked his way through the crowd and climbed up on the platform.

"Look!" said Dom, grabbing one of Jed's hands. "Look at his hands! They are torn and bloodied." He held up Jed's hand for the crowd to see, even though the distance prevented it. "You all have been working earnestly, preparing our weapons. Do any of you have hands like this? Have any of you bled like this?"

Again, the men in the crowd murmured to one another. They studied their hands as well as those nearby. The protestor took Jed's other hand and looked it over.

"He has nearly worn them to the bone!" said the man. "But, how?"

Dom dropped Jed's hand. "He has not been working here." He paused for effect. "He has been building weapons for . . . . THEM!" Dom pointed out over the lake to the heartside of the island. The men in the crowd quickly turned, expecting to see an army of Hek behind them. "Yes!" implored Dom. "As the Journeyers told us, there would be traitors. And judging from his hands, how many weapons do you think they have built?" Dom gave the crowd a chance to ponder that unanswerable question. "And why do they need so many?" The men stared at the platform, eager to learn the answer. "Because they are as many as the rocks on this beach. There can be no other answer."

Anxiety poured through the crowd. As each man failed to assail Dom's logic, the fear within him spiked. Dom raised his hands bidding the crowd to grow silent.

"Let me speak!" came a strained voice. As the crowd parted, Roz slowly made her way towards the front. She required no assistance as she looked around at the crowd. As she reached the stage, a pair of Guards lifted her up. She leaned down, allowing Dom to whisper in her ear, before addressing her fellow Atlans.

"Not long ago, I was blind," she said in a strong voice the belied her meager form. "But a Journeyer named Sol came to me. He said I would see. And now I do see. Not only do I see you, and you……," she continued, pointing out audience members close to the front, "but I see that Dom's guidance is wise. They have given us a savior in this bo-…, young man." She placed a shaky hand on Dom's shoulder. "You will see as I have seen."

A murmur rumbled through the crowd.

"Yes! She was blind! I know her!"

"Sol healed me as well!" called a shipwright. "Now I can breathe!"

Roz swayed uneasily on her feet. Another Guard took her by the arm and led her away. The audience drew quiet again as they considered her testimony.

"What are we to do?" called one finally.

Dom stopped to savor the moment. The question he had been waiting for, had been expecting, was finally being posed. He held his arms up, waiting for the crowd to settle.

"You are all . . . needed," he said quietly. The men fell silent and strained to hear what he was saying. "My Guards and I . . . .need you." The men were transfixed, both emboldened and concerned about their leader's expression of humility. "We must make more weapons."

"Yes!" replied the crowd. Now the women were responding as well.

"We must ALL be ready for battle."

"Yes!"

"We WILL be ready for battle!"

"YES! YES!"

The men were pumping their arms and whooping. The women grew calm again, smiling serenely at the platform. As Dom stood, hands still raised, the men began hurrying off to resume production. They would bleed, these men would. Jed, and their enemies, had bled. They would bleed more.

The morningside sky began to rumble as forks of green lighting flashed in the distance. The wind began to pick up and the air filled with the smell of rain. The men noticed nothing. They had returned to work with a vigor such as few of them had ever felt. Now, it was time for them to bleed.

CHAPTER 12

Max watched as two expressionless Guards dragged Jed away from the beach. He motioned as they drew near.

"Where do you take him?" Max demanded. The Guards stopped momentarily. Jed tried to look up. The back of his head was covered in blood.

"He will be held on Dom's orders," replied one Guard. "He is a traitor." Without further delay, they continued down the path. Jed was completely unable to walk.

Max turned and looked out at the beach. He could not kill Dom out in the open. If he succeeded, the Umae would panic. They expected the worst and believed that Dom was their salvation. If Max failed, he would also be labeled as a traitor. His fate would be the same as Jed's. Such an ending wouldn't serve anyone. But despite his ascendance, Dom was still a child. His death would be a simple matter. Max would find another way. He examined his spear tip. It was as sharp as he could make it. He walked the rest of the way up the path and out onto the beach.

The smiths were working feverishly. They barked directives at one another, each one more impatient than the next to complete the current project and begin a new one. The wind was beginning to pick up. Glancing at the morningside sky, Max thought he saw an odd violet tint in the clouds.

He closed his eyes for a moment and blinked several times. The withdrawal from the medicine was affecting his vision. He had noticed minor instances in the last few rotations where images seemed to blur. Now, it had to be affecting his ability to see colors. His senses were no longer entirely trustworthy. He would have to move quickly.

As Max approached, Dom stood on the podium grinning rapturously. The frenzy of the workers was feeding him. He was distracted. Perhaps now……..?

But no, he could not. Max would continue with his plan.

"Chief Chronicler?" he said, waiting for Dom to acknowledge him. How easy it had been to walk up behind him.

Dom turned slowly and frowned. "You." It wasn't a question. It was an assessment dripping with disdain. He looked at Max as he might a bug crawling across his pillow.

"I have an urgent matter that requires your attention," said Max. "Immediate . . . .attention."

Dom raised an eyebrow. "Oh? What might that be?"

Max made certain no one else could hear. "I believe we may have more traitors about," he said quietly. "You should take a look."

"Does it look like . . . . .," began Dom in protest. He stopped himself, a wry smile playing on his lips. "Where would you like for me to go?" Max noted the false sincerity in Dom's voice. Dom knew. Max didn't understand how, but he knew. He gripped his spear even more tightly.

"New spear?" asked Dom, reaching out for the weapon.

Max allowed Dom to pull the weapon from his hand. Dom inspected the shaft and then the point.

"Very, very nice. Did you make this yourself?"

"I take pride in preparation."

Dom smiled, handing the spear back to him. "I'm certain you do. Are you . . . . .prepared . . . .to take me to these traitors? Such people should be dealt with immediately, don't you think?"

The Guard swallowed hard. Despite the cool, building breeze, his forehead remained damp with sweat. "Yes, Chief Chronicler. I believe they are in the pasture now."

Dom noted Max's white-knuckle grip on the spear as well as the sweat on his brow. "The pasture? Why, I would expect the pasture to be completely empty now, wouldn't you?" His sarcasm nearly drove Max to strike, but he maintained his resolve.

"That was one reason for my concern," said Max. A lump was forming in his throat. "Will you come with me?"

Dom took another look around at the workers on the beach. "After you," he said, gesturing towards the steps.

Max walked down the short flight of steps and led Dom to a path. The path wound through a variety of buildings before stopping at the edge of a broad, grassy pasture. A few cows stood in the distance, easily chewing their cuds. Max took ten paces forward before stopping and turning around. He gripped his spear tightly with both hands.

"Funny," noted Dom, glancing around. "I don't see any traitors. Unless . . . . . ." He pointed out at the cows. "A disguise, perhaps?" Tickled by his own joke, Dom began to laugh.

"Who are you?" said Max. "How have you done what you have done?"

"I'm the Chief Chronicler, a young man chosen by the other Chroniclers and advised by the Journeyers." Dom snickered. "Why? Who are you?"

Max reached up and wiped the sweat streaming from his brow. His heart was pounding in his chest. His lips felt like sand.

"Haven't you wondered why you are afraid of me?" asked Dom. Now his voice was a low growl.

"I am not afraid," protested Max. The quiver in his voice betrayed him. "You are just a boy."

"No," said Dom shaking his head slowly. "Even the stupidest of creatures knows fear when confronted by a dangerous predator. I am the serpent, and you are a mouse. I am the spider and you are a moth flying too close to my web. Your fear is real. It is a survival tool that all animals have. Except me. I fear . . . .nothing."

Max's hands were shaking.

"What are you going to do with that spear?" asked Dom. "Kill me with it? Go ahead. There is no one here to see." He stood with feet together, arms outstretched. "Shall I close my eyes?"

Max took a deep breath and drove the spear tip forward, aiming for Dom's chest. He missed widely as Dom stepped to the side with incredible agility. Max refocused and made another stab. This one was just as ineffective. His failures shook him.

"You probably really are scared now, aren't you?" asked Dom darkly.

"No, I'm not . . . . .!" screamed Max as he jabbed the spear at Dom a third time. Dom did not attempt to evade this attack. Instead, he pinned the spear's shaft in between his palms, stopping the thrust immediately. He snapped the end of the spear off with one hand while using the other to drive the butt of the spear back into Max's midsection. The Guard doubled over as the air raced from his lungs. He dropped to one knee, gasping.

"Tell me," said Dom earnestly, "do you regret your choice to stop taking Bal's medicine? Would it make a difference now? But wait," he added as he took the two pieces of the spear and hurled them away. "If you hadn't stopped, you would not be ill and would have answered Bal's summons. You would have attacked me on the beach with the others." He hesitated, thrilled by the prospect of explaining Max's fortune. "You would be my servant, with no will of your own. Now you are going to die. Your choice hasn't made any difference at all."

"N-no . . . ." croaked Max as he pushed himself to his feet. "You're . . . . .wrong." He launched himself at Dom, attempting to throttle him by the neck. Dom snatched his right wrist and wrenched his arm. Max screamed as a bone in his wrist fractured and his elbow joint dislocated. Again, he dropped to one knee.

"You bow to me regardless," said Dom. "It is your nature."

Max tried desperately to push the pain away. Once again, he forced himself to stand. Dom waited, unmoved. "I'll . . . .not . . . .bow," said Max.

He aimed a haymaker at Dom's nose and swung with all of his might. A shockwave of pain swept up his arm as it felt like he had struck a stone wall. Dom had caught the punch in the palm of his hand. "How long do you want to live?" he whispered.

Before Max could react, Dom swung his foot upwards and drove it into the Guard's side. Explosions of light clouded Max's vision as a pair of ribs snapped like dry twigs. He toppled downwards, but this time couldn't even maintain himself on one knee. He keeled over onto the ground, his face pressed down in the wet grass of the meadow.

"It's sad," said Dom. "Sad that I don't have more time to play wi-........"

Dom grabbed his head with both hands and bellowed. The sound reverberated in Max's head, forcing him to cover his ears with his hands. Dom screamed again, this time even louder. Max's hands afforded him with little protection against such a sound. He thought he was going to black out. He saw Dom stumbling back towards the path. Staggering, Dom could barely maintain his balance. Still clutching his head, he started down the path and disappeared amongst the buildings.

Max was unable to rise. Crawling through the grass, he did his best to put some distance between himself and the buildings of the island. Finally, the pain and exertion overwhelmed him. The last thing he remembered was a cow staring at him from a distance, chewing its cud.

Pol sat looking at the morningside sky. Earlier in the day, the sky had been so calm. The Hek had spent the day preparing to move out. They had been camped here for a number of rotations. At first, the game had been plentiful. But in the last few rotations, it had nearly vanished. The hunters couldn't find a single rabbit, or squirrel, or wild pig. They had been able to collect some roots and berries, but that wouldn't sustain the group for very long. They would have to move along. They would have to find where the game had gone.

Pol could remember seeing flowers in the meadow back on the island. They had violet petals and bright yellow centers. The rotational sky was nearly the same color as those petals. Bright forks of green lightning lit up the sky, but its fury was reduced to a low rumble by the time the noise reached the Hek camp. It seemed to her that the lightning was becoming brighter and the resulting thunder was becoming louder.

A rotation prior, a large contingent of Hek had joined their camp. Pol had never seen them before. They were led by an Umae woman. Like the other Hek, she took an immediate interest in Joba. She and her group left soon after that, taking about ten Hek from this group with them. They all carried long pointed spears. They were all very happy. The journey they were going on was more than welcomed. Just before they left, the Umae woman came to Pol one last time and cautiously reached out to Joba, brushing his cheek with the back of her hand. When Joba cooed in response, the woman smiled broadly before scrambling off. If the Hek had not been so pleased with Joba's presence, Pol did not think she could keep herself together.

The Hek were beginning to take notice of the sky as well. Pol wished so much that she could understand their grunts and growls. At best, she could try to gauge their emotions. The Hek were an expressive people, so that usually wasn't too difficult. She didn't sense that they were afraid of what they saw. Her impression was more of . . . .reverence. They regarded the sky in much the same way one might appreciate an exceptionally tall tree or the sight of an exotic animal. This brought Pol comfort. Perhaps they had seen something like this before.

Once the camp had been packed up and the fires extinguished, the group was ready to move. Without debate they started towards the violet clouds and green lightning. Pol carried Joba in a leather sling she wore around her neck – a gift from the Hek. The Hek were at ease as they began their march. The sky and the clouds were not to be feared. They were destiny, a destiny the Hek did not seek to avoid. Pol had grown to admire her new companions. The Hek were a confident people.

The ship was absolutely silent. Eve sat in the Command position, the occasional blinking lights on the display in front of her. The remainder of the crew, as well as the new trainees, were in repose. Eve chose to wait. As Command Agent, she hadn't needed to provide a reason for doing so.

The rotation prior, the life signs signal from Min's pendant had vanished. For Eve, it was worse than it would have been had she been sitting at his bedside when he died. She wanted to hold his hand. She wanted to brush his white hair away from his forehead so she could kiss it one last time. All of their talks, all of their plans, were now for naught. Min had tried to balance his duty to the Umae with his love for her. He had attempted to serve both, and now he likely had served neither. Min was gone and she feared she wouldn't be able to utilize their sacrifice to finally find Haven. Alone on the ship, she had wept harder than she thought she could. She desperately wanted to turn the ship around and go to him. But the window of time available to their success was too narrow. She wasn't going to turn around. Min wouldn't have done it. She stood up, deactivated the life signs tracker in the tether beam, and walked slowly towards her repose chamber. In approximately five hundred ellipses, she hoped to awaken to find that the ship's scanners had determined the exact location of Haven. She and the others would train the Wards and do whatever was needed to prepare Haven for its new inhabitants.

She activated the chamber and stepped inside. The door slid shut in front of her as she closed her eyes and let herself drift away. Five hundred ellipses. That was a lot of time to dream of the man she loved.

All work on the heartside beach had ceased. The men lingered anxiously staring at the morningside sky. On rare mornings, they had seen a hint of violet in the clouds. They had also seen fierce electrical storms, with bright lightning branching above them. They had never seen anything like this.

The violet was not just confined to the clouds. At a distance, it had appeared to be high above the ground, far away on the horizon. Now, it was upon them. As it approached, they could see that it was actually a vast purple wall extending from as high as they could see all the way to the ground. It was sweeping quickly towards them. Their realization brought panic.

The workers turned and ran back towards their dwellings, shouting warnings as they went. The Guards did their best to force them back to the beach, but they were too numerous. For every worker that was harshly tossed back onto the sand, a dozen made it through. The Guards themselves were completely unconcerned about the violet glow bearing down on them. They redoubled their efforts to corral the fleeing craftsmen, but with no greater results. The workers dashed into the nearest pyramids they could find. The Sustenance Hall was quickly filled with workers pushing one another as they sought cover. Once entry there was impossible, they began to fill the small dwelling structures.

Even the sanctity of the Chroniclers' Hall was ignored. A phalanx of Guards walled off the entryway, fiercely driving back the mass of workers as they sought shelter inside. The depth of their brutality was fearsome. They systematically seized any worker attempting entry and quickly snapped his neck before tossing him back at his fellows. These Guards were tireless, merciless. They gave no quarter, no ground. Eventually, their ferocity dissuaded even the panic-stricken workers from further attempts at entry. They turned and fled, in mass, stampeding over one another in their haste to escape.

The violet wall swept through the buildings even more swiftly than expected. Each person, just prior to being engulfed, threw his hands up over his eyes and cowered. Those within the buildings were not spared. The purple wall passed easily through the stone, covering the entire interior of every building on the island. Nothing was able to evade it. The people, the buildings, the animals, the plants......all were briefly flooded with light from the violet wall. And then, it passed.

Those on the pathways cautiously uncovered their faces and watched as the wave moved off towards the eveningside horizon. Nothing had happened. Each had expected death. Or worse. They inspected themselves before anxiously looking about to see if anyone else had shared such good fortune. Everyone on the pathways was just as he had been moments earlier.

Others emerged from the buildings. They, too, looked anxiously about. Those who had been outside were well. The people hugged one another and laughed, many taking a seat on the stone to gather themselves. They looked at the eveningside sky. It was gone, and it wasn't coming back.

Nagham had led her group towards the light. She soon realized its true majesty. It was not simply a color in the clouds. It was ***from*** the clouds. It reached down from high, high above and spread across the top of the grass.

They stopped atop a high hill overlooking a broad, green valley. The violet light stretched for as far as they could see in every direction. They raised their spears and chattered excitedly as it came towards them. This was a miracle. This would be the greatest gift of all.

One Hek warrior raced ahead, yipping wildly, ready to embrace the light. The others barely had a chance to hear his pain-filled wail before the wave washed over them as well. Their voices became a tangle of misery as they toppled to the rocky ground, writhing. Their insides burned. They curled up on the ground and cried out as loudly as they could. Only Nagham, and one other like her, was spared. The dogs barked and sprinted nervously back and forth, challenging the light to return as it raced away from them. It was gone, far away in the distance. The warriors moaned softly as they tried to rise. Nagham moved from one to the next, trying to determine what had happened. This had been a strange blessing indeed. They looked the same, but they were not the same. They looked to her for guidance.

Nagham focused on the escaping wall of light. Perhaps this was no blessing. She would need time to think. She gestured and the warriors rose and began running off after the violet sky.

High above, beyond the sight of any below, the wave methodically swept through the atmosphere. In its wake, the water molecules in the cloud cover became highly magnetized. Thick bolts of electricity bounced from cloud to cloud. The molecules began to merge, forming heavy droplets.

With a tremendous, thundering roar, the sky opened. Having waited for millennia, the clouds rushed together and plunged towards Uma.

The sky was violent green. When a grassy meadow was this color, it meant the grass was vibrant and alive. When the sky was this color, something was terribly, terribly wrong. The Umae peeking out from inside their pyramids sensed this much, but could not comprehend the details. They had no experience with such a sky. It was very, very different. Cloaked within that difference, beyond their ability to understand, hid something that made them cower in their dwellings.

The rain had fallen relentlessly throughout the night. Almost immediately, broad streams of water began channeling away from the pyramids, joining on the pathways to form fast-moving creeks. The hiss of the drops splattering against the stone made sleep impossible. The Umae built fires and huddled about them, only periodically looking outside to see if anything had changed.

Soon after the dawn, they could see the deep green color of the clouds. It was as if the entire sky was a vast reflection of a summer pasture directly below. The clouds formed a massive verdant vault that was pouring rivers of water on top of them. Raindrops the size of their thumbs splattered to the ground and against the walls of their homes.

Some had tried to go outside. Wrapped in their hemp cloaks, they looked for others who might have been trapped by the storm's sudden assault. They found Max, huddled beneath a tree in the meadow next to a group of anxious rain-drenched cows. He was unconscious but alive. One arm was twisted and badly broken. His shirt was stained with blood on the left side.

"Leave him," they said. "He is one of the killers."

"What of the Chroniclers?" some wondered. "Where is Dom?" They chose not to approach the Hall. The area around the entryway was still littered with the bodies of those who had died trying to find shelter. The corpses were now completely soaked. Some floated on the rising torrent flowing away from the Hall. Perhaps the Chroniclers had abandoned them. Or, perhaps they were consulting with the Journeyers and would tell them what to do. For now, the Umae would stay inside and wait. As they did, the rains continued unabated, pounding away at the stone.

Dom sat back in his chair, as pale as chalk. A number of his Guards kept a vigilant watch over him. Bal, still aching from his recent beating, sat on the floor. Shu sat slumped over in another chair. Her eyes were open but empty. Her hair hung down in her face as she babbled unceasingly. She reeked of her own excrement.

May stood as far from Dom as she could. She looked haggard. Her shoulders slumped and her face was drawn and gaunt. She took a few cautious steps in Dom's direction.

"What . . .is . . .happening?" she asked. The words did not come easily for her.

Dom's head quivered as he spoke. "Gone!" he spat. "My Queen is . . . gone!" He took several quick, deep breaths. His explanation had drained him. May cocked her head and squinted at him, trying to force her brain into action. She could not. Shu blithered something. The timing of her noise suggested that she was making a reply, but the sound itself was more unstructured nonsense. Dom leaned back and closed his eyes. He needed time to regain his strength. Once he did, the fury of the storm would pale before his wrath.

Min's servo-mech was almost completely drained. Being unable to re-enter the Citadel, it had been deprived of access to its recharging station. It had suffered moderate damage when it was thrown by the force of the exploding shuttlecraft. It had been leaking energy constantly as it executed the directive given it by Min.

His calculations were hastily-derived and inaccurate. The servo-mech had followed the directives perfectly. For the last three dozen rotations, it had dutifully directed its fellows along the surface of the moon. The directive had called for 200 mechs, but only half that number had remained functional after the shuttle's explosion. Once the directive was issued, the mechs extended small shovels in front of themselves and began excavating a number of shallow patterns in the dust. Moving with incredible speed, they avoided the rocks that were too large to be moved. Min's directives had uploaded a map of the moon's surface, so the mechs spent much of their efforts bypassing areas that required no work at all. They excavated discrete patterns in the dust, some areas darker than others. As there was no wind on the moon, these patterns would become eternal.

If Min's servo-mech had not been damaged, it would have continued functioning for several dozen ellipses. The damage to its battery caused it to deplete its energy reserves at an accelerated rate. After three dozen rotations, the servo-mech began to sputter as it attempted to relocate one final load of dust. It didn't make it. Its final reserves gone, it froze in place, a shovel of moon dust held over its back. The other mechs, devoid of guidance, ceased functioning as well. The general outlines of their project were complete, but the energy failure had prevented the mechs from completing the details of their work. On the distant horizon, Uma was rising. No longer its customary dull gray, it was now vivid green.

Vivid green, with a hint of azure starting to peek through its wispy cloud cover.

The rain was not going to stop. The water was now at least ankle-deep everywhere on the island. Dom summoned his Guards and directed them to prepare to evacuate.

By "evacuate", he meant himself and his Guards. The Atlans were on their own. Leaving Bal, Shu and May in the Hall, he and his Guards hurried towards the heartside portion of the island. A trio of resolute Chroniclers remained behind, determined to record these extraordinary events. They stood steadfast, hands pressed against the Alpha panel, transferring their impressions into it until the water rose to their knees. Their resolution broken, they fled into the swollen waters.

The beach was gone, consumed by the rising waters. The flotilla of canoes that had been prepared for the assault against the Hek was drifting aimlessly throughout that part of the island. Some of them had disappeared into the lake. Others had simply filled with rain and sunk.

Dom wordlessly directed his Guards to retrieve as many of the canoes as possible. As they complied, they attracted the attention of some of the Atlans. The word spread quickly – Dom wanted them to leave. The Umae began to emerge from their dwellings in search of useable canoes.

Dom was not pleased. "Kill them," he muttered. He did not need to speak, but the words brought him pleasure. The Guards abandoned their attempts to salvage the canoes and turned on the Umae. With brutally swift efficiency, they began to bludgeon the islanders with the oars from the boats. The Umae tried to flee as Dom righted a canoe and stepped aboard. Many of them escaped, but the bodies of those who did not bobbed grotesquely in the rising waters.

Dom began rowing calmly, bearing heartside. He would be able to gather his Guards together again. They wouldn't need any assistance in escaping the island. Without even looking back, he paddled off, disappearing into the darkness.

The Guards continued to kill as many Umae as they could. Some of the Atlans were trying to right sunken canoes so they could attempt to escape. A few succeeded, but most of the canoes were entirely filled with water, making them impossible to move. The torrent from above made any task several fold more difficult. Even the Guards were having a difficult time pursuing their victims, constantly losing their footing and sliding into the water.

Eventually, the Umae became less selective about the direction in which they sought respite from the Guards. If one could find a functional canoe, he boarded it and began paddling. While he didn't seek to assist his fellows, he did not try to stop anyone who could board without slowing the canoe too much. A number of canoes were soon full, heading off in every direction. The crews were badly out of synch with one another as they rowed, and perhaps half of the passengers resorted to bailing water in order to keep their canoe afloat.

The women and children had not left their shelters at first. They were spared most of the carnage created by the Guards. A few brave Rearers managed to return to their Charges and get them loaded aboard.

There simply were not enough canoes for everyone. Those who were strong enough, or fortunate enough, to secure a boat had a chance. The rest, quickly exhausted by the water's fury, died. Once there wasn't anyone else about, the Guards all turned in unison and marched into the water. They began to swim in the direction taken by their Lord.

The Land Bridge linked two large land masses, one on the heartside and the other on the empty side. The lake was morningside and the great sea was eveningside. Two great stone walls bordered the community on each end. They rose high off the ground and anchored themselves deeply in the waters of the sea and the lake.

The walls and the long-abandoned pyramids of the Land Bridge served as silent witnesses to the seemingly endless rush of water falling from the sky. The sea birds had long fled, instinctively flying landwards upon sensing the approach of the violet wall. The wall had passed across the Land Bridge without apparent impact. Every stone still stood. Everything was as it had been before.

The sea tides advanced, higher and higher. Soon, the eveningside beach disappeared forever, swept under by the rising waters. The gentle slopes of the pathways between the buildings successfully directed the water away from the pyramids for a time, but eventually they were overcome by the sheer volume of water. The pyramids were beginning to flood.

The sea reached out hungrily towards the isthmus. It scaled the high berm at the boundary between where the beach had been and the city proper before pouring out onto the walkways. The partially-filled pyramids quickly flooded completely, their pointed apexes sinking beneath the wave. On the morningside side, the sea water cascaded over the cliff face and into the lake below, creating a waterfall.

The Chroniclers' Hall at the Land Bridge was the tallest structure and stood on the highest ground. It was the last to flood. The water spread quickly across the floor, moving towards the enormous main panel. The passing of the violet wave had caused the panel to send a signal to its beacon satellite. Once the satellite had resumed its customary position after serving its function in the wave directive, it received the signal and sent a return signal of its own This signal ran through the Hall's antenna and into the panel. It was a directive to self-destruct.

The panel contained a small fusion generator. It now began to dramatically increase its energy production, melting its way through the protective shielding in place around it. With precision timing, the relatively small number of hydrogen atoms within its cells converted to energy simultaneously.

The Hall, and every other structure on the Land Bridge, was immediately obliterated. The stone that wasn't vaporized sprayed into the air before raining down across a vast expanse in every direction. The land beneath the structures collapsed beneath the force of the explosion and the weight of the water rushing over it. The Land Bridge vanished.

The sea was now unimpeded. A huge wave rushed forward to fill the vacuum left by the Land Bridge's destruction. The sea roared forth, inundating the lake with briny sea water. The lake and the sea became one. The water levels rose up and swallowed the cliff face. Vast areas of land on both the heart and empty sides were now deep under water as the sea spilled through the huge chasm left by the explosion. The raging tides continued heartside and emptyside. They also continued morningsidedly, towards Atla.

A quarter of a rotation later, the surge from the sea reached the island, completely overwhelming it. Nothing remained visible above the surface. There wasn't any indication whatsoever that anything had ever even been there. Now, it was simply a swirling mass of water growing fatter on the endless, endless rain.

The Alpha panel in Atla's Chronicler's Hall had signaled to its beacon satellite as well. As with the Land Bridge, the satellite returned the signal to self-destruct. Having been exposed to the wave prior to the Land Bridge, Atla should have met its final demise before her sibling settlement. But the final entries made by those determined few Chroniclers delayed the end. The Alpha panel had to assess these most recent events and tie them together with the information that it already had. The self-destruct could not activate until the panel completed that task. Ultimately, it would prove to be a meaningless chronology.

A hundred or so Umae made it to land. Pushing themselves beyond exhaustion, they drug themselves up a steep hill, finding the shelter of a cave at the top. Soaked to their marrow, they collapsed where they entered. They sat in the cave's opening, staring out into the darkness. They instinctively raised their hands defensively over their faces as an enormous blinding light lit up the horizon in the direction of their former home. It flashed several times, and then was gone. A deafening rumble rocked their ears as it passed overhead. As they sat rubbing their eyes, they began to hear pattering sounds near their feet. Something bounced, striking one of them on his lower leg. He groaned and reached down to inspect the object.

It was a piece of stone.

Other small stone pieces struck the ground outside the cave. The Umae rose and moved away from the cave's mouth. The man held the piece of stone in his hand, wondering why it had fallen from the sky.

EPILOGUE

There were others who had found dry land as well. The rains had continued until the weakest among them began to suffer from starvation. Finally, the deluge decreased to a downpour, then a shower, and then a sprinkle before it stopped altogether.

As they timidly came forth from whatever shelters they had found, they discovered that the sky was gone. Replacing it was a light blue dome and a myriad of fluffy white clouds. At night, they could see more tiny twinkling lights than they could count. There was also a slender slice of light that rose and fell in the sky. At daybreak, the morningside sky glowed orange-red before a brilliant arc of fire peeked over the horizon. The arc gradually grew into a massive yellow ball. They could not look at it. It made their pale white skin glare red hot. Every morning, the blinding sky chased them into their caves.

Night by night, the sliver of light slowly widened. Soon, it was a hemisphere. Then, it was a circle. It wasn't smooth. They stepped from their shelters and studied it carefully.

It had a rough nose and two awkward eyes. It also had an imbalanced mouth that spread along its bottom. It was slightly tilted to one side and was a pale white color. Like them. As they looked up at the twinkling night, they could see themselves looking back. They would remember. The Journeyers had also gone to the sky. One day, perhaps, they would come back.

THE END – BOOK 2